FIRE ON THE MOUNTAIN

ISBN: 978-1-7336429-1-0

Meathouse Publishing
MeathousePublishing@gmail.com

FIRE ON
THE MOUNTAIN

A NOVEL

JAMES
KIRKLAND

meathouse
PUBLISHING
Echo Park

"We now return our souls to the creator,

as we stand on the edge of eternal darkness.

Let our chant fill the void

in order that others may know.

In the land of the night

the ship of the sun

is drawn by the grateful dead."

- Egyptian Book of the Dead

Chapter 1

I was in Maui, locked in a jail cell twenty miles from an active volcano.

Aloha.

Haleakalā is a massive volcano that forms more than seventy-five percent of the island of Maui. Its name means "House of the Sun" and its peak reaches ten thousand feet above sea level. Below, it goes far deeper, some three miles into the Earth's core. Haleakalā had been dormant for over four hundred years.

Until a week ago.

My name is Dave Pasch. I was in town to cover the Maui Invitational with my broadcasting partner, two time NCAA and NBA Champion, Deadhead, and human three-ring circus, Bill Walton. We were told by many people, assured by many experts, that we were not in danger. The tournament would proceed as scheduled. Apparently we'd all be just fine because Haleakalā is a "shield volcano." That means the lava is thin and can travel for great distances down its shallow slopes straight into the ocean. "Composite volcanoes" are the ones you have to worry about. Mount St. Helens. Mount Vesuvius. Krakatoa. They were all composite volcanoes. A shield volcano is not likely to explode catastrophically.

Not likely?

Not comforting.

I could see Haleakalā out of the small, barred windows of the cell. Ominous. Crimson. Glowing. I couldn't literally feel the heat from the volcano, not at this distance, but you'd be crazy to think I didn't feel... something.

Something deeply unsettling. Something powerful had been awakened. Something primal. It was everywhere on the island and it seemed like we were all affected by it. Violence and mayhem were in the tropical air. Dogs barked throughout the night. Birds spooked and squawked. It was fear. A fluttering in the guts that tells you to run. And run fast. But I had nowhere to run. I was behind bars. And I was not alone.

I looked around the concrete box of battered and beaten men. A sea of black eyes, bloody noses, busted lips, and missing teeth. A tall, sinister man with a curtain of greasy hair walked around in little circles in the middle of the cell. His circles got wider and wider as he purposely bumped into people, silently daring them to do anything about it. A ragged, disgusting junkie scratched at the track marks that dotted his arms like dark constellations, rocking back and forth, badly needing a fix that wasn't coming. A chubby, salt-and-pepper-haired businessman in a brand-new Hawaiian shirt was curled up on the floor in the corner, shivering like a hurt dog. He had shit himself.

A giant, shirtless man with muscled arms sat with his hands on his knees, proudly showcasing his bloody knuckles. His entire upper body was so covered in tattoos I could hardly see unpainted skin. He caught me looking at him and stared back at me with eyes of hate. I looked away.

The smell was disgusting. A nauseating mixture of bodily fluids and filth. Someone started to curse. Shouting the same expletive over and over again like a hex. Someone told him to shut up. That person was told to shut up. There was screaming. Shoving. The packed cell ready to erupt like the volcano in the distance.

This was the worst night of my entire life.

Then it got worse.

The giant, tattooed man with bloody knuckles hadn't stopped staring at me. In fact, after he caught me looking at him again, he said, in a terrifyingly calm voice, "What are you looking at?"

I said nothing.

I looked down, hoping he'd just ignore me. But he didn't. He stood up and walked over to where I was sitting. My heart dropped into my stomach. Every bloodshot eye in the cell was on us as he stopped in front of me. The toes of our shoes were almost touching.

"Stand up," he said, almost gently. His breath was hot, like air from a muffler.

I didn't want to stand up. I knew that if I stood up I would get in a fight and I would lose that fight. I would lose that fight very badly. I closed my eyes again. I was in Hawaii, damn it. I was supposed to be having a good time. I should be at a luau with a lei around my neck, watching hula dancers juggle fire.

"I said, stand up."

There was nowhere to run. Nowhere to hide. I was in jail. Under lock and key.

And the worst thing?

I was guilty.

Two Days Earlier...

Chapter 2

You ever just know you're going to have a great night? This was one of those nights. Absolutely nothing could go wrong. I was wearing a Tommy Bahama Hawaiian shirt I bought for the trip. A bold, bright yellow with coconuts and surfboards. I had just passed through the buffet and had a plate piled high with roasted pig, Hawaiian macaroni salad, and purple sweet potatoes in one hand, and an ice-cold beer in the other. The Hyatt Regency had pulled zero stops on the luau they threw to welcome the teams participating in the Maui Invitational, college basketball's premier kickoff event.

The coaches had all drifted over to a table in the middle of the room. I saw an empty chair right between Mike Krzyzewski and John Calipari. Bingo. That's Dave Pasch's chair. A year ago, I would have just walked on and sat at an empty table in the back of the room. A wallflower, longing to sit at the cool table. But not anymore. Tonight, I would feast on pork and legendary basketball stories.

I had changed since the events that transpired a little over eight months ago. Walton and I had been calling the Pac-12 Tournament in Seattle when an old teammate of Walton's approached him after a game. He was desperate. His daughter Abigail had been kidnapped and he couldn't go to the cops for help. Bill and I agreed to help look for her. Together, with our new producer, Stephanie Walker, we succeeded in finding Abigail. We were in the process of taking her back from her well-intentioned, but horribly misguided kidnappers when we were overtaken by some extremely not-well-intentioned bikers who held us at gunpoint on a rainy cliff high above Puget Sound. They planned to kill us, take the ransom money, and dump our bodies into the ocean.

But that didn't happen. Because I fought back. I lept into action. Literally. I launched myself at a biker named Toucan who held a gun to my head. I headbutted him and broke his nose, saving my life and the lives of five other people, including Bill Walton.

The experience changed me. Since then, I've been more confident. Decisive. A new man. Pasch.0. And Pasch.0 was walking right to his chair at the cool table. Coach K was holding court. He held a margarita in his hand that was dwarfed by the 2015 NCAA Men's Basketball Championship ring on his finger. He had just launched into a yarn about the '92 Dream Team. Something about a heated, week-long argument between Lenny Wilkens and Larry Bird about the pick and roll. This was going to be good.

But, right before I sat down, I felt a tap on my shoulder.

"Pasch. Let's go. This party sucks."

I turned to see my broadcasting partner, Bill Walton. Always quick to embrace island life, he was wearing a Hawaiian shirt with red, blue, and green tropical flowers and at least five leis.

"Bill, I'm not going anywhere. This is the best party I've ever been to in my life."

"Pasch, please! They have this party every year. It's lame! Come on, I'm taking you someplace way better. A real party. The party of the year. Maybe the century!"

I looked back at the table. I cursed under my breath.

"What party?" I asked. "What party could possibly be better than this?"

Waltons face went cheshire. "It's a surprise!"

Curiosity is the gasoline that runs the engine of my mind and Walton had just filled me up with premium.

"Come on, Bill. What party could possibly be better than this?"

"There's only one way to find out, Dave."

I couldn't believe it, but I was leaving. I put the plate down and took one last look at the coach's table. Of course it was the moment they all burst out laughing at the end of Coach K's Dream Team story. Damn it, Walton.

As we left, we passed our producer, Stephanie Walker, and her husband, Colonel Cabrera. They had met during the years Stephanie spent producing hard-hitting news in war zones, before starting a family and downshifting to the relative safety of college basketball. She was smart, funny, and still looked like the hotshot Notre Dame point guard she once was. Her husband Elvin was an Army Ranger whose charming personality helped me forget the fact that he could kill me with his thumb. I complimented him on his vacation mustache, which he seemed to have grown in the blink of an eye.

Walton invited them to come with us. But, being sane people, they politely declined.

"It's our anniversary. We're not going anywhere with you two idiots," Stephanie told us while draping an arm around the Colonel. His red Hawaiian shirt with palm trees and parrots was unbuttoned halfway down his hairy chest. They both looked like they had indulged in some tropical drinks. The Hawaii effect.

"Happy Anniversary! What a superb place to spend it!" Walton boomed.

"Thanks, Walton. Check it out, Elvin got us heartbeat rings." Stephanie showed off their beautiful matte black, high-tech rings and explained how they were able to feel each other's heartbeats wherever they went. Very romantic. On our last anniversary I got my wife a gift card for a massage. Note to self: step it up, Pasch.

"My mother got us an even better present. She's watching Ana while we're here." The Colonel beamed. "I mean, don't get me wrong. I love my daughter with all my heart. But we get to stay in bed all week!"

"He means sleep in," Stephanie said, pulling our minds out of the gutter.

"Oh, absolutely," The Colonel confirmed. "We haven't slept 'till nine o'clock in three years. Having a kid is like having a tiny drill sergeant living in your house, screaming at you every morning. We are going to enjoy this."

We left the happy couple and I followed Walton out of the room, ignoring the tickle in my brain that was telling me I was making the biggest mistake of my life.

Chapter 3

Ten minutes later we were 1,500 feet in the air and climbing. I was in a seaplane piloted by a dirty old hippie named BB, who insisted his name was spelled without periods.

"Like the gun." He winked.

BB had a long white beard and white hair pulled back into a ponytail. He wore a faded Shell '76 gas station baseball shirt, swimming trunks, and Chuck Taylor high tops he had cut into sandals. He was an old friend of Walton's. I have met hundreds of them over the years. They were all the same. They all loved the Grateful Dead and hated hygiene.

BB smiled at me. He had a gold tooth.

He made me nervous. I was still recovering from our ocean takeoff. The little seaplane's pontoons slammed against every wave in a rough sea and, for awhile, I didn't know if the plane would go airborne or break into a thousand little pieces.

"Can you please just watch where you're going?" I asked as gently as possible.

"Dave, have no fear! BB is the best pilot on the islands! You're in good hands!" Walton said from the back of the plane. He was sitting in a lawn chair duct taped to the floor. "BB was in the Air Force! For goodness sakes, the man flew for Air America!"

"You mean American Airlines?"

"No! Pasch, you fool! Please! Air America was the CIA's private airline. During the Vietnam war, BB ran support for secret operations along the Ho Chi Minh trail in Laos and Cambodia. It was all wildly illegal and still classified. BB's the legend of a story that can't be told! The tragedy! The glory!"

BB cackled. He looked and sounded just like the Crypt Keeper, the skeletal host of the campy series that showed spooky movies on late-night television. I was seriously regretting my decision to leave the Hyatt as the clouds in front of us thickened. After a few minutes, as we kept gaining altitude, I slowly realized they weren't clouds. It was the smoke from the volcano. Haleakalā was right in front of us. An impossibly huge bowl of fire. I could see the auburn glow of lava spilling down the east side of the mountain as we approached from the north.

"Um, hello?" I said. "We're headed straight for the volcano?"

"Hell yeah!" BB said proudly. "Enjoy the view, brother! This is a special treat. It's super illegal for planes to fly this close to an active volcano!"

"Aloha Haleakalā! This is incredible! Mother nature, look at her go! Busy making more Hawaii!" Walton leaned between BB and me to get a better look. "Dave, did you know this is how the Hawaiian islands were made? Creation through destruction. The circle of life! The ring of fire!"

I begged BB to turn the plane around. Or turn in any direction. But he did neither. He just kept flying us straight towards the volcano, now less than a mile away. I could feel the heat coming from it. The temperature inside the plane went up twenty degrees in a matter of seconds. Sweat poured from our faces. I looked at BB and he seemed entranced. He was slack jawed, almost hypnotised. After a few more moments I could no longer see sky or land through the front window of the plane, just a red ocean of boiling lava. I saw BB's hands pushing down on the stick, steering us right into the mouth of Haleakalā. I gripped the side of the plane with my hands. The metal was hot.

"Pull up," I screamed. "Pull up!"

"Calm down, Dave!" Walton said. "You're ruining the ride!"

"Pull up the damn plane right now or I swear to God I will throw you both out the door and land it myself!" I was screaming. I might have been crying.

"Hey, Dave!" BB said, smiling. The idiot was actually smiling. "You wanna fly the plane, be my guest!"

BB let go of the stick. He put both arms over his head and laughed. This was it. I was going to die. And, as I've always imagined, it was all Bill Walton's fault. I froze, paralyzed. I saw my wife's face. Then, miraculously, just as we made it to the edge of the crater, the plane began to rise. BB's hands were still in the air but we were going up. We were going up fast. Like God himself reached down and grabbed the plane in his hand.

"What's happening?! How are you doing this?!" I yelled.

"Thermal soaring!" BB explained. "Hot air rises and so do we! We took a free ride, brother!" BB grabbed the stick and finally turned us away from the volcano and down the west side of the mountain, opposite of where the lava was flowing. We landed on a tiny airstrip on the coast. The small wheels under the seaplane's pontoons felt every single bump in the runway. I had my eyes closed and was fervently praying when we finally came to a halt. We made it. Alive. But I looked over at BB and decided right then and there that I would never forgive the dirty little hippie for scaring me like that.

Chapter 4

The tiny airstrip where we landed was more like a mini-airport. It had a gas pump and even a small terminal where a dozen or so people could comfortably wait for a plane. Next to that was an airplane hangar. BB opened the door to the hangar and turned on the lights to reveal a giant, old Boeing 737 with Air Force Fun painted along the side in fading letters.

"Oh, no. No more plane rides, please. Where is this party?"

"No, Dave. The party's right here on Maui. We're driving. That's the Pope's private plane."

I looked at him. "There's no way that hunk of junk is the Pope's plane. Plus, I happen to know the Pope's plane is called Shepherd One not Air Force Fun."

The two hippies laughed at me.

"No, not that Pope," Walton said. "The Pope is our friend's nickname. We're going to his birthday party. That's the surprise. You're gonna love it, Pasch!"

Ugh. I should have known. Walton pulled me away from an awesome luau to go to some stupid birthday party for another dirty old hippie. BB opened the door of a Toyota Land Cruiser parked under the wing of the plane. It was from the 80's, boxy and green. BB lowered the driver's side visor and a set of keys fell into his hand.

After a bumpy few minutes on dirt roads that carved through thick mountain jungle, the road stopped twisting and turning as a guard house appeared. BB braked in front of a sturdy boom gate that looked strong enough to stop a tank. A high chain-link fence topped with concertina wire stretched into the jungle on both sides. It was like entering a military base. Weird.

BB rolled the window down as two men exited the guard house. They were both Polynesian, with the stocky, muscular build of rugby players.

"Hello Swiss Guard!" Walton shouted from the passenger seat.

The men wore tan linen pants and blue polo shirts stretched to their maximum capacity. The polos had an emblem on them that read, "Paniolo Hale." BB and Walton greeted the two men like old friends. Their names were Ani and Ahi. Ani had a shaved head and a cauliflower ear. Ahi had long black hair to his shoulders, which I assumed covered at least one cauliflower ear of his own.

"Mr. Pasch. Nice to see you. I hope you have a good time tonight," Ahi said.

"Oh, they told you I was coming?" I asked, confused.

"No, dude. You're famous. We know who you are," Ani said, smiling.

I laughed. Already starting to feel more at ease. Ahi hit a button and the boom gate rose.

"Thank you, Ahi and Ani!" Hollered Walton as BB gently guided the Land Cruiser onto the property. The narrow jungle road continued for another hundred yards or so then opened up to reveal... well, paradise.

A palatial estate sprouted from the side of the mountain, looking like the world's most expensive tree house. Large tropical vines hung from the house, showcasing hundreds of the beautiful white hibiscus flowers associated with Hawaii. The grounds were immaculately maintained, looking like a garden you would see outside a museum. Festive lights were everywhere, creating a party atmosphere.

We got out of the car and joined the party. Hundreds of people were coming and going from the big house on the hill. The place smelled like flowers and delicious food, depending on the breeze. Someone was walking toward us, smiling. It was legendary basketball-coach-turned-hippie, Don Nelson. I almost didn't recognize him. I still remember the old-school coach he once was. A heavyset, red-faced maniac fueled by coffee, alcohol, fast breaks, and winning.

"Nellie!" Walton said as he embraced the man who now looked more Gandalf than Bobby Knight. "It looks like Maui is treating you well!"

"Bill, I love living here. I just love it. Everything used to piss me off. I mean everything. Now, nothing does. I feel great. Peaceful. Oh, speaking of…"

The Hall of Fame coach pulled a small mason jar from the pocket of his black blazer. He unscrewed it and took out a large green bud of marijuana that glimmered under the lights like it had been dipped in sparkle glitter.

"The latest batch of Nelly Kush," he said as proudly as a grandfather holding his grandson. "Frankly, it's my masterpiece." He reached into another pocket and pulled out three tubes. "These are for you guys. One each."

As he handed us the tubes, I realized they each contained an enormous marijuana joint. Just huge. They were roughly the size and shape of ice cream cones.

"Save 'em for a special occasion."

I tried to give mine back but Nellie refused to take it. Walton and BB assured me I was being rude so I stuck it in the pocket of my red Arizona Cardinals windbreaker that I grabbed before we left the hotel. BB popped his tube open and announced there wouldn't be many occasions more special than "right here, right now."

They lit up the gargantuan joint and a cloud of smoke surrounded them like Pig Pen's dust. That was my cue. Whenever Walton and his friends lit a joint, I always walked in the opposite direction seeking fresh air. With Walton involved, it was usually a pretty long walk.

Chapter 5

I walked down a garden path cut into a grove of bamboo. I took out my phone and called my wife to complain about the turn my night had taken, courtesy of Bill Walton.

"David. Why do you listen to that tall, crazy man?"

I laughed. I didn't have a good answer for that question. I never did. We talked some more, I told her I loved her and then we hung up as I came across a little wooden bridge that forded a stream that splashed down the mountain into a small pond. I paused for a moment on the bridge to look down at the giant koi fish swimming near the surface. The sound of the water pouring over the rocks was very relaxing. I walked on and found a little tiki bar along the path, seemingly oddly placed in the middle of this zen jungle. I sat down next to an older, silver-haired man in a deep green Hawaiian shirt with yellow pineapples and ukuleles. He was finishing a cocktail and looking up at the stars. I looked around.

"Is there a bartender or do I just get my own drink?"

"I think it's self-service," the silver-haired man said as he got up. "But allow me."

"Oh, you don't have to do that."

"No worries. I need a refill and it's as easy to make two as it is to make one. You okay with a Mai Tai?"

"Sure," I said. Damn. I just wanted a beer.

"You don't sound like you're sure."

"Sorry." I smiled. Busted. "I don't really like sweet, fruity drinks."

The silver-haired man laughed.

"Well, my friend, your first mistake is thinking of the Mai Tai as a drink. The Mai Tai is not a drink. It's an idea." He said, smiling. "The idea of paradise. What everyone dreams about. A perfect beach, the sun going down, Bunny Wailer singing in the background. A Mai Tai in their hands. It's a dream you can drink."

"A dream?" I asked. "About what? Novelty umbrellas?" He laughed again. A warm, loud laugh. He looked at me.

"Did you know that the cocktail umbrella was invented right here on this island by an enterprising young bartender who wanted to save the ice in his drinks from melting in the hot sun?"

"Is that true?" I asked.

"Could be." He laughed again. "The truth about truth is that in history, as the years unfurl, it's the best story that survives, not the most accurate."

As he spoke, he filled a silver cocktail shaker with rum and various juices, fitted it with a glass and began to shake it over his shoulder, turning his ear toward it like a musician listening to an instrument. His hands moved like a magician. Graceful, hypnotic, surprising. He clanged the metal shaker against the bar and twisted off the glass with no effort at all. He poured the concoction into two tall, glass tumblers and garnished them with a flourish of lime and a sprig of mint.

"Here you go. No umbrella," he said, handing it to me. "Cheers." We clinked glasses. I took a sip and was blown away. It was the best cocktail I ever had in my life. It was tasty and refreshing with the perfect amount of kick from the rum. I thanked my spontaneous bartender and moved on, heading in the direction of the unmistakable chatter of an excellent get-together. I met up with Walton along the winding path after passing a friendly woman who offered me a big, warm smile as she walked by. After she turned the corner, I stopped in my tracks.

"Wait a minute. Was that Meryl Streep?"

"Indeed! A wonderful philanthropist!"

"Uh, Bill. She's also an amazing actress?"

"Inconsequential!"

Walton and I headed up to the house, passing more celebrities in music, arts and politics than I'd ever seen gathered in one place. It was like my head was on a swivel. The security at the front gate was beginning to make a lot more sense. Who was this Pope character?

The house had huge, floor-to-ceiling doors that were all opened to a giant patio. It felt like we were still outside on this perfect night. There was a pool on the patio, which was currently covered by a glass floor that people were dancing on. It reminded me of the dance floor in Bedford Falls that opened to a pool that Jimmy Stewart and Donna Reed fell into. Whoever this Pope guy was, he really did have a wonderful life. And unlike George Bailey, he seemed to be rich in both money and friends.

We were met at the door by a short, thin Korean man who greeted Walton by handing him a kombucha on a silver tray that looked heavy in his frail arms. I don't know how old he was, but I would have believed he was anywhere from fifty to ninety and he couldn't have weighed a hundred pounds soaking wet. He was completely bald and wore a long-sleeved Hawaiian shirt. It was solid black with very subtle embroidery that gave it depth and texture. He wore matching black pants and black shoes. Walton put a hand on his shoulder. It was like covering a walnut shell with a frisbee.

"Samangja! How did you know I desperately wanted a high-alcohol Kombucha?!"

"Bill, it's literally all you ever drink," I whispered out of the side of my mouth.

"Pasch, this is Samangja! The Pope's... well, I don't know what to call you."

"I am Mr. Paul's butler."

"Butler? No! God, no! You're not a butler, you're the force that holds Pope's universe together! Samangja you are gravity." Samangja blushed adorably at Walton's thunderous praise.

"Welcome, Mr. Pasch. Please let me know if there's anything I can get you. Anything at all."

Samangja smiled and headed off. He shuffled more than walked, taking small, careful steps as if his shoelaces were tied together. I watched him help a guest who had spilled wine all over himself. It was Yo-Yo Ma.

Chapter 6

Walton and I went out to the patio. Walton spread his arms, showing me the extent of Pope's estate. It was extraordinary. Right on the coast, his land was bordered only by the ocean to the south and to the west. To the north, I could see nothing but fields and jungle for miles and miles. And, to the east, right behind us, was Haleakalā. We joined a group of people watching the volcano. The deck offered an incredibly close-up view of the smoke slowly rising into the black clouds above. I knew first-hand from our recent near-death flight over the volcano that the lava was flowing to the other side of the mountain. I just wish I was as confident as everyone else seemed to be that the lava wouldn't eventually spill over to our side.

"Pasch did you know that this type of eruption is called a 'Hawaiian eruption?'"

"Yes, Bill. And if the volcano was in Alaska, it'd be an Alaskan eruption."

"Incorrect! I was referring to the gentle flow of lava, not the state in which it's located!"

"I was just kidding, Bill."

"Pasch, you shouldn't joke about volcanoes! It's bad luck!"

"You're right about that."

I turned to see a man who, according to his uniform, was Commander Kirby of the US Navy. He cut a dashing image in his dress whites, tan skin and crooked smile.

"Joking about volcanoes can offend the goddess Pele. And trust me, that's the last thing you want to do. On the big island, there's a gallery in Volcano Village that displays the letters of people who took volcanic rocks back to the lower forty-eight and were then beset by a string of terrible bad luck so rotten, they'd send back the lava rocks with a letter of apology to Pele."

"Exactly! Pasch, apologize to Pele!" Walton demanded.

"Maybe later," I said to Walton as I turned to the Navy man. "Nice to meet you, Commander Kirby, I'm Dave Pasch."

"Oh, I know who you fellas are. I'm a big fan. You can call me Roy," he said, shaking our hands as his Southern accent kicked in.

"So, Roy. How do you know the Pope?"

"Oh, the usual. We met while we were both stranded in the middle of the Pacific Ocean during a tropical cyclone."

I laughed. Commander Kirby sipped his drink as the people around us turned to listen to his story.

"So, there I was. Sailing around Kauai in my catamaran. I had just broken up with my girlfriend and, in my opinion, there's nothing that puts a man's heart back together like the blue ocean, a six pack, and a fishing pole. So, I was out there, clearing my head, not catching anything but a buzz, when a big storm came in from the west and I decided to head in. I was almost home when I heard a faint SOS call on my radio. I caught the latitude and longitude before the transmission dropped out. I knew I should just get the heck out of there but, because I'm an idiot, I turned around and headed straight into the storm."

Commander Kirby took another sip of his drink and continued his story.

"Now, when the sea turns angry, it doesn't waste time. Waves got so big, I quickly realized I had made a horrible decision. But I kept sailing towards the coordinates until I came to a capsized 40-foot cruiser. It was a beautiful boat. Even upside down. Pope and his buddy BB, whose name is spelled like the gun, had climbed on top and were holding on for dear life. I pulled alongside as best I could and threw them a rope just as a rogue wave hit us. I don't know what happened, but when I finally came up for air, my catamaran was heading down Davy Jones' way. I tell ya, it sank faster than Jack Dawson when Rose kicked him off that door. So, I swam over to the cruiser, climbed up there with Pope and BB, stuck out my hand and said, "Hello there, I'm Commander Roy Kirby and I've come to rescue you.""

We all laughed. I looked up and realized there was now a crowd around Commander Kirby as he finished the story.

Everybody was smiling and hanging on every word. I did a double-take when my eyes passed Warren Buffett and Miley Cyrus.

"Now, Hawaii officially has 137 islands, most of them inhabited. After clinging to that capsized cruiser all night we woke up on one of 'em. I still don't know which one it was, and if anyone finds it, please bring me back my car keys."

More laughter.

"We spent two days on that island before our good friends in the Coast Guard found us. And in those two days, Pope, BB, and I survived on the freshest seafood I've ever had in my life and became great friends. Though, I would have traded either one of them for a keg of beer and a lemon."

I laughed along with the rest of the large group that huddled around Commander Kirby. I gotta give it to him, that was a pretty good story. Maybe even better than Coach K's Dream Team story.

I'll never know.

Chapter 7

I finished my Mai Tai, savoring it to the last drop. I didn't realize how hungry I was until I spotted the line for the buffet. I still hadn't had dinner. I excused myself and got in line behind a woman I couldn't help but notice. She was tall, tan, fit, and wearing a stunning "Deep V" dress that glided over her shoulders and plunged to her belly button. We exchanged smiles.

"Amazing, isn't it?" She said, looking around.

I nodded. "Heck of a party."

"No, the house."

I followed her eyes to the ceiling.

"Carved koa wood. One of the rarest trees in the world. You can't even cut them down anymore, you can only harvest fallen trees. Very expensive."

I nodded.

"The Pope built this place from the ground up. When he bought the land, it was just a cow pasture with a hut. The old paniolo sold it to him for cash. And for years he built and rebuilt and added on to what he calls Paniolo Hale. That means 'Cowboy House.'"

She gestured at the house and laughed.

"Yeah, right. Designed by I.M. Pei. Complete with a restaurant-quality kitchen, spa, home theater, state-of-the-art recording studio and a guest house Secret Service-approved for sitting Presidents. Yee-haw."

We moved down the buffet line, though calling it a 'buffet' didn't do it justice. It belonged in a Renaissance painting.

"You know, I tried to buy this place from the Pope last year. I had big, respected investors all lined up. We were going to convert it into an eco-hotel. This would have been the lobby," she said, gesturing to where we were standing. "The rooms would have been built right into the sides of the mountain. Very organic. Trees wouldn't be cut down, of course. They'd be moved. If possible. We did all the environmental surveys. It was all going to work. We made him a very generous offer and he, like, got offended."

"Yes, well, it's also on the side of an erupting volcano," I said. "Maybe not the best place for a hotel?" She smiled at me like I was missing it completely.

"Life in Hawaii is beautiful precisely because there is an element of danger to it. People drown every day. Drive off the roads into ravines." She nodded to the volcano. "Living next to earth's ticking time bombs forces you to appreciate, to feel gratitude, for life."

"Wow. I never thought of it like that." I paused, trying to think of something to say that was smart and cool. "So, you from here?"

Ugh. Nice job, Pasch.

"My mom is. My dad's from Detroit. He came here on vacation, met my mom, and never went back home."

"Aww. How romantic."

"Yeah. It'd be more romantic if he wasn't already married. But, it is what it is."

"Mmhmm."

At the end of the buffet, David Chang himself handed me a cut of pork shoulder that looked like it had been slowly roasting for a month.

"Whoa." I turned around and whispered, impressed. "David Chang."

"Yeah, he does all of Pope's events. Does it for free, as well, from what I understand. The Pope was one of his first big investors." She shrugged. "I find everything a bit salty."

This was a hard woman to impress. Before we headed off in our different directions, she handed me her business card.

Nalani Richardson. Realtor.

"Nice to meet you. If you ever think about buying property on Maui, let me know. Maybe not today. Tomorrow. A week from now. A year from now. Ten years from now. Hawaii can have that effect on people. Eventually it'll pull you back. When it does, give me a call."

"We'll see. I like to be surrounded by a few thousand more miles of land at all times."

"Keep the card. You never know."

Nalani winked and disappeared in a sea of powerful, beautiful people. She fit right in.

Chapter 8

I was starving. I sat down and dug into an incredible meal. If you ask me, it was the perfect amount of salt. I gave David Chang a thumbs up. I don't think he saw me. I smiled as Walton joined me at the table with his own plate of food.

"So, Dave. Having a good time, or would you like to go back to the conference room at the Hyatt?"

"Okay, okay. I surrender. You were right. This is amazing."

"I told you! Always trust me, Pasch! I have never steered you wrong!"

"Bill, that is not true. But, I have to ask. Who is the Pope?"

"Oh man, this cat doesn't know who the Pope is?"

I frowned as BB joined us at the table. Judging by his plate of greens, he was a vegetarian. Another reason not to like the guy.

"Where do I begin?" Walton wondered.

"How about the beginning?" BB giggled. Clearly the effects of Don Nelson's joint were coursing through his mind and body.

Walton smiled. "The Pope grew up in San Francisco. Back then he was just Jon Paul. The nickname came later."

"I assume around 1978?"

"Exactly! How did you know?"

"Pope John Paul? First and Second? 1978?"

Walton just looked at me and shrugged. I shook my head. Marijuana.

"Anyway, Jon Paul's dad ran a radio station up there. KCSM in San Mateo. He grew up at the station, surrounded by music, DJs, and musicians. He loved tinkering with the equipment. He was always taking stuff apart and putting it back together. That kind of thing. He was a brilliant student, but bored by school. Eventually he dropped out of college and dropped into the Haight Ashbury scene full-time."

"Early sixties. Haight Ashbury. Talk about right place, right time. Why do the legends always end up at a legendary place at a legendary time?" BB chimed in.

"He followed the dancing bears!" Walton said.

"The bears are always dancing!"

They toasted drinks. I did not. As is my standing policy in regard to Grateful Dead references.

"Since Jon Paul had access to a bunch of recording equipment, Bay Area bands, of which there were many, kept asking him to record them. Demos. Concerts. Whatever. He'd get paid in pizza or beer or weed and was happy."

Walton leaned in, excited.

"In fact, around this time, Jon Paul recorded a few shows for a little band called Mother McCree's Uptown Jug Champions. Later they changed their name to the Warlocks and, my friend, do you know what they changed their name to after that?"

"Gee Bill, was it the Grateful Dead?"

Walton was stunned silent. He was very upset.

"Yes, Pasch. It was the Grateful Dead," he said quietly then pouted, loudly sighing in my direction as BB took over the story.

"So, while hanging out and recording bands and having fun, Jon Paul kept tinkering around with microphones. He'd been doing it his whole life, and eventually he put one together that revolutionized the music industry. I tell ya, if you hear a song from the 70s or 80s, it probably was recorded on one of Jon Paul's mics. He made a ton of money. Millions! That's when he bought his own plane."

"Air Force Fun?"

"Yes!" Walton said, taking the story back. "Jon Paul was still crashing on his friend's couches when he bought a 737. He outbid a guy trying to buy it in Memphis. His name was Fred Smith and he wanted the plane for a business he was starting up. The Pope felt bad for outbidding him and bought him another plane. He also invested in his fledgling company. Turned out to be a very smart investment, Dave. Do you want to know the name of the company?"

"FedEx?"

It was a long while before Walton would look at me again.

"I'm sorry, Bill. I just know who Fred Smith is. Please finish the story. I swear. I won't say another word."

Walton still wouldn't look at me. BB picked the story back up.

"So, I had just come back from Vietnam. I was hanging around the airport in Memphis looking for a job spraying crops or somethin' when a thirty-year-old homeless multi-millionaire hired me to fly him around the world recording all my favorite bands."

"So Jerry!" Walton boomed.

"Very Jerry," BB said, echoing Walton's Deadhead philosophy to describe all luck and coincidence as being "Jerry."

Walton had either stopped being mad at me, or forgot he was mad at me, and launched back into the story.

"So, the Pope was on top of the world. And that's when he met Tandy."

"May she rest in peace," BB said, touching his heart.

"She was a wonderful woman, a perfect yin to his yang. They got married. Had a son."

Walton looked around and pointed out a guy with a carefully trimmed beard and round glasses who had tattoos poking out from the sleeves of his black t-shirt.

"Arlo Paul. He's in town for the party. He lives in Manhattan."

"Guy's a piece of shit."

"BB!" Walton chastised, then turned back to me. "Sadly, BB's not wrong. But to lose your mother at such a young age..."

Walton's eyes got moist.

"Tandy was killed in a car accident when Arlo was five. Got hit by a semi. Guy had cocaine in his system." Walton paused, still stung by the memory. "Remember, Pasch. No powders, pills, or needles."

"Or marijuana or hallucinogens," I said.

Walton and BB shook their heads at me in pity.

I shook mine right back.

"The Pope was destroyed. He threw himself into his work. He ran his company. He sat on the boards of major corporations. He advised presidents. Kept recording. Always advancing technology. It never stopped. Everyone wanted their song 'blessed by the Pope.' But it took its toll on him. He was running on empty.

"After years and years of this, we finally convinced the Pope to take a vacation. To Maui. And, thankfully, Hawaii quickly worked its magic. He started taking walks every day. And every day he walked a little longer, walked a little farther. One day he didn't come back. We freaked out and came looking for him. And found him right here, on the side of this mountain, at--"

"The Cowboy House."

"Pasch, will you please let me tell the story?!" Walton boomed.

"Sorry. Go on."

"That's it. That's the story. The end. Good-bye."

I apologized. He huffed at me.

Then the lights went out.

Chapter 9

A spotlight hit the center of a stage that had been set up in the living room. My silver-haired bartender approached the microphone to thunderous applause.

"Hey, I know that guy," I said to Walton. "He made me a Mai Tai."

"Pasch, you fool! That's the Pope!"

"That's the Pope?"

"Of course! Jon Paul, the legend! The man of the hour! Hallowed be his name!"

"Thank you so much for coming to my birthday party," the Pope said into the mic. He sounded great. I can only assume he did his own sound.

"For my 75th birthday I've decided to give a gift. I want to give back to the state that has done so much for me. Hawaii took me in, gave my soul shelter, taught me the true meaning of mahalo. And now I want to give something back, before the day I say the big aloha."

The crowd shouted "No!"

Someone yelled, "Seventy-five more years!" It was Walton.

That got a laugh from the Pope. "Maybe. Why not? But when that day comes, whenever that day comes, I've decided to gift this place. To this place. I'm donating my entire estate to Hawaii on the condition that it become a state park. Open to the public so everyone can enjoy it the way I have. So, to my good friend Kelly Kaluhiokalani, the honorable Governor of the great state of Hawaii, the Cowboy House is yours."

The Governor, a warm, gregarious woman with a silver streak in her brown hair, walked on stage and hugged the Pope to a raucous standing ovation.

"Okay, that's more than enough of me talking," the Pope said, stepping back to the microphone. "Now, please, enjoy yourselves. There's plenty of food, drink, and now we are very lucky to be entertained by my good friend, Moses Boulevard."

Wow. I raised my eyebrows at the mention of the name Moses Boulevard. He was the kind of famous it would take effort not to know. My kids will go crazy when I tell them I was at a party with Moses Boulevard. He was a huge star. Not necessarily my kind of music, but it was super cool he was here.

"Pope knows Moses Boulevard?" I asked.

"Oh yeah. He's staying in the guest house while they record a new album. Very cool. Nice dude. Gets high," BB said, with an insane amount of spinach in his teeth. I couldn't even see the gold tooth anymore. I hated this guy.

Moses Boulevard launched into his first song and a crowd of people, including a woman who may or may not have been Diane Sawyer, rushed the stage and started jumping up and down with their phones in the air, recording the show.

The Pope worked his way through the room, shaking hands and eventually arrived at our table. We all stood to congratulate him. Walton and the Pope enjoyed a long hug, then Walton introduced me to the man of the hour. I found myself suddenly feeling nervous.

"Happy Birthday, Mr. Paul," I gushed. "Sorry, I didn't know who you were earlier. Thanks for the drink. It was delicious."

"It was my pleasure, Dave. I'm a big fan of yours. Just not as big a fan as this lady right here. Guys, this is Governor Kaluhiokalani," he said as she approached. "She is officially your number-one fan. She was thrilled to find out you'd be here tonight and might have me kicked off the island if I didn't introduce you."

I had to give it to him. The Pope turned me from a nervous geek into a confident big shot in about three seconds flat. I shook hands with the Governor, who was surrounded by an entourage of her own.

"Dave Pasch, so nice to meet you. I'm a huge, huge fan. I'll be at the Kentucky/Chaminade game tomorrow afternoon, but I'm bringing headphones so I can hear you and Walton call the game. I wouldn't miss it. I'm going to enjoy watching those bluegrass boys go down."

I thanked her, though I didn't have as much faith in the success of the Governor's hometown Chaminade team as she did. While talking to the Governor, I noticed the Pope turn to BB and ask to speak to him privately for a second. Why anyone would want to speak privately with that stinky little weirdo is beyond me. BB nodded stiffly. He seemed uncharacteristically quiet and nervous. I watched as the scruffy pilot walked off with the Pope.

I didn't see anything else because that's when Moses Boulevard launched into his hit song, Last Bullet. Even I knew that song. I heard it played in stadiums and arenas during almost every game I announced for the past decade. And now I was hearing it live. I joined the crowd that had rushed the stage. In the fray, I got elbowed in the head by a particularly excited fan.

It was Diane Sawyer.

Chapter 10

"With just three minutes to go, Cal is down eleven points to Gonzaga."

This was shaping up to be an inauspicious start for the University of California, Berkeley in the Maui Invitational.

"Come on, Golden Bears! Where is your roar?! Are you in hibernation?! Dave, did you know bears do in fact often wake up during hibernation to eat and relieve themselves? They're so much like us!"

Sometimes it was best to just ignore Walton.

"Freshman point guard Kenny 'Woosie' Montague brings up the ball for Cal. The five-star recruit dribbles to the top of the key and Maki Sakamoto, Cal's seven-foot senior, is calling for the ball in the post. But Woosie pulls up and shoots another three."

At least, I thought it was a three. Calling these games was tricky because of all the different lines on the court. In addition to three different three-point lines for the basketball court, the Lahaina Civic Center also had yellow lines for a volleyball court and a mysterious third, red-lined court for a sport I didn't recognize. When in doubt, I always kept an eye on the referees to see what was and wasn't a three-pointer. Turns out, it was a three, but it didn't go in.

"Woosie is struggling from the field, but not from lack of trying."

"This is absurd! Feed it to the big man! He posted up a guy half his size. The mouse was in the house! Dave, I have mice in my house. It's a terrible problem. It's hard to get rid of mice humanely. But it's the only way! We're all God's creatures! Who's to say who's in charge? Perhaps my wife and I should be put in glue traps and released in a field! That would be nice. A pleasant vacation!"

As Walton ranted about mice, Gonzaga grabbed the rebound and stretched their already impressive lead with a fastbreak dunk. I tried to get Walton back on track.

"Bill, the Golden Bears need to wake up or they will find that aloha means goodbye here in the Maui invitational."

"Pasch, you fool! No one says goodbye at the Maui Invitational. Every team plays three glorious games!" I winced. It still stung when Walton called me a fool, even after a thousand times.

"Yes, Bill. Cal would still play, but I'm sure they'd prefer a shot at winning the tournament to playing in the loser's bracket."

"There's no such thing as a loser's bracket! They're playing basketball in paradise! They're all winners!"

"Okay, Bill." I conceded the point. "Gonzaga moving the ball around nicely. Dunlap with the ball in the corner. He shoots, and-- it's blocked by Sakamoto!"

"Rejection! Return to sender! Address unknown! Blessings to the men and women of the US Postal Service! Overworked and underappreciated since 1775! And on a personal note, I'd like to say thank you to my mail carrier, the intrepid Gwendelyn! Neither snow nor rain nor heat nor gloom of night stays that courier from the swift completion of her appointed rounds! Amazing! Thank you, Gwendelyn, for all that you do."

Walton was in rare form, which meant he was in very normal form.

After the blocked shot, Woosie grabbed the loose ball and initiated a fast break. Sakamoto ran down the middle of the court. He was wide open for an easy bucket, but Woosie pulled up and took another long three that again missed its mark. Walton went apoplectic.

"What did I just watch?! Please! Feed it back to the big man after a block like that! Reward him! He ran the length of the court and was ready to throw it down! This is a travesty! I need to wash my eyes out with apple cider vinegar."

"Gonzaga hits a three, to go up fourteen with under two minutes to play, and Coach 'Fast' Eddie Bianchi is showing his frustration on the sidelines."

Fast Eddie was a fan favorite, easily recognizable with his white hair gelled in place like a helmet, along with his gold chain and year-round tan. He was screaming at his players, assistants, and the heavens in equal measure as he called his last timeout before the game slipped away.

"Okay, guys. We're staying here during the timeout." Stephanie's voice came through our headphones. "Give me some of that sweet, sweet filler. Come on, Pasch. Hit me with a 'you know, Bill.'"

I smiled. Stephanie made calling the games fun.

"You know, Bill…" I heard the video truck cheer in my headset. "The knock on Fast Eddie is that, while he's a great recruiter, he's perhaps a little loose with the discipline. His teams are known for having fun, on and off the court. Bill, it seems like you would have loved playing for Fast Eddie."

"Incorrect! Nothing could be further from the truth! I craved discipline! Excelled under it! I assure you, John Wooden was not fun to play for. Every practice was pure torture from beginning to end, and I loved it! Thanked him for it! Structure! Discipline! Freedom and experimentation was for my personal life!"

"Fast Eddie has never won a championship, maybe why he came out of retirement this year for another shot."

"Maybe a man's motivations are his own, Pasch, and it's insulting to speculate about them."

I stared into the camera. My signal to Stephanie that I was reaching the end of my tether with Walton. Stephanie threw me a life preserver by cueing up a graphic of Fast Eddie's coaching history complete with a nifty "Fast Eddie" race car graphic. In the few seconds we watched the graphic, I was able to catch my breath and get a second wind.

"Bill, Fast Eddie is a legend for his 'Fun and Gun' style of play. However, he has been criticized for his clock management. He rarely has timeouts at the end of the game, when he needs them most."

"Do you know how many timeouts John Wooden called in my career at UCLA?" Walton said, and folded his arms over his chest, absentmindedly crushing his leis.

"How many, Bill?" I sighed.

"One. And it was by accident. He was scratching his hand and the ref thought he was calling a timeout. He was furious. He wouldn't let us sit down and he said nothing for three minutes. We just stood there sweating. We were up by thirty, as usual."

The horn sounded and the game was back. Thank God.

"Woosie inbounds the ball to Kelly Prows, and the Cal junior immediately launches a long three that hits the back of the rim, and Gonzaga is off on yet another fast break. Dunlap goes to lay it in and-- Ouch! Sakamoto takes him out with a hard foul. Oh, no. Dunlap flies into the stands. I hope he's alright."

The crowd's reaction was not positive.

"That's Sakamoto's fifth foul and it's an ugly one. He fouls out with a minute left to play and the fans are really letting him have it on his way to the bench. You hate to see that, Bill. But thankfully, Dunlap appears to be alright."

"Completely unnecessary hard foul! With the game out of reach? Frustration misplaced!"

"Sakamoto leaves the game with nine blocks, twelve rebounds and... wow... only seven points. He's had a dominant game, but hasn't scored much."

"It's sad! It's like watching a dormant volcano! He needed to erupt like the mighty and powerful Haleakalā! And not with dirty fouls, but by throwing it down!"

"Well, Bill. It's hard to throw it down if you don't have the ball."

"Yes! It's a travesty of epic proportions! The best player on the court has been rendered useless by his own team! It goes to show you, every big man is at the mercy of his guards. I thank all the guards in my career who fed me the rock and let me throw it down. Greg Lee! Henry Bibby! Geoff Petrie! Dave Twardzik! Lionel Hollins, Dennis Johnson! Blessings! Mahalo! Thank you for the ball. Thank you for my life!"

The rest of the game was uneventful. Woosie Montague finally drained a couple of threes to keep the margin of victory under twenty points. The teams left the court and we started packing up our things in the brief downtime between games.

I turned my phone back on. As my screen popped to life, I was surprised to remember it was only eleven-thirty in the morning. The games started early in Maui and there were three more to go. We'd have a nice, long afternoon break before calling the last game of the day between Kentucky and Chaminade.

"What is going on?!" Walton said, looking at his phone. "I have fifty missed calls and texts!"

While Walton was trying to figure out what was happening, BB appeared in the front row of the stands.

"Walton!" He yelled. "Hey, Bill!"

BB was acting crazier than last night, which is saying something. The idiot climbed down over the railing into the restricted press area. He kept calling for Walton while squeezing by the great P. J. Carlesimo, who was none too pleased that a scraggly hippie was disturbing his post-game radio broadcast. I watched P.J. cover his mic and gesture at his producer, Kyle, to call security. I certainly wasn't going to stop him.

BB ran up to Walton, who, with one look at his friend's face, knew something was terribly wrong. "BB. What is it?"

"Bill, the Pope is dead."

"What?! What happened?!"

"Somebody shot him, man. Shot him at his house this morning. He's dead. The Pope is dead."

Walton looked at his phone, dumbstruck. This was the news that was pouring in from calls, texts, and emails.

"No. No! Who would do that? Who would shoot Jon Paul?!"

"Do the police have a suspect?" I asked.

"Yeah, man," BB said, looking around the arena. "They got a fuckin' suspect. Me!"

That's when I noticed, near the top of the stands, two police officers working their way down through the parting crowd. I looked around. There were cops coming down from every exit, heading right for us.

BB grabbed the front of Walton's Hawaiian shirt, his face pale and desperate. "Bill, you gotta believe me, man. Whatever you hear. Whatever they say. I didn't do it."

At once, a dozen hands grabbed BB and pulled him away, into the bowels of the arena.

"I didn't do it, Walton!" BB yelled. "I didn't kill the Pope!" The words echoed around the gym as they hauled him off.

"You fools! You're arresting an innocent man!"

"We don't know that, Bill. We don't know anything."

"Well, Dave," Walton said, clenching his fists, "then it's time we found out everything."

Chapter 11

Walton and I headed straight for the video truck, which the network had borrowed from a local Maui TV station. The door was open and most of the crew had filtered outside, enjoying the Hawaiian weather in the break between games. Nick Patel was sitting on the stairs to the truck, soaking up the sun and looking cool in his shades and brand-new Nikes. Of course, Nick's Nikes were always brand-new. I don't know what Nick's job title was, but when the score in the corner of your screen goes from 86 to 88, that was Nick. He was eating shave ice, a local "delicacy" of frozen sugar water which, in my humble opinion, was the worst thing Hawaii had to offer.

"Aloha, big red. Mr. Pasch. Want one?" He said, holding up his shave ice. It was rainbow colored. It looked like he was eating a clown's head. "Stephanie hired a guy with a cart to make these for us. She's the best."

"We don't have time for shaved ice, Nick! A legend has been murdered and they want to hang an innocent man!" Walton said brusquely.

"Wait, what?"

Walton pushed past a confused Nick into the truck where Stephanie was quietly working in the calm, professional environment with which she always surrounded herself. A candle was lit on the table. Wherever we went, it always smelled nice in the video truck. Today was pineapple and coconut. Stephanie looked up from her computer.

"Bill, I was just reading about your friend, Jon Paul. That's awful. What happened?"

"That's exactly what I intend to find out. Come on, we're going to the crime scene right now."

"Bill, I can't just leave. We have three more games to cover this afternoon. You know we all have jobs to do that don't just exist while you two are announcing games."

I saw Bill react. I'm not sure he knew that.

"Stephanie, please. We're a team! We need your help!"

Stephanie took a moment, clearly wanting to handle this delicately.

"Bill, what happened in Seattle was different. A young girl needed help and there was a reason we couldn't go to the police. But, as you well know, things got out of hand. We almost died, Bill."

"Your safety is paramount to me! That will never happen again! Let's go! Come on!"

"No. Seattle was my last Bill Walton adventure. I won't put myself in danger like that ever again. My priorities are my family and my job, Bill. That's it. I can't get involved." She looked back at the article on her computer. "Besides, I was reading the news. Reuters said the police already have someone in custody."

"Reuters is not news! It's PR for oil and gas companies. Please, the United Kingdom funded them in the '60s and '70s to push their anti-Russia propaganda! But yes, my friend was arrested. But he didn't do it! We have to find out what really happened! Stephanie, you must engage! You must answer the call!"

Stephanie looked at Bill with a steely resolve.

"Bill. I'm out."

Walton sank. This was obviously a rough morning for the big man.

"Okay, if that's the way it is. Dave and I will handle this. Come on, Dave."

We left the truck as Stephanie called after us. "Hey! I want your butts in your seats at five-thirty for the six o'clock game!"

"We'll be there," I assured her.

"And Walton!" Stephanie called.

Bill stopped and turned back.

"I'm sorry about your friend."

Bill nodded gratefully and we headed out of the truck.

"Door open or closed, Steph?" I asked her on the way out.

"Closed."

Chapter 12

I drove us to the Cowboy House in my rental car, a ruby-red Ford Mustang with a V-8 and four hundred and sixty very wild ponies under the hood. It was a convertible, which wasn't ideal for me. I had to wear my complementary Maui Invitational hat to protect my head from the sun so Walton could enjoy the infinite amount of headroom. Not that he was enjoying himself at the moment.

I powered us down the Honoapi'ilani Highway, thirty-five miles of bending, breathtaking coastal road. The mustang tore into curves like a machete through a coconut. The engine was throaty and angry sounding. Like it had a chip on its shoulder. God help me, I sure do love that Detroit muscle. Walton, however, seemed unimpressed with our current speed, which was already well over the limit.

"Pasch! Can't this thing go fast?!"

As a response, I dropped my foot down even further. The car surged forward and we were pushed back into our headrests. I turned up the radio. Elvis was singing "What Now My Love." The strings and achy Elvis performance of this epic ballad seemed to harmonize with the Mustang's power and the smooth Hawaiian highway. Despite the circumstances, I was enjoying myself. Then I saw Walton start fiddling with the radio. I knew what was happening and, while my attention was focused on a sharp turn I was taking a little too fast, he connected his phone and started playing, guess who?

The Grateful Dead.

I sighed as Jerry Garcia went on about having seen where the wolf slept by the silver stream or whatever, but I knew it wasn't the right moment to fight over the radio. Let Walton have it. I tuned out the music and focused on the open road ahead. It certainly kept my attention. The Lahaina Civic Center is on the northwest coast of the island. The Pacific Ocean was on our right as we headed to the southwest corner of the island. The drive took us an hour. A lot longer than our flight last night, not that it was worth it. I'd drive for days to avoid taking another flight with BB.

Walton guided me as we pulled off the highway onto a two-track that lead up into a half-dozen switchbacks, where the road turned sharply and doubled back on itself, again and again, to climb the steep mountain. After ten minutes or so, we reached the guard house.

"Ahi, Ani!" Walton shouted, getting out of the car even before I had a chance to stop the Mustang. "What happened?!"

"BB killed him, man. He shot him," Ani said.

"Impossible!" Walton pleaded.

"Sorry, bruddah," Ahi said, gesturing to the wall of security cameras we could see through the windows of the guard house. "We've gone through all the footage. He's the only one who could have done it."

"Show me," Walton said. Ani and Ahi led us into the guard house to the state-of-the-art security system.

"Wow. I guess the Pope took security pretty seriously," I said. "He didn't seem like the kind of guy who would live behind all these fences and cameras."

"It wasn't for him, Pasch. Please!" Walton said. "It was for his guests. Some of the most famous and powerful people in the world have stayed here. Rock stars! Captains of Industry! Presidents! Prime Ministers! And he valued their safety. Far above his own! Now please, Pasch, let them tell us what happened."

Ahi sat at the controls to the security system as Ani gave us the rundown.

"Okay, last guests left at two-thirty in the morning. After an event like this, it was customary for us to do a full sweep of the main house, guest house, and grounds before everyone went to bed. With Moses Boulevard in the guest house, we were on full alert. Especially with what's going on with him these days."

"Ah, Ellen Pishkin?" I asked.

They nodded. As famous as Moses was, everyone knew about her these days. She was on my Apple News Feed every morning. Ellen Pishkin was a troubled woman who was in love with Moses. In fact, she was convinced they had been married by God. She started showing up at the front row of his concerts in a wedding dress, then, alarmingly, started showing up at his home. Moses filed multiple restraining orders, but they didn't work. Then, tragically, a few years ago, Ellen Pishkin snuck into his apartment while Moses was asleep and stabbed him. Her plan was for both of them to die in bed that night and live together in eternity. Thankfully, her plan didn't work. Moses survived and, with a medieval dagger sticking out of his back, restrained her until the cops showed up and arrested her. But, two weeks ago, Ellen Pishkin escaped from the psychiatric hospital where she was being held. Nobody knew where she was.

"There you have it!" Walton said. "She must have snuck onto the grounds and killed the Pope!"

Ani and Ahi shook their heads.

"Give us more credit than that, Bill. No way we would've let that happen," Ahi said. "Besides, this morning she Tweeted a picture of herself getting off a plane in Maui, saying she was coming for her husband. She was on that flight during the murder. She couldn't have done it. The point is, last night we were on high alert."

"So, after the last guests left at two-thirty, we searched every inch of the main house and the grounds. It was clean. At three o'clock, we cleared the guest house before Moses went to bed." Ahi pointed to the pretty little building separated from the main house, providing privacy for both host and guest.

"Arlo and Samangja were in their bedrooms in the main house while Pope was down in his studio. The Pope never slept much. He'd chill out down there all night, tinkering with stuff, listening to music. When we said goodnight, a little after three o'clock, he was safe and sound. There was no one else on the property."

Ahi clicked through the footage of dozens and dozens of cameras showing every square inch of the grounds.

"But this was all after BB left! He flew me back to the hotel at one o'clock! Pasch insisted on taking a taxi, because he hates fun, but when we left, Pope was alive! BB couldn't have done it! Case closed!" Walton said, confidently.

"Sorry, buddy. BB came back," Ahi said as he pulled up the footage of BB driving up to the gate in the boxy old Land Cruiser. "Right there. BB pulls up at 5:03."

Walton watched with dread as BB, clear as day, pulled up to the gate.

"I signed him in. I was still on duty while Ahi got some shut eye." Ani nodded to a room in the back of the guard house. "BB said he had to talk to Pope. That wasn't unusual. They'd hang out for hours in the middle of the night. Used to life on the road, I guess. But what was unusual, is that BB was only in there five minutes. After that, he came right back out." Ahi fast-forwarded the footage and there was BB hurrying out of the studio. Almost running.

"Then he took off. Didn't even say goodbye. That was also weird. He always said goodbye." Ani said.

After a long beat of silence, I turned to Walton.

"He didn't do it," Walton insisted, but quieter.

"I hate to ask," I said. "But should we look at the footage inside the studio?"

"Can't." Ahi shook his head. "No cameras inside the house. Pope's rules. He wanted his guests to be safe but he didn't want to live under a lense. All the cameras are on the grounds, not in the house. But BB is the only one who came and went. Moses didn't leave the guest house until just after six o'clock. Right here."

They showed us Moses slowly walking from the guest house in a robe, opening the door to the studio and, without walking inside, stepping back in horror. There was no sound, but it seemed like he was screaming.

"I was right here when it all happened. I woke up Ahi and we came running. We found Pope's body. We would have resuscitated him if we could but... he was too far gone."

"Did you hear the gunshot?" I asked. It was funny, I believed in my heart BB killed the Pope, but my brain was still looking into every nook and cranny of the situation, trying to find any loose end it could.

Ani thought. "Well, no. But it's a sound studio. It's completely soundproof. He's had Dave Groll in there banging on the drums for hours and you couldn't hear a thing if your ear was pressed against the wall. Which mine was. I'm a big fan."

"Where was the gun?" I asked, still looking for loose ends. "Did BB bring it with him?"

"No. It was in the studio. It was in a glass case, like a display. Moses gave it to him when "Last Bullet" sold a million copies. It was a Smith & Wesson .44, an old Western gun mounted over a single, platinum bullet. BB smashed the glass and shot Pope with it."

"That didn't happen," Walton insisted.

I looked to Ani and Ahi. They seemed as convinced in BB's guilt as I did.

Ani motioned to the screens. "I don't know what to tell you, Bill. Pope was alive at three o'clock and he was dead at six o'clock. BB was the only one who came and left during that time."

"Can you get to the studio from inside the house?" I asked.

"Yeah. There are two entrances to the studio. One from inside the house and the one outside."

"So it could have been Samangja or Arlo!" Walton said, happy to finally have other suspects. Then he sank as he realized the only other suspects in Pope's murder were the people closest to him.

"Bill, do you really think Arlo killed his father? Or Samangja killed anybody?"

"No! I don't know! I'm just letting my mind explore the possibilities! I'm sick of these little screens. The screens can't replace the eyes. And ears. All six senses. Come on, Pasch. Let's investigate the crime scene."

Ahi and Ani stood up.

"Whoa, Bill. You shouldn't go up there."

It was too late. Bill stepped over the giant boom gate as easily as I would step over my kid's skateboard. He headed up to the house with a full head of steam and me, as always, in his wake.

Chapter 13

Yellow crime scene tape was strung across the doorway to the sound studio. Walton tore through it like a marathon runner. I paused before following him inside, knowing I was crossing a threshold of far more importance than a simple doorway.

The studio was beautiful. To my left, an old leather couch sat against the wall. Fresh island flowers sprung from a vase resting on a large, antique coffee table. The walls were crowded with artwork, framed posters from old concerts and a large oil painting featuring blocks of deep red against coal black. One wall was devoted to framed gold and platinum records. There was a giant mixing board to my right with a thousand little buttons and knobs facing a studio that could have fit a large band or a small orchestra. There was also a smaller vocal booth where the singers would go. On the floor of the studio, just as I walked in the room, was broken glass. Above it, on the wall, was a sturdy picture hanger hook in the middle of a large, blank space. The gun and the case were gone. The cops must have taken them in as evidence.

I finally worked up the courage to look at the one place I had avoided looking. Walton stood silently over the blood stain on the carpet. It was next to the chair by the mixing board. Jon Paul had clearly been sitting at the controls when he was shot.

"Who are you, and why are you in my crime scene?"

We turned. Standing in the doorway was a man in polished leather shoes and a pair of crisp black pants with a Hawaiian shirt tucked into them. I had never seen a Hawaiian shirt tucked in before. And it was as subdued as a Hawaiian shirt could be. Dark gray with wavy black lines and white flowers. The man's black hair was sprinkled with gray and pulled back into a tight ponytail. Walton and I were stunned into silence at his arrival.

"I'm Detective Palakiko of the Maui Police Department. I say again, who are you, and what are you doing in my crime scene?" He didn't raise his voice, but I heard each word clear as a bell.

"Detective, I'm Bill Walton and this is my partner, Dave Pasch. Jon Paul was my dear friend and we are here to help you find out who did this."

"Brian Baxter did this. We have him in custody."

"Wonderful! So you released BB?!"

"Uh, Bill. I think Brian Baxter is BB?" I suggested.

Walton thought about that and nodded.

Marijuana.

"Well, BB didn't do it. He has assured me of his innocence. You've made a terrible mistake, but it's a mistake we can help you correct. If we work together, I assure you we will find out who did this."

"We?" Detective Palakiko said, seemingly trying out the syllable for the first time in his life. "No. We won't be working together. I have another idea. I will work this case and you will spend the night in jail for interfering with a criminal investigation. Take them away."

Uniformed cops rushed into the room, swarming Walton and me, and they dragged us to the police cars parked outside. Walton screamed "fascists" over and over again as I saw my career flash before my eyes. Getting arrested and missing the next game, and maybe more, wouldn't make me any friends at network headquarters. That's if Steph didn't break into prison and kill us first.

"Wait, wait!" I screamed. "We're broadcasters! We're calling the Maui Invitational! We have a game to do tonight!"

"Not anymore," said Detective Palakiko. "Get them out of here!"

"Then you're going to have to explain that to the Governor! She's our biggest fan!"

The cops pushing and pulling us to the cars seemed to lose energy at the mention of the Big Kahuna. I went with it.

"It's true. She was at the party last night. She'll be at the game tonight. If we're not there, she's going to want to know why, and I'll be very happy to tell her who arrested us for just wanting to know who killed her very good friend!"

I was panting, out of breath. I talked for a living and rarely thought twice about the words coming out of my mouth. But this time, my career was on the line. Detective Palakiko held up his hand and the officers stopped.

"Is this true?"

"They do call the games, sir. The big guy played in the NBA. Won a championship with the Celtics," one of the cops said, nodding to Walton and then looked to me and shrugged. "Him I don't know."

Thanks a lot.

"I also won a championship with the Blazers, not that it matters. I competed. I won every time I tried my best. That's what I cherish in my heart, not the rings and trophies."

For the love of God, Walton. Not now.

"It's true," I said. "You can call the Governor. Or I can. I have her private number. She gave it to me last night."

I was lying. It wasn't the first time I went "all in" on a bluff. Usually there were a couple bucks at stake in a poker game. In this game, it was my freedom. I steeled my expression. Just like I did when I was holding nothing but a pair of threes. I tried to believe the lie. I had a full house. Aces over kings.

Detective Palakiko paused, taking a long, deep breath. It seemed to take forever, as if he was waiting as long as humanly possible before having to say the words he was about to say.

"Release them."

I sank with relief. Thank God.

"How long is this tournament?"

"Three days! The Maui Invitational ends the day before Thanksgiving every year! How can you not know that?! How can someone who doesn't know that possibly be trusted to find my friend's true killer?!" Walton bellowed as he ripped his arms away from the cops who held him.

I stared daggers at Walton, begging him not to poke this particular bear right as I was about to bluff our way out of the woods.

"Fine. Call your basketball tournament. But hear this: the second it is done, I want you off the island immediately. And, until then, I want you to steer clear of this investigation. If you interfere, in any way, shape, or form, I will lock you in jail myself. Even if that upsets our beloved Governor."

"Sir, you've got yourself a deal. You won't hear from us again. Thank you very, very much," I said as I grabbed Walton and dragged him to the car before he could say anything to change Detective Palakiko's mind. I fired up the Mustang and got us the heck out of there.

Dark clouds appeared about halfway through the trip home and, in an instant, warm tropical rain started to fall in ladle-sized drops. I had to pull over to the side of the road to put up the convertible's roof. I felt bad for Walton. With the top up, the Mustang was cramped, even for me. Walton was forced to lean the seat back and lie down for the trip back to the arena. He said nothing the entire time. I never heard Walton so quiet. He talked constantly. He talked in his sleep. The man's voicemail box was filled with his outgoing message. The reality of the Pope's death had finally hit my friend with its full weight.

"You know, Bill..." I said, breaking the silence as we arrived at the arena. "I could call Steph and get someone to fill in for you."

Walton didn't reply for a long time. The windshield wipers were the only noise.

"No," he said, finally. "I'm calling the game."

Maybe it's for the best. Maybe it would help take his mind off things. Maybe.

Chapter 14

"The jump shot hits the front of the rim and the rebound is jammed home! Wow, he really threw it down, eh Bill?"

"I don't know," Walton said. "I guess." Then he was quiet. The game was definitely not taking his mind off things. His mind was right smack-dab on top of things. I tried to steer him into a topic of conversation.

"That was freshman Gareth Reynolds, an athletic freak of nature who is a key part of this much heralded recruiting class. Kentucky seems to reload every year, Bill," I said. Walton said nothing. It was like fishing in a pothole after it rained. I tried again. "Do you have a problem with the one-and-done rules, Bill?"

"Why should I, Dave? We're all one-and-done here on this earth. One life and that's it. How will you spend it?"

"Calling basketball games with you, Bill. Like this exciting one."

"Will you get a good shot in this, your one possession? We all have a shot clock over our heads. Tick tock, Dave. Tick. Tock."

I was speechless. He had been like this for the entire game. As the game wound down, Walton proceeded to recite the entire lyrics of a Grateful Dead song from beginning to end. Completely ignoring the game. It was a little troubling how few fans on social media noticed anything strange. Stephanie kept egging me on, in my private feed, to pick up the energy. I rarely do that sort of thing, but I do believe at some point after a dunk, I may have screamed "hotchie motchie!" Not my proudest moment on air. It wasn't a good telecast. At one point I looked into the stands and saw the Governor take out her headphones. Even our biggest fan turned us off.

Thankfully, there couldn't have been many people watching. Kentucky predictably walloped Chaminade, the small, private university from Honolulu. After the game, I guided Walton out of the arena as quickly as possible. He was like a zombie. I ran over and thanked the Governor for coming, but was really thanking her for saving our butts. She'll never know it, but without her we'd be in jail right now.

Once outside the arena, I opened the car and, with the press of a button on my key fob, put the top down on the Mustang. Walton just stepped into the car without opening the door. He truly was a giant man, but so very fragile. Physically and, today, emotionally.

I drove us the short distance back to the hotel. If Walton was in bad shape, I wasn't doing too much better. It had been a long day. I was exhausted and hungry. I ran down the menu of the Hyatt Regency Poolside Bar and Grill in my head. I had been on the hotel's website all week and had the menu memorized. My sights were set on the Umalu Burger: Potato Bun, upcountry lettuce, tomato, pickle, and whatever a "maui onion" was, I wanted it. And yes, my friend, I would be adding bacon and avocado.

I could see the Hyatt in front of us, shining like a beacon, when Walton spoke his first words since the broadcast.

"Take the next left."

"Not yet, Bill. The Hyatt is just up a little farther."

"We're not going to the Hyatt, Dave. Turn left."

"Bill, we are two minutes from the hotel. And I am starving. I haven't eaten since breakfast and it's been a long day."

"We're going to a restaurant, Dave. Pika's. Trust me, it's better than the Hyatt."

"Bill, I checked Yelp and TripAdvisor, both of which confirmed the Hyatt has all the best-rated restaurants in the area. So, you're wrong. Whatever Pika's is, it's not better than the Hyatt, which is where we are going."

"Pika's, Dave. Trust me. It is…" Walton paused, then corrected himself. "It was the Pope's favorite place. I want to have a drink there to toast my friend. Please."

Damn it. Damn it, damn it. Damn it!

"Sure, Bill. Of course."

I took the left, toward the coast, while the Hyatt taunted me in the rear-view mirror. I weaved down a small country road. Off the beaten path would be an understatement. The farther we went, the less road we were driving on. By the end, we were spinning our wheels on sand as I parked the Mustang in a makeshift lot next to a dozen or so other cars. We walked up to a beachside restaurant on stilts that glowed warmly in the darkness. Music was floating outside, competing with the sound of waves crashing on jagged rocks.

We climbed the old wooden stairs to a porch that wrapped around the restaurant. A small sign hung from the roof. It was light blue, and hand-painted in white, was the word "Pika's" in cursive. It wasn't a big place, maybe twenty tables, but it was cozy. The kinda place that felt familiar even if you were walking in for the first time. Walton greeted some friends he recognized standing by a table that had a picture of the Pope on it, surrounded by candles and flowers.

"Pope's favorite table," Walton explained as we took another table with a view of the ocean. An older man with a shaved head and a surfer's physique wearing a chef's apron walked up to us and greeted Walton with a hug.

"Pika, this is my partner, Dave Pasch. He'll want the burger. I'll have whatever's freshest from the bounty of mother ocean's bread basket." Pika nodded. He didn't write anything down, which always made me nervous. "High alcohol kombucha?" He asked Walton.

Walton nodded, gratefully. "Dave? Beer or Pinot Gris?"

"Actually, I'll have a Mai Tai."

Walton turned to me, surprised. I did tend to order the same thing wherever we went. But tonight, I wanted to switch it up.

"Pope made me a Mai Tai at the party last night and it was the best drink I've ever had. If we're going to toast him, I'd like to toast him with that."

Pika smiled. "Well, since I taught Pope how to make a Mai Tai, I think you'll like mine."

"Make it two, Pika." Walton smiled.

I looked around. I recognized a few people from the party, all coming to pay their respects. As was my habit, I picked up my phone to check out the restaurant's Yelp score.

"This is so weird, Bill. This place looks great, but it has a ton of bad reviews. Look, it's only rated one-and-a-half stars," I said, showing Walton my phone.

Walton smiled.

"It's an inside joke. All of Pika's regulars leave awful reviews to keep the tourists over at the Hyatt. Don't believe everything you read on your little screen, Dave."

Moments later, a server brought our drinks. Walton and I toasted, and I was pleased to discover Pika's Mai Tai was just as perfect as the Pope's. I took another sip, melted into my chair, and relaxed for the first time that day. I was already planning ahead to my second Mai Tai as Bill told me Pika's story.

"Pika was the head chef for a big chain hotel until he finally saved enough money to open his own place." Bill gestured to the restaurant. "He struggled for the first few years. Frankly, Pika is an amazing chef but an awful businessman. Pope was one of Pika's few loyal customers, and when he found out he was going out of business, he bought the place on the spot. The Pope made a few smart, subtle changes, let Pika focus on nothing but the food, and the place has thrived ever since. For a loyal, local crowd." Walton smiled at my phone and I put it away. "Pope tried to give ownership of the place back to Pika about a hundred times, but Pika always insisted Pope remain the owner. Said he was his lucky charm."

Our food arrived and, even with raised expectations, I couldn't believe how good it was.

"Oh my," I mumbled, not wanting to stop chewing. "This is incredible."

The double cheeseburger was simple, without any fancy gimmicks to distract from the flavor. It tasted true. Honest. A simple, house-made bun. Two fresh, flavorful patties cooked perfectly medium and lovingly embraced by melted cheese. Fresh butter lettuce stacked with pickles, mayo and ketchup. Each and every french fry was a work of art. Thin. Golden. Crispy. Salty. And served with a ramekin of a delicious spicy mayo sauce that kicked me right in the taste buds.

"Thank you mother ocean, for your bounty, for your sacrifice." Walton said before digging into his Mahi Mahi, which looked and smelled like it was swimming in the ocean about five minutes ago. Another pair of Mai Tais hit the table without us having to order them. Walton and I enjoyed a wonderful meal together and, if just for a second, I think he was able to forget the day's horrible events.

Chapter 15

After dinner, we were at the bar, perhaps over-indulging in Mai Tais, when Walton and I were approached by an attractive woman in her sixties as she entered the restaurant. She walked in heels like she was born in them. She wore a cream-colored business suit, the kind a senator would wear. I soon found out it was also the kind of suit a very high-powered lawyer would wear. Walton introduced us. This was Michelle Vignault, the Pope's personal attorney. I remembered seeing her at the party. I also recognized her from CourtTV. At one point she must have defended a Kardashian or something. She exuded confidence and intelligence. If something went wrong, this was definitely who you wanted in your corner.

"Hey, Bill." They kissed cheeks. "We just came back from the police station."

"Wonderful!" Walton said. "So, you're representing BB?"

"Represent him? He's lucky I didn't strangle him. The son of a bitch killed Jon Paul. We told that Detective Palakiko enough to put him away twice."

"No, not you too! He didn't do it!" Walton pleaded. "Why would he? He had no reason to kill, Pope!"

"I'm afraid he did, Bill."

I turned to the woman who had come in with Michelle Vignault, a short, short-haired, Hawaiian woman in board shorts, flip flops, and yet another Hawaiian shirt, though hers was much more well-worn than the ones I had been seeing from me and my fellow tourists. It was frayed at the edges and had images of a beach at sunset. The sun, palm trees, the sky a faded purple. Over and over again. She introduced herself to me.

"Lala Kapule. I was Pope's business manager, and I can prove that, three days ago, BB stole a hundred thousand dollars from the Pope."

"No! I refuse to believe it," Walton said. "It doesn't make any sense. Why would you steal from a man who would give you anything you asked for?"

"I don't know, Bill. But he did. And the idiot did it all at once, when he could have just slowly bled Pope for whatever he wanted. I had it set up so BB could go down to First Hawaiian and take out whatever he needed. Five thousand, ten thousand dollars. No big deal. He did it all the time. Usually for repairs on Air Force Fun or for party favors for a night like last night."

"Party favors?" I wondered aloud.

"Marijuana, Dave. Please. Pope would buy weed by the pound, and he and his friends would go through it in a weekend. Just listen and save your childish questions for later!"

I seethed, then downed a little too much Mai Tai and, what the hell, ordered another. That'll show him.

"So, three days ago, Friday afternoon, BB goes to the bank like normal," Lala continued. "But this time, instead of five or ten thousand dollars, he takes out a hundred thousand dollars."

"And they gave it to him?" I asked, hoping I didn't slur.

"Sure. A hundred thousand dollars wouldn't break the Pope, but I noticed it and confirmed it with the manager of the bank, who personally gave BB the money. I asked BB about it and he told me it was for the party, but 'it was a surprise' for the Pope, so I shouldn't tell him about it," she said, giving us a withering look.

"Bull. Shit." Michelle interpreted for us as the bartender brought the ladies a couple drinks they never had to order. They must have been here a lot with Pope over the years. Michelle had a pina colada and Lala took a local beer, a Big Swell IPA.

"Low and behold, I didn't notice a hundred-thousand-dollar-surprise walk through the door of the party," Lala said. "I told Pope everything. He assumed BB had a very good reason for taking the money and said he would talk to him about it."

"The Pope did take BB aside at the party, remember, Bill?" I said. "Something was definitely off."

"Exactly. Pope confronted BB about the money, and six hours later he was dead," Michelle said. "Bill, he had motive and opportunity. He's the only one who went in and out of there that morning. Even if I believed BB, which I don't, I wouldn't touch this case with Robert Shapiro's dick stapled to a ten foot pole."

I shuddered at her imagery.

"No!" Walton exclaimed. "Impossible! Okay, maybe BB took the money, but it had to be for a good reason. And he didn't kill Pope. He couldn't! BB wouldn't hurt a fly!"

"Bill. C'mon. BB served in Vietnam," Michelle said. "He hurt hundreds and hundreds of flies."

"That was the war! He was a pawn in Lyndon B. Johnson's deadly chess game with the Soviet Union!"

"Don't you mean, Vietnam?"

"Quiet, Pasch! Please. I can't give you a history lesson right now! Michelle, BB's actions in the war are ancient history."

"Okay, then. What about the time he killed someone, right here on Maui, nine years ago," Michelle snapped back.

"What? He killed somebody?! Bill, why are we wasting our time trying to clear this murdering lunatic?"

"Dave, he wasn't convicted. He was innocent!"

"Bill, there's a big difference between not convicted and innocent," Michelle said. "Trust me, I know. I defended BB as a favor to the Pope. I got him off, but it's one of those cases I don't like to think about."

"It was self defense! A crazed, bloodthirsty drug dealer tried to kill BB and steal his money!" Walton screamed.

"A lot of people think BB was the crazy one. And the other guy was dead, so we only heard his side of the story."

"The best story survives, not the most accurate."

"What?"

"Nothing," I said. It struck me, I had only known Pope for a few hours but I could already quote the man.

"BB did it. And I told that greasy bastard that, this time, he was on his own."

I liked Michelle.

"When you talked to BB, did he confess?" Walton asked.

"No. He says he didn't do it."

"Then he didn't do it!" Walton exclaimed. Like it was the most obvious thing in the world. Michelle, Lala and I shared a look. I felt bad for Walton. I hated to see loyalty like this abused. Bill turned to Michelle, pleading. "It wasn't BB. It had to be someone else!"

"Bill, if it wasn't BB, that only leaves Arlo or Samangja," I reminded him.

Michelle and Lala exchanged a look.

"You know what I think about that, Michelle," Lala said. "Arlo could have done it and, after last night, he had a very good reason to."

"Disagree, Lala. Your theory is flawed," Michelle quickly countered.

"What theory?" Walton pleaded.

Lala took a swig of her beer and laid it out. "Arlo didn't know Pope was donating his estate to Hawaii. He thought he was going to be inheriting it. He found out at the party, like everybody else, and he was furious."

"And the thing is…" Michelle was willing to concede, "Jon Paul died before everything could be finalized. We were going to draw up his new will today and have him sign it. But... we never got the chance."

Lala nodded. "Pope didn't have a ton of money in the bank. He had plenty to live on, but he constantly donated the bulk of his income to a variety of charities and non-profit organizations. Until last night, the estate was the only thing Arlo was inheriting. Then he wasn't inheriting it. But now... he does."

Michelle shook her head. "Arlo didn't do it. He's an asshole, but there's no way he could kill his own father. No way. He wouldn't get his hands dirty."

"We should at least look into it," Walton said. "We have to."

"Bill, I know how you feel about BB," Michelle said, gently. "But he's guilty. He did it. I talked with him. I'm a world-class bullshitter and I know one when I see one. BB wasn't telling me the truth."

"But he loved the Pope with all his heart."

"Come on, Bill. This is not the first time a man killed someone they loved."

Michelle and Lala said good-bye and went into the restaurant to get dinner as Walton and I digested the new information. Information that, for me, sealed BB's fate. But I could tell Walton was invigorated by the possibility of a new suspect in the murder of the Pope.

Arlo Paul.

Chapter 16

I paid our check. Walton's streak of "forgetting his wallet" was reaching a Cal Ripken Jr. level of endurance and consistency. I was adding the tip and signing my name when I heard an all-too-familiar voice in my ear.

"You knuckleheads better be sober by game time tomorrow."

It was Stephanie. She wore a tropical evening dress and wry smile. She was holding hands with the Colonel and standing with a group of friends. The Colonel seemed even more inebriated than last we saw him, which was an impressive feat. He motioned to himself and his three buddies.

"Walton, Pasch! Meet the Army/Navy game!" The Colonel bellowed.

"Army/Navy game? Aren't the four of you about eighteen players short?"

The Colonel laughed and explained that the "Army/Navy game" was their annual golf tournament between old friends. It was the Colonel and his Army buddy, Major Jason Swygard, versus Captains Aaron Singh and Dylan Green of the U.S. Navy. It was clearly a friendly rivalry that was taken very seriously.

"See?!" The Colonel shouted to his buddies. "I told you I knew Bill Walton and Dave Pasch!"

I smiled. "That's funny, I brag to my friends that I know Colonel Cabrera."

Everybody laughed. I love gassing it for a friend. We all shook hands with the golfing foursome and their wives, and as they left the restaurant, Stephanie lingered to say good-bye.

"Good night, guys. And Walton, thanks for the tip. This place is great."

"Anytime, Stephanie. More importantly, we've had a break in the case! We have a new suspect--"

"Uh-uh. No. Bill, I already told you," Stephanie cut Walton off, "I'm out. Let the police handle this."

Before Walton could protest, Stephanie left to break up a shirtless wrestling match that broke out on the porch between representatives of the Army/Navy game.

"Okay, Dave. Once again, it's just you and me," Walton said, still stung by Stephanie's rejection. "Gather your wits. We must speak to Arlo this instant! To the Cowboy House!"

"I wouldn't recommend that, bruddah."

I turned around, surprised to find Ahi and Ani, the Pope's security team.

"What are you guys doing here?"

"Arlo fired us. Didn't even give us severance. He said it was the cost of sitting on our asses while BB killed his father."

Ani and Ahi looked more ashamed than angry.

"That's absurd," Walton assured them. "Listen to me. Do you think, for one second, Pope would have wanted you to stop BB from coming to see him?"

They shrugged, conceding Walton's point.

"And, more importantly, BB didn't kill him! It was Arlo! We have theoretical proof and we have to confront him with it this instant!"

"Don't do it, boss," Ani said. "Detective Palakiko put his own men at the gate to keep an eye out. If you step one foot on the property to talk to Arlo? Aloha."

Pika interrupted Ahi and Ani's warning with a tray of glasses and a tall bottle of very old scotch.

"If you want to find Arlo, he goes running in the mountains above the estate every morning. Very early. He doesn't sleep much, that boy. Just like his father," Pika said.

"That's about the only way he's like his father," Walton scoffed.

Pika thought for a moment.

"Arlo is different from his father in many ways. But, it can be hard to be the son of a great man."

"So true," Walton said, immediately flip-flopping, as he did so often. "Mercury is closest to the warmth of the sun but dwarfed and burned by its magnificence!"

Pika put the glasses down and poured us all neat splashes from the old bottle. We took them in our hands and followed Pika's lead as he held his up.

"To our friend, John Paul. He saw this world and he made it better."

We toasted and drank. It was smoky, peaty stuff. Worthy of the man we were honoring. Walton spent the next hour greeting old friends as they came and went, all trading stories about the Pope. It was a surprisingly festive atmosphere. A Hawaiian wake, I guess you'd call it.

Eventually, we said our good-byes and, after our many, many Mai Tais, we decided to leave the Mustang and walk back to the hotel along the beach. It was a beautiful, moonlit walk. Along the way, after one of the best meals of my life, I decided to leave Pika's a Yelp review. I gave it one star.

Chapter 17

The barrel of the gun in my face looked as big as a manhole cover. I was kneeling on the edge of a cliff, my back to the ocean. I heard the waves crashing in the darkness far below me. Walton distracted them. The bikers turned to look at him. This was my chance. I planted my foot on the ground and lunged forward, but I'm wearing dress shoes. They slip in the mud and I fall on my face. The bikers laugh. Toucan, the big ugly one, puts a boot in my side and kicks me over onto my back. "Nice try, Pasch," he says as he lowers the gun and BANG!

I woke up.

A nightmare. I've had them a lot since surviving the events on the edge of the cliff that night. I was covered in sweat and panting like I had just run a marathon. Heart hammering. I gave silent thanks for the hiking boots I bought on a whim in the Seattle Hyatt. I listened to my gut and it saved my life. Walton would say I "followed the dancing bears."

I say I "listened to my gut."

I wouldn't be able to go back to sleep. My body was ready to fight for my life, but I was alone in a hotel room at three in the morning. I got out of bed and grabbed a bottle of water from the minifridge, then did the one thing that could calm me down in moments like these.

Push-ups.

When the nightmares first started happening, I was doing ten push-ups before going back to bed. Then it was twenty. A hundred. Then I stopped counting. I just did push-ups until I was tired enough to go to bed. Tonight, it would take awhile.

Breathe in. Down.

Breathe out. Up.

Repeat.

After a good long while, maybe an hour, I was finally ready to go back to sleep. I grabbed another bottle of water, slid back the glass door to my balcony, and stepped out into the warm night air. I looked down and watched the wind push through the palm fronds like an invisible hand. We were on the 22nd floor and had a magnificent view from the south side of the resort. To my right was the Pacific Ocean. I could see Pika's down on the beach, finally closed for the night. And far, far off in the distance... Well, I couldn't quite see Mount Haleakalā, but I could see the glow. The smoke.

Hiking boots instead of dress shoes. Life instead of death. It's crazy, so many little things had to go right for us to survive Seattle. Hundreds of tiny, little things. Like a cosmic game of Plinko, every bounce had to go in our favor and, fortunately, it had. It boggles the mind. The odds were astronomical. And here I was, doing it all over again. Walton and I were on a slippery slope. I could feel it. And I didn't like it.

"Pasch, what are you doing?"

I screamed and literally jumped in the air, my bottle of water flew from my hand and, after a few beats, gently thudded on the ground far below.

Chapter 18

"You shouldn't litter, Pasch."

"Bill, you scared me half to death."

I turned to Walton, who was on the balcony next door. He had dragged his mattress out there to sleep outside. He looked like the hippie meat in a mattress taco.

"Can I come over?" He said, as he was already standing up and folding his daddy-long-legs across the gap between the two balconies. I looked down all twenty-two stories. "Bill, it's a long way down. Just use the hallway. It's a four-second walk."

"I don't have that kind of time, Dave. Life is too short!" He said, as he grabbed the guard rail of my balcony and, with minimum effort, stepped over the gap onto my balcony. He pushed past me and into my room. He found two cans of Pau Hana

Pilsner in my mini bar. He took them out, kicked the door closed, and rejoined me on the balcony. I grabbed a beer out of his hand and opened it before he could fail to offer me one. He smiled. We clinked cans and leaned against the railing of the balcony, taking in the breathtaking view under the full moon.

"Dave, tell me about this Cal team," Walton said, breaking the silence. I was surprised. I thought he would be talking about any of the numerous things worthy of note and reflection from the last twenty four hours, not the loser of the game we called.

"Well, Bill. What do you want to know?"

"What can you tell me about the big man? What's his name?"

It's funny how Walton's mind works. He could tell me the name of each and every one of Jupiter's 79 moons, but not the name of a single player in the Maui Invitational.

"Sakamoto," I said, sipping my beer. My eyes transfixed on Haleakalā in the distance. "Maki Sakamoto. Born and raised in Japan. Grew up wanting to be a baseball player, until, as a 6'10" sophomore in high school, he finally accepted where his talents lay. He focused on basketball, won the All-Japan High School Tournament his senior year, and was invited to the Nike Hoop Summit, where he turned more than a few heads. Went to Cal to play under their former coach, Scotty Wrightson. Sakamoto could have gone pro last year, but he got hurt, Wrightson got fired, and yesterday was the first we've seen Sakamoto playing under Fast Eddie. He doesn't seem like a good fit for Fast Eddie's 'fun and gun' system."

"System," Walton scoffed. "I despise systems. John Wooden had a system, it was called excellence! If John Wooden was to coach a sport that he had never seen, and didn't know the rules of, he would still lead that team to a championship. Guaranteed. Why? Because of excellence. And what's up with Stephanie? She's being weird," Walton said, effortlessly shifting from first to sixth gear in the conversation, as he so often did. "Why isn't she helping us with this case? We're out here fighting for my friend's life and she's enjoying a nice, relaxing work vacation."

Yes, she certainly was. I was jealous. She was having a great time, and I was standing on a balcony with a lunatic at four o'clock in the morning.

"I don't know, Bill, she's got her husband here. It's their anniversary. I think she just doesn't want to get involved. And honestly, maybe she's right," I said, tentatively. "I mean, why are we doing this, Bill? This isn't like Seattle. It's different. Maybe we should just leave this one to the police."

Walton paused, looking at the volcano in the distance.

"Dave, do you know how the Grateful Dead got their name?"

"Yeah. Sure," I lied. Hoping that would stop the story I knew was coming.

"It was a dark and stormy night in Palo Alto, California. 1965," Walton said, as the wind dramatically picked up in the palm trees under our balcony. "Jerry Garcia, Bobby Weir and Billy Krutzman were sitting around smoking some DMT."

"I'm sorry, what?"

"Dimethyltryptamine, Pasch. It's a chemical compound created by the pineal gland when we are born, when we die, and when we're in deep REM sleep. It's not the point of the story. Please!"

"Okay, okay. Sorry, go on."

"So, it was a normal night on 1012 High Street in Palo Alto."

"I'm sorry. Stop," I said. "Jerry Garcia actually lived on High Street?"

"Yes, Pasch, but that's not important to the story! What is important is that they were trying to come up with a name for the band, and Jerry, inspired by the thinning of the veil that one experiences when smoking DMT, picked up an old Britannica World Language Dictionary. He closed his eyes, flipped to a random page and put his finger down."

Walton closed his eyes and recited the definition by memory.

"GRATEFUL DEAD: The motif of a cycle of folk tales which begin with the hero coming upon a group of people ill-treating or refusing to bury the corpse of a man who had died without paying his debts. He gives his last penny, either to pay the man's debts or to give him a decent burial. Within a few hours he meets with a travelling companion who aids him in some impossible task, gets him a fortune, saves his life, etc. The story ends with the companion disclosing himself as the man whose corpse the hero had befriended."

Walton opened his eyes. "And Jerry said, 'Hey man, how about the Grateful Dead?'"

"Huh," I said, considering. "That's actually a pretty cool story."

"NO! It's much more than a 'pretty cool story,' Dave. It's fate. It's beauty. It's a train bound for glory. It's Jerry himself!" Bill took a sip of beer. He looked at me.

"Dave, we have to find Pope's killer. We have to pay his last debt and give the man a decent burial, so the Pope's soul can become one of the grateful dead." I swear, at that moment the wind picked up. A gust went through the palm trees and sent them to and fro like giant green heads headbanging in slow motion.

"Bill, the Pope was a great guy. The best. But BB? I… I just don't see it. The facts all lead to him doing it, and, I'm sorry, but I'm not sure he told you the truth."

"Pasch, Please," Walton said. But without the same enthusiasm that he usually did. "He's innocent. He swore it to me. I believe him. I have to."

"But…"

"Pasch, you're with me, right? We are a team. Right?"

I tried to think of a way out of this. I was in Hawaii. I didn't want to spend all my free time chasing down dead ends on a road to nowhere. Stephanie backed out, smartly. Why couldn't I? I looked up at two huge, puppy-dogs eyes and sighed, defeated.

"Yeah, Bill. We're a team."

Bill hugged me. Something I was very uncomfortable with, but I relented. Then he wordlessly smashed his empty beer can into a walnut-sized lump in his hand and tucked it into his pocket. If nothing else, the man was a dedicated recycler. He then stepped back over to his balcony, where he lay back down on the mattress and whispered-yelled, "Goodnight Pasch!"

I got back in bed, leaving the balcony door open to enjoy the warm night air. It wasn't long till I heard the warbly guitar and staccato rhythm of the band that picked its name out of the dictionary coming from Walton's trusty bluetooth speaker. After years with Walton, I could name just about every bootleg concert he played by the first song. This was the Honolulu Civic

Auditorium, Jan 23rd, 1970. The Pope probably recorded this one, I thought, before drifting off to sleep.

I was right.

Chapter 19

Walton powered his bike up the mountain. Peddling. Pumping. Not fast, but steady. His long legs like pistons. He could go on forever. Walton's bike was massive. Built of aluminum, titanium, and carbon fiber. It looked like it was a part of him. Half man, half machine. In a way, it was. He was connected to it, snapped into the petals via his bike shoes, specially made by an Italian company to fit his size 17s.

Atop his bike, the big man cut a visage like knight-errant in lycra armor. Wrap-around sunglasses gave him a cycloptic look. His face looked made of stone, albeit stone covered in white sunscreen that he didn't rub in properly.

I was a good half-mile behind him, trudging up the hill on a 10-speed bike the hotel gave me that was, I think, intended for an adolescent. It was six-thirty in the morning. I watched Walton thunder up the mountain. The sun rising over Haleakalā was his backdrop. The sky was a thousand shades of red and orange. It was quite a sight.

The distance between us was growing. One revolution of Walton's pedals seemed equal to eight of mine, but I was enjoying myself. The fresh air and exercise were good for me. I allowed myself to enjoy the view, and tricked myself into thinking we were on a leisurely bike ride in Hawaii, not riding up the side of a volcano to track down a murder suspect.

The angle of the incline was a challenge that demanded my full concentration. Neither I, nor my bike, was designed for it. But I kept pedalling, determined not to surrender and walk the bike up the hill. That's something the old Pasch would have done. But Pasch.0 powered on. I kept my head down, trying to ignore the burning pain in my legs and focused on my hiking boots as they went round and round. The hiking boots were now well worn and fully broken in. I loved them. I had worn them a lot since they saved my life, and they had called to me this morning when I got dressed. Something about diving back into another mystery, I guess. I wanted to be standing on solid ground. Or at least biking on it.

With my head down, pumping away, I didn't realize Walton had stopped his bike until I passed him. I gratefully stopped pedalling and coasted a slow, wide U-turn and saw Walton was standing behind Arlo Paul, who had stopped running to catch his breath. He was bent over, hands on his knees, panting. His back was to Walton as he looked down at the ocean, far below us, wearing a gray Wolaco running shirt with matching gray shorts and gray Nike Zoom Pegasus running shoes. His phone was strapped to his bicep with an armband, and he wore wireless Powerbeats earphones.

"Long distance runner, what you standing there for?!" Walton beckoned. Surprised, Arlo turned around and took out his earphones.

"Walton? What are you doing up here?" He said, between gasping breaths.

"I was hoping to talk to you, Arlo. I'm devastated by what happened to your father. I'm so sorry." Walton put a giant, sweaty hand on Arlo's shoulder. Arlo backed away, disgusted. "Who's the dork on the kid bike?"

Well, that was a cheap shot.

"That's my partner, Dave Pasch. We'd like to ask you some questions about Sunday night. What you may have seen or heard."

"I didn't see anything. I was in my room all night. Then I woke up and heard BB killed my father. That's it. I gotta go, I want to keep my heart rate up."

Arlo put his earphones back in and jogged off. I thought we were wasting our time, but I had to admit that his attitude seemed weird. We're talking about the cold-blooded murder of his father, and he wants to keep his heart rate up? Walton and I got back on our bikes and rode beside him while he ran. Thankfully, we were going back the way we came and we were able to coast our bikes downhill. My brakes squeaked slightly.

"Arlo! BB didn't kill your father! I'm sure of it!" Walton called to him.

"He's the only one who could have done it!" Arlo shouted back.

"Well, there were two other people in the house who could have done it," I offered. Arlo stopped running and turned off his music with a touch of his finger.

We finally had his full attention.

Chapter 20

"Wait a second, you assholes think I killed my father?"

"Of course not!" Walton said, backpedaling on both his bike and the conversation. He looked over to me and I nodded. We had planned out a strategy and it was time for me to rip off the bandaid.

"I think you did it," I said. "Admit it, you were upset when your father gave the Cowboy House to Hawaii instead of leaving it to you."

"Upset? I wasn't upset. I was fucking furious. Classic move by my hippie fucking father."

"Whoa. Do not speak ill of your father," Walton warned.

"Fuck you, Walton. And fuck him."

Walton almost fell off his bike. He swerved and caught himself. Arlo continued.

"Asshole gives away the one thing he had left to give to me. The man just gives millions and millions of dollars away every year. Pissing away my inheritance on his do-gooder hippie bullshit. But when I ask him for help? He gives me jack shit. I'm starting a business that's going through some problems. Growing pains. Nothing unusual. But it's a great business."

"What's your business?" I asked, wanting to keep him talking.

"We're buying up student loans. Millions of dollars worth, and we'll triple the investment on the interest from collections." He kept running, talking over his shoulder at us. "All you need is money and patience. The longer you wait, the more you make. We're going to make a killing. But, my partner on this was just arrested for insider trading. Totally unrelated, and it's all bullshit, probably, but the government froze his accounts and spooked the hell out of the other investors. Everyone bailed, and now I have to re-raise all the start-up capital. That's after I already dumped every cent I had into it."

Arlo stopped running, and in a moment, his hard eyes turned soft.

"Hey, Walton. Between your NBA and broadcasting money, you've gotta have a helluva pile of cash stashed somewhere. If you want to come in, I personally guarantee you will triple your money in five years."

Walton shook his head.

"No thanks. That doesn't sound like the kind of business I want to be a part of."

"Jesus. That's exactly what my dad said. Almost word for word. I guess you hippies all think alike." And, like a switch, Arlo's eyes turned dark again. A tingle went up my spine. There was a cold fury behind those eyes I didn't like.

"Bastard refused to help me by day and, by night, gave away my entire fucking inheritance. The fucking Pope. Mr. fucking Perfect. Well, he wasn't a perfect father, I can tell you that. He was always there for everybody but me."

"That is not true," Walton said, fiercely.

"What would you know, Walton? You were just another one of his stoner music buddies. Cruise in, hang out, toke up, listen to some tunes, jam or whatever. Yeah, Pope was the man. Raising a kid? He was a piece of shit."

"Enough!" Walton pleaded. "Look, I know we all mourn in our own ways, but your way is terrible!"

"So, you were mad at him," I interrupted, hoping to fuel the heat of this conversation into a confession. I didn't know what I was doing, but it worked for Tom Cruise in A Few Good Men. I gave the little creep everything I had. "You were pissed off. And rightfully so! I'd be pissed off if I were you! I also hate hippies!"

Walton gave me a look as Arlo stopped and turned to me.

"Yeah. I was fucking mad."

"And, now that you own the Cowboy House, you're not going to give it to the State of Hawaii, are you?"

"Fuck no. That was crazy." Arlo scoffed. "I'm not giving away a twenty-five million dollar property to become a fucking state park. That's literally insane. I'm going to sell the shit out of that house and use the money to launch my company."

"So, it sounds to me like your father's death was the best thing that could have happened to you. Almost makes it hard to believe you didn't kill him."

Arlo finally realized where I was leading him. And he didn't like it.

"Fuck you. Am I glad he didn't get the chance to leave me with absolutely nothing? Sure. Did I kill him? No. BB did. Be sure to thank him for me."

Walton made a primal sound that hurt me to hear. I felt his pain. As a father, it saddened me that a man as great as the Pope had a son who hated him this much. I was going to have a nice, long chat with my kids today and tell them how much I loved them.

"And, not that I have to explain myself to you two dickheads, but I couldn't have killed my father."

"Thank you for saying that. He was a beautiful man," Walton said, gratefully.

"No. Fuck that. I mean, I literally couldn't have done it. Physically. If BB didn't kill my dad, that means he had to have been killed after BB left. Between five and six o'clock in the morning, right?"

I nodded. Walton was still reeling from Arlo's last comment.

"Well, I was on a video conference that entire time with people on the east coast. I was on it at five o'clock when BB showed up and I was still on it at six o'clock, when I heard Moses screaming his head off and all hell broke loose."

So, Arlo Paul had an alibi. I still didn't trust this guy. Or maybe I just didn't like him.

"The whole thing was saved and put up on the firm's website, so all their investors could log in and watch it. Rosenfeld & Moskos Investments. The cops confirmed everything. So, to you, Mr. Rent-a-bike, and to you, you big, cheap, hippie bastard, I say, fuck off. Feel free to come back and visit the Cowboy House during the tournament next year. It'll be a hotel and you can rent a fucking room."

Arlo put his music back on and ran off with his middle finger in the air. I couldn't believe this was the Pope's son. The apple fell so far from the tree, it rolled down a hill and landed in a big pile of, excuse my French, poop.

Chapter 21

Going down the mountain was different then coming up. It was worse. I had both my hands squeezed on the brakes as hard as I could, and I still wasn't slowing down. In fact, I was speeding up. The hill was too steep. I was going faster and faster until I was nearly out of control. There was literally nothing I could do. I hated it.

Meanwhile, Walton was having the time of his life. As always. He was riding with his hands raised over his head, howling like a mad wolf. I started to panic. Right as I was looking for the softest, safest spot to purposefully crash the bike, the road finally, mercifully, evened out and my brakes were able to catch, slowing me down to a blessed stop.

Walton just kept going. He reached the bottom of the mountain well ahead of me. I took my sweet time getting there, luxuriating in having full control over the bike again.

"Heck of a ride, eh Pasch?" Walton said before squeezing a water bottle into his mouth. His spandex stuck to his body in uncomfortable ways. Especially when he stood ramrod straight with his shoulders back, which was always. I averted my eyes.

"Sure. Next time we'll switch bikes," I said as I hopped off the rental and pulled my underwear from the very depths of my colon.

"Let you ride Althea?! Never!" He said, patting his bike like a horse as we tossed our helmets in the back seat of the Mustang and strapped the bikes to the rack the Hyatt had given us.

We made it back to the Hyatt in good time. I took a nice, hot shower and ordered some yogurt, fruit, and granola from room service. After the bike ride, I felt like being healthy. I ate on my balcony while having a long chat with my family on the phone. I told my wife I wished she could have made the trip. Stephanie and the Colonel had the right idea. Maybe next year.

After telling my wife, and each of my kids, that I loved them with all my heart, I went down to the lobby to meet Walton, who had apparently skipped the shower and just sat in the hotel jacuzzi for an hour. No soap was applied. Just chlorine. He just toweled off and applied some of his crystal deodorant, which, in my experience in dealing with Walton's body odor, was like pouring a thimble of water on a four-alarm fire.

We walked into the video truck well before our next game, another early morning affair that started at nine-thirty. Most of the crew lingered outside. I greeted one of our editors, Big John, who was nursing what looked like a pretty bad hangover. Nick was already inside the truck on his laptop, phone, and iPad at the same time. He was, if nothing else, a quintessential millennial. He had the same sneaker resale website on all three screens. It appeared he was bidding on a pair of basketball shoes on one screen while bidding against himself on the others. It didn't make sense to me, and, since I didn't care, I didn't ask.

"Nick, the Video Wizard!" Walton boomed.

"On the ones and twos, big red, on the ones and twos." Nick and Walton laughed for reasons that were unclear to me. Nick then turned to me and politely said, "Good morning, Mr. Pasch."

"Good morning, Nick," I said. Nick and I had stopped trying to attempt banter years ago. It just didn't work for us. Walton and I turned to Stephanie who was at her station in the center of the room. Today's candle was mango. I sensed a theme.

"Wow. Early for the production meeting. Thanks, guys. That means a lot to me." Stephanie smiled sardonically. "What do you want?"

"We need your expertise on a matter of the utmost importance."

"Great, Bill. What college basketball-related matter can I assist you with?"

"Stephanie, please! We just need you to confirm an alibi for us."

Stephanie rolled her eyes, frustrated. "Bill, I told you, I'm out. I gave you my reasons, please respect them."

Walton looked to me, exasperated.

"Stephanie, Bill and I respect your reasons for sitting this one out. We do. Me, especially." Walton shot me a look I ignored. "But this will be easy, I promise. We just need you to check out a video conference Jon Paul's son said he was on during the time of the murder. There's apparently a link to it on the website for Rosenfeld & Moskos Investments," I said, looking at the notes I typed in my phone so I'd remember. "I tried to log in but the site wouldn't let me."

"Guys, you're not hearing me. We're about to do four games today. I have an entire day of work ahead of me, and, since no one is in any imminent physical danger, I am going to focus on that and then have a nice, relaxing meal with my husband. That's it. For the last time. I cannot help you. So stop asking."

Walton and I were stunned silent. She really wasn't going to help us?

"I might be able to help."

We turned around, surprised to hear Nick offering his assistance.

"I know that company. Rosenfeld & Moskos. My dad invests with them. I actually think I could get in there and check that out." Nick paused, looking at Stephanie. "If that's okay with you."

"Nick, if it doesn't interfere with your job, I don't care what you do."

"Cool. Then I'm in."

"Thank you, Video Wizard! You have truly saved the day!" Walton thundered.

I gave Nick all the information we had as Walton dramatically turned back around. "Stephanie, I just want you to know…" He paused. It seemed like he was honestly trying not to cry. "Your refusal to help us, to help my innocent, imprisoned friend, saddens me to the very depths of my soul and I may never forgive you for it."

The room was silent for a long moment, then the crew came in. We all sat through what I would call the most awkward production meeting of my entire career. And, if you've never been to a television production meeting, let me assure you, that's saying something.

Chapter 22

"Another wide-open layup and Chaminade is up nine! Cal is stunned with five minutes to go. Listen to this crowd, Bill!"

"What?! Dave, I can't hear you, the crowd is too loud!"

The gym was hopping. The locals were going nuts, and every fan not there for Cal was relishing the potential upset. The Governor was there with her daughter and they were both screaming their heads off. Fast Eddie paced the sidelines, furious. He was wearing a festive blue and gold Hawaiian shirt festooned with hula girls that did not reflect his current mood. The prideful coach did not want to lose to the small, local school.

"Bill, do you know the last time Chaminade has beaten a Power Five Conference school?" I asked, knowing that, if Bill didn't know the answer, Stephanie would put it in my ear so I could look much smarter than I actually am.

"I don't know. Never? Yesterday? Who cares?!"

"It was actually 1982, against number one Virginia." Thanks, Steph. "Another team that featured a dominant big man, Ralph Sampson. As Chaminade prepare to take down Cal and Maki Sakamoto, they seem to be quite the David to these Goliaths," I added with a flourish.

"Please, Pasch, the story of David, who slew the giant with a small stone, is obviously a parable for the amanita muscaria mushroom. The Philosopher's Stone! Read a book, Dave!"

And there's Walton making me sound like an idiot while referencing hallucinogens. Quite a feat in a single sentence.

"I will tell you this, if Ralph Samson lost to Chaminade," Walton continued. "He must not have not received support from his teammates."

Uh-oh, I knew where this was going.

"Basketball is a team sport, Dave. And so is life. The sacred bond of teammates should never be broken."

Walton was clearly talking to Stephanie instead of calling the game.

"Look at this game. When a teammate needs help, the Chaminade players respond. They are playing for each other, a beautiful and important thing. One finger cannot win a fight alone! All one finger can do is point and blame! But five fingers, clenched together in a fist, can wield a mighty blow!"

I tried to steer Walton back on point, but, as usual, he was having none of that.

"These Chaminade players didn't refuse to be part of the team today, they embraced it! They accepted the challenge. In my playing career, I never decided when I was or wasn't on the team. I was always on the team! The team and I were one!"

"Walton, didn't you decide to not be on the team in Portland?" Stephanie shot back in our ears.

"Different circumstances! How dare you, Stephanie! I was gravely injured and badly mistreated! Betrayed by people I thought were my friends!"

"Bill, you dummy, they can't hear me! Don't talk to me, or about me, on air! FOCUS ON THE GAME!" Steph yelled, while also turning up the volume on our feed. Bill and I both winced and pulled off our headphones. Her point was made.

"Sakamoto, the seven-footer from Osaka, posting up Chaminade's diminutive center. Sakamoto has to have a good six inches on him. He's calling for the ball. Woosie Montague waves him away to clear the lane for a drive. Sakamoto puts his head down and moves out to the corner. Woosie drives, Euro steps and… loses the ball! Another turnover for the freshman guard and, if possible, this crowd is getting even louder!"

"This is insanity! Feed the big man!" Walton bellowed.

Chaminade went the other way and scored easily. Fast Eddie's specialty was never defense and this team certainly wasn't playing any. The whistle blew, though you could barely hear it in the arena. Fast Eddie called a timeout, and to Walton's intense dismay, benched Maki Sakamoto for a small ball lineup. I dare you to find anyone who liked the idea of "small ball" less than Bill Walton. But, to Fast Eddie's credit, it worked. The smaller lineup made an immediate impact as their speed disrupted Chaminade. They forced a few turnovers and got some easy buckets.

"This lineup seems to be working. Bill, is Maki Sakamoto's future for Cal this season going to be on the bench?"

"If it is, I weep for the future, Dave. I weep for all of us. A team without a big man is like a night sky without a north star. It is directionless! Polaris! Ursa Minor! The little bear! The Golden Bears need you now more than ever!"

Cal's small ball run gave the team a spurt, but it was too little, too late. The clock was against them and their comeback bid ran out of time. The crowd was on their feet, going absolutely nuts.

"Last few ticks of the game, Woosie launches a half-court shot that misses everything and the upset of the year has already happened in Maui. Chaminade wins and the Silverswords will have plenty to be thankful for this Thanksgiving!"

"Glorious! Celebrate, Cinderella, celebrate! Put on your glass slippers and dance!"

The crowd swelled. It was an ocean of noise. A spine-tingling release of enthusiasm and joy. The camera caught the Governor in the stands, crying and hugging with other fans. An image that was sure to get her re-elected for another term.

"What a feel-good story for Chaminade!" I said. "But losing to a D3 school has got to mean trouble for Fast Eddie Bianchi and the Cal Bears. Is this rock-bottom or is there further for this team to sink, Bill?"

"Pasch, please! Enjoy the moment! Let Chaminade celebrate! Focus on the positive! Why must you always look at the rain instead of the beautiful rainbows! Aloha Dolly Parton!" Walton screamed as I watched the Cal players and coaches make a hasty exit out of the arena. All but Maki Sakamoto, who was still sitting on the Cal bench, all by himself, watching Chaminade celebrate.

Chapter 23

I'm a Hyatt man. But, even I had to admit, the Four Seasons Maui was something special. It felt like another world. A paradise within paradise. It was situated on a stretch of picturesque beach in Wailea, a section aptly named "the golden crescent."

We had another break between games, and Walton insisted we talk to Moses Boulevard to find out what he may have seen or heard the night Pope was killed. Moses had apparently relocated from the guest house down the road to the Four Seasons after his friend and host had been brutally murdered. Understandable, to say the least. I kept an eye out for Detective Palakiko. If he showed up, I was hoping we could convince him were were just checking in on a friend, not investigating Pope's murder. But, thankfully, there was no sign of the angry detective.

We walked through the stunning lobby, which was cavernous. Like a palace, except in place of a throne was a reception desk. Large paintings and statues of modern art were everywhere. A wooden table in the middle of the lobby was adorned with the largest bouquet of flowers I had ever seen. It dwarfed Walton as he passed by. The ocean crashed in the near distance. A peaceful sound that was drowned out by a very unpeaceful one: the sound of Walton walking across the marble floor. He still hadn't changed out of his bike shoes.

He clomped and clicked like a football player through a locker room. And yes, he was also still in his spandex bike shorts. Since the cameras only filmed us from the waist up, he hadn't changed. And sadly, a pair of bicycle shorts was far from the weirdest outfit Walton had hidden under the table over the years. I'd say the top three strangest were, in no particular order, a Scottish kilt, matador pants, and absolutely nothing but a terrible rash of poison ivy from ankle to belly button he refused to explain while insisting it couldn't be covered by any clothing whatsoever. That was a very long night.

I followed behind Walton a good distance, hoping people wouldn't think we were together. I happily joined in on the "can you believe this guy" looks going around. Finally, we passed through the lobby and headed out back to the pool, where Moses told Walton he would be waiting for us in one of the private cabanas.

It turned out the cabana wasn't just private. For Moses, the entire pool was made private. We were pleasantly surprised to find

Ahi and Ani in charge of his security detail. We greeted them warmly and congratulated them on their new gig.

"Yeah, well, as you know, our services were recently made available, and we happily agreed to help Moses when he asked us," Ani said.

"We have the whole place locked down. Everywhere Moses goes, there will be a perimeter around him. Six guys you can see, another six you can't," Ahi said while Ani took a step back to track a couple who were walking by.

I was starting to see how Ani and Ahi worked. Only one of them paid attention to us at a time. If one was talking to us, the other was scanning the area around us. They didn't miss anything. Every door that opened, every person that walked by, garnered their complete attention. Well, one of theirs. While the other continued a perfectly seamless conversation. They were still on full alert for the dangerous and elusive Ellen Pishkin.

"You know, we would have caught her today if Arlo hadn't kicked us out. She showed up to the Cowboy House this morning. Walked right up to the dang guard house and started asking questions. The idiot cop at the gate thought she was just some fan and turned her away," Ani said as Ahi held up his cellphone, which displayed the footage from the guard house security cameras.

"By the time we called the cops and told them, she was gone. So frustrating," Ahi said as he swiped through his phone to show off the access they still had to every camera on the property. "But we know she's in the area. She's close. It's freaky, man. But we're on it."

A chill went down my spine. Things were crazy and getting crazier. I looked up at the volcano. The plume of black smoke rising from Haleakalā was getting darker.

Chapter 24

Walton and I left Ani and Ahi and found Moses. It was easy enough. He had the entire place to himself. He and a couple of his friends were occupying a cabana at the edge of the infinity pool. Moses was wrapped up in a fluffy white robe. He was with a beautiful woman and a very in-shape young man who were wearing almost nothing, both rolling giant marijuana cigars and piling them on the table. They seemed to be having a good-natured competition as to who could roll them bigger and faster while looking more insanely beautiful.

"Moses, thanks for seeing us. We wanted to stop by and share our sympathies."

"Thank you, big man. You know I loved the Pope. Loved that man. And I never expected in a million fucking years that he would get shot. I could have named literally a thousand other people I'd expect to get shot ahead of the Pope."

"Did you notice anything unusual that night?" I asked as we all sat down in the comfortable cabana furniture.

"Man, I'll tell you what I told the cops. I didn't notice shit."

"Excuse me, Mr. Boulevard. Your breakfast?" We looked up. There was a hotel employee who was clearly very excited to be the one who got to bring Moses his breakfast, though it was already well past noon.

"Thank you so much, can you set it up over there?" He said, nodding to the next cabana.

"Right away, sir."

"Sir? Come on, Phoebe. Call me Mo."

"Right away, Mo."

Phoebe was positively beaming. Moses had made her year just by reading the tag on her uniform and using her name. Nice guy. Phoebe pushed the cart away with gusto, and Moses turned back to us, seriously.

"I woke up early. Pope liked to work mornings. Said that's when the good stuff happened. Something about the energy we get in dreams. He said the longer you're awake, the more you lose it. So, I got up. Walked over to the studio, and he was dead on the floor. First dead body I ever saw. I freaked out."

Moses saw my surprised reaction and seemed disappointed in me.

"What? You think I'm used to seeing dead bodies? You think all rappers are gangsters, Dave Pasch?"

"No. Not at all. Well, I mean. You did write a song called Last Bullet. I figured..."

"You figured I was from the streets? Dude, I'm from the suburbs. Private school and little league soccer. My dad was an accountant, man. I never saw a dead body before, and I don't want to see another one ever again."

He led us over to the neighboring cabana as Phoebe finished removing all the metal domes from the serving trays. It seemed there was every type of breakfast food imaginable. Pancakes, French toast, fresh fruit, fluffy scrambled eggs, toast, muffins, croissants, and all manner of juices and coffee to wash it all down. At Moses' insistence, we fixed ourselves plates. I was thrilled. My "healthy breakfast" just made me hungrier. Being healthy sucked. I piled a plate high with scrambled eggs, toast, bacon, and brought back a pancake for the table. I'm a big fan of the table pancake. Walton took a very large bowl of fruit and ate it with his hands. Moses only grabbed a croissant and a cup of coffee. It seemed the impressive spread was just for us.

"Baby, can you hand me one of those?" Moses asked, nodding to one of the giant marijuana cigars stacked on the table. I turned to the attractive woman as the shirtless, fit man grabbed one, put it in Moses' mouth and kissed his cheek. Moses read my surprise.

"Didn't know about that either, Dave Pasch?" Moses said, smiling.

I shrugged and smiled. "To be fair, I don't know much about you at all. All I know is my kids love you."

"For real? Thanks, man. Tell them I love them, too." I smiled as Moses sat back in his overstuffed wicker chair, took a sip of coffee and lit what even Don Nelson would have called a huge doobie. He took a big drag, and offered it to me.

"No thanks," I said. "I don't smoke that stuff, and Bill and I have a game to call later today, so he can't either." At that, Bill took the enormous joint and sucked half of it down in one gulp. Walton's lungs were, apparently, like everything else, super human.

"Pasch, please. Don't be rude!" He said, passing it back to Moses who had turned contemplative.

"You know, I was nobody when I showed up at Pope's doorstep. I was nineteen years old. Been performing around Atlanta for a few years. People knew me, but I was still nobody."

He paused, picked up his phone and typed something into his memo page and put the phone back down.

"I had songs, I was ready to record, and since I was arrogant as hell, I only wanted to do it with the very best. And that's the Pope, right?"

Moses leaned forward in his seat. In that moment, he looked more like a wide-eyed kid than a global superstar. "So, I saved up for like a year, borrowed the rest from my dad, and got a cheap-ass flight to Maui. Finally got here, and went straight from the airport to where I kinda thought the Pope lived. I pieced together the location from pictures I had seen in magazines and stuff. Stories I read. Man, I wandered around the side of that mountain all day." He laughed.

"I had blisters on my feet when I finally rolled up on Ahi and Ani at the guard house. I told them I wanted to record with the Pope. They called up to the house and he came down. The man came down to meet some dumb-ass kid who just walked up to his house wanting to record with him. A nobody. He asked me to sing him something and I totally panicked. Forgot every song I ever wrote. My mind just went blank so I made up somethin' on the spot. I mean, thank god 'Pope' rhymes with a ton of shit, right? When I finished, he smiled and told Ani and Ahi to open the gate. Best moment of my life."

Moses sat back, smiling at the memory. Or maybe the marijuana had kicked in. Maybe both.

"I learned so much recording with him, and just hanging out with the man. He put me up in the guest house. I'm nobody, and I'm sleeping in his guest house with a freakin' picture of Muhammad Ali on the wall. A picture of him in the room I'm in. Blew my mind. We'd work all morning, all day, and at night we'd chill. Just smoke and watch westerns in his little theater. Popcorn and everything. Now, I'm an Unforgiven man. But Tombstone was Pope's favorite. And when Last Bullet sold a million copies, when my first album went fucking platinum? I got him that gun and that platinum bullet."

"A Smith & Wesson .44, right? Just like the one Wyatt Earp carried," I offered.

"Man, that was the gun Wyatt Earp carried. The Model 3 he used to shoot Frank McLaury at the OK-fucking-Corral. Bought it from a collector in Tucson. That's what really fucks me up, though. I can't believe he was killed with the gun I got him."

"Moses," Walton chastised, "Pope loved that gun. Don't you dare accept responsibility for this. It was a beautiful gesture he cherished dearly."

Moses shrugged, sadly.

"Man, BB should fry in the electric chair while getting the needle. I do not give a fuck."

"Moses, I understand why you feel that way, but he didn't do it," Walton said. "He promised me."

"Oh, he promised you?" Moses said, getting a little angry. "If he didn't do it, then who did?"

"We are working on a theory that his son may have done it. But he has an alibi," I said, lamely.

"It's gotta be Arlo!" Walton insisted. "It's not BB and we all know it couldn't have been Samangja. Moses, you know Samangja. I've known Samangja for years. Believe me, it could not have been Samangja!"

"Okay, you know him so well, did you know Samangja isn't his real name?"

Walton's mouth literally dropped open.

Chapter 25

"Now, normally I wouldn't chew another man's food…" Moses continued, "But, under the present circumstances, y'all should know. Samangja's real name is Johnny Soon-Park, and Johnny Soon-Park?" Moses paused for dramatic effect. "Johnny Soon-Park was an assassin for the mob in South Korea."

Samangja was an assassin? I'd be less surprised if Moses told me he was an alien. What was even more surprising was how Walton reacted to this news. He didn't say a word. He just stood up and walked back through the hotel and waited in the car until I arrived a few minutes later, having politely said my good-byes to everybody.

"Take us back to the hotel, Pasch. That man is clearly insane."

"Heh. Maybe too much marijuana?" I offered, trying to help.

"No, Pasch! Weed doesn't cause insanity! It cures it! Whatever is wrong with his brain has nothing to do with the calming effects of the cannabis flower!"

"Okay, Bill. Fine. Whatever you say."

I started the car and put it in reverse.

"Stop the car, Dave."

"Bill, what are you--"

But he was gone. Walton got out of the car and click-clacked his way back through the hotel. I caught up with him as a slightly confused Ahi and Ani nodded us back into the pool area. Walton marched back into the cabana and pointed a long, boney finger at Moses.

"You're telling me that Samangja, the sweetest, most gentle human being I've ever met in my entire life, next to John Wooden and my own mother, was an assassin for the Korean mob?!"

Moses chuckled and continued his story as if there had been no interruption.

"Samangja only talked about it once. Me, him, and the Pope we were up late one night, that first week. We got to talking about shit we regret. Bad shit we did. You know how it is, trading off stories. I go, Pope goes, and then my man Samangja just fuckin' drops this whole crazy story on us. Even Pope didn't know. You looking for a gangster, Dave Pasch? Johnny Soon-Park was a fucking gangster. He was deep in the mob. There, they call it the Kkangpae.

"Since he was eleven years old, they had him working. Making deliveries, keeping lookout, dealin', stealin', whatever. He grew up hungry, tough, and strong. Years later, he's about sixteen. Hasn't been to school in two years. Hasn't seen his family in five. Head of the gang tells him, you want in? All the way in? It's time for you to prove yourself. They give him a gun and tell him to go shoot this guy. They don't tell him anything else. Here's the gun, there's the guy. That's it. What they don't tell him is that it's a suicide mission. They don't expect him to survive. They sent him to kill the head of some rival gang. Sent him into their fucking headquarters to die.

"But Johnny Soon-Park doesn't die. Johnny Soon-Park walks in there and kills every last motherfucker in the place. My guy runs out of bullets and starts killing dudes with their own guns. Uses up those bullets, and ends up stabbing the main dude in the neck with a fork! Rips out a grown-ass man's carotid artery with a damn utensil. Sixteen years old. Becomes a legend. Spends the next ten years as their top enforcer and makes his boss the most powerful, feared criminal in Seoul."

Walton scoffed. Making that exaggerated "pfft" sound.

"You don't believe me?"

"It's impossible!" Walton thundered. "I've seen him nurse an ant back to health! That human being could not have been the mob's most feared assassin."

"Exactly." Moses laughed. "That's the whole point of the story, Bill. He's a completely different person now. When he left Korea and came here, he swore to God that he killed his last man, fired his last bullet. That's what that song was about. That wasn't about me. I told you, I'm no gangster. That song was about Samangja. 'Last Bullet' was about Johnny Soon-Park."

Walton just blinked as Moses lit up another giant marijuana cigar.

"Look, man. I think BB did it. And I hope he goes down for it. But… If he didn't do it… If BB really didn't do it? I'm not sayin' Samangja did…"

Moses paused. He took a huge puff of the joint, held it for a few beats and slowly let it out.

"But that motherfucker definitely could have."

Chapter 26

When a human being dies, it takes eight to twelve hours before rigor mortis sets in. The muscles are frozen in place. The skin loses color. The body drops from 98.6 degrees down to room temperature, and the face becomes a mask. An expressionless expression. For an open-casket viewing at a funeral home, like the one Walton and I were in, all bodily fluids are drained and replaced with a formaldehyde-based chemical solution. The face is styled. Make-up and hair products are added to make the person look more "natural." It doesn't work. Death is a hell of a thing to look at and it cannot be disguised.

The dead man we were looking at was a stranger. His friends and family stood in line to take one last look at him. What a strange tradition. A record was playing on a turntable. A scratchy, old recording. Just a ukulele and a woman's voice singing sadly in Hawaiian. After entering the building, Walton and I stopped in our tracks at the scene before us. Then we gathered ourselves, nodded solemnly to the few people who looked to us, and moved on.

We found Samangja in a room full of caskets. They were all for sale. A few were on the floor, in full display. Their top half doors propped open so you could see the colorful silk lining and pillows inside. Many more half-caskets stuck out of the wall, split vertically down the middle. Copper, bronze, maple, oak. Different colors. Different materials. Different prices. All meaning the same thing: the end. The big sleep. The long good-bye. The dirt nap. El grande adios. The permanent sayonara. The endless siesta in the wooden tuxedo.

Samangja was looking at the caskets. He wore the same thing he had at the party. Black pants and his black, long-sleeved Hawaiian shirt. He seemed even smaller in daylight. And older. We walked into the room and greeted him. Samangja was here to have Jon Paul's body cremated. Being in a funeral home was creepy enough. Knowing what was happening in the other room made it downright grotesque.

Walton got right to the point.

"Samangja, I think the police arrested the wrong man for Pope's murder. I think BB is innocent," Walton said, softly. "I can see why the police think it was him. In their eyes, he had a motive and he was one of only three people who could have possibly done it. Him, Arlo, and you. Arlo couldn't have done it because he has an alibi. That only leaves you, Samangja. But you couldn't haven't done it, either. You're not capable of killing anyone. Right?"

Samangja looked to Walton, then sighed and let his head drop. As if he no longer had the strength to hold it up a second longer. Walton shook his head.

"I didn't believe the story I was just told about a man named Johnny Soon-Park," Walton said, "until right now."

Samangja sat down in a dark, velvet armchair. It was somewhere between black and purple. In any other circumstances, it would have been a very comfortable chair. But Samangja was far from comfortable.

"Samangja, I can't believe you lied to me all these years. Samangja isn't even your real name?!" Walton said, getting a little loud. I put my hands out in a calming gesture. Not here. Not now.

"I know this will be hard for you to understand, but I was not lying when I told you my name was Samangja. That is who I am. The man I was… Johnny Soon-Park." He paused. He clearly hadn't said that name in awhile, and it caused him pain to say it again. "That man is dead. And I thank God he died. Johnny Soon-Park was a horrible man. He was violent. Angry. He was evil." Tears fell from Samangja's face. He did nothing to stop them. He just told us his story.

Chapter 27

Johnny Soon-Park spent a decade killing for money. Sometimes for pleasure. Sometimes out of pure boredom. And, somewhere in the violent mayhem of his life, he managed to fall in love. Not because the woman he met was some kind of saint who saved him. Because she was just like him. And they enjoyed their lives together. He killed people. She accepted that. Supported that. Even enjoyed it. Johnny Soon-Park would come home covered in blood and brain, and she would help him wash it off. Burn the clothes. Patch his wounds. Lie and scream at the police when they came to question him. It was normal to them. And they lived well. Lived in luxury.

But then, quite by accident, they had a child. Johnny Soon-Park was furious at the inconvenience of having a baby. But, the first time he held his daughter's tiny, innocent, body in his arms, everything changed. In that moment he knew he could never kill again. He couldn't shake the thought that everyone he had killed was once a baby, just like the one he held in his arms. Helpless, crying, perfect.

Soon after his daughter was born, Johnny Soon-Park took all his money out of the bank. A substantial amount. And he took his daughter and her mother to a random place in South Korea. He wouldn't say where. But it was purposefully random. He just opened a map, closed his eyes, flipped the pages and put his finger down. He took his family there, and bought them a house and new identities. All paid for in cash. He got the house all set up for them with everything they could possibly need, and spent as much time as he could with his daughter. Then he left. He had to. He said he would come back if he could, but not to expect him. They cried many tears and shared one last night as a family. Then, he went back to Seoul.

Johnny Soon-Park went to his boss. The boss of bosses, Mr. Kang. He told him, respectfully, that he was done. That he wanted out. He told them he would pay them. Sacrifice whatever they asked. But he had killed his last man. They were in Mr. Kang's office, an extravagant shrine to his power and success. Mr. Kang got up from behind his giant desk, walked over to Johnny Soon-Park, and accepted his terms. He told him if he wanted out, he was out. They shook hands and, as soon as he was gone, Mr. Kang ordered his men to kill him. As a message: nobody left Kkangpae. Not even Johnny Soon-Park.

But, Johnny Soon-Park survived. Barely. It would have been easier for him to kill the men who tried to murder him in the street as he left the building. But he had made his vow: he would never kill another man. He was already a different person. But he was still strong. Not the frail man who sat before us. Johnny Soon-Park was powerful. He got away from the assassins, but he was gravely injured. Shot, stabbed, and beaten, but alive.

They knew he had escaped. Johnny Soon-Park had cheated Mr. Kang of his message, and they would never stop looking for him. He could never go back to his family. They would eventually find him and kill them all. So he left. Beaten, bleeding, and near-death, he escaped Korea. He had nothing on him but his watch. A very expensive watch, for he had only very nice things back then. He traded it for passage on a fishing vessel headed east. He managed to survive the trip, though he didn't know how. His wounds got infected. No one cared. No one treated them. No one fed him. No one gave him water. He was lucky they dumped him on the dock in Honolulu instead of just dropping him in the ocean.

He roamed the streets for days, weeks, eating out of trash cans. Drinking out of puddles. He got sick. He was delirious. Finally, he was so exhausted, in so much pain, he gave up and fell down into a gutter to die. That's when the Pope found him. Unlike the thousands of other people that day, Jon Paul didn't just walk by the sick, smelly, disgusting man. He stopped and helped him. Jon Paul took him to a hospital and paid for everything. Johnny Soon-Park was cared for. His wounds were treated and he regained his health, but never his strength. That was gone forever. Part of his old life. He lost so much weight, the doctors thought he was surely dying. But he wasn't dying. Just shedding his old skin. Like a snake.

Johnny Soon-Park was finally healthy and ready to leave the hospital, but he had no papers. He was in America illegally. The Pope and his lawyer, Michelle Vignault, handled everything. All they needed to know was his name. He obviously could not tell them who he was, so he told them his name was Samangja.

"In Korean, Samangja means death. It means loss. I didn't lie to you, Bill. Samangja is who I am."

Bill nodded.

"The day they released me from the hospital, Mr. Paul came back to visit me. He offered me some money to help me get back on my feet, but I refused it. Instead, in my timid, new English, I asked him for a job."

Samangja smiled at the memory. It was good to see him smile.

"And I worked for him ever since that day. Happily. Up until then I had lived only for myself. For my own greed. To serve my own desires. Fueled by rage. From that day on, I lived to serve others. Fueled by love. By caring. And, in doing so, I found a semblance of peace. I never saw my daughter again. Or her mother, who passed a few years ago. But I was able to see my daughter grow up on social media. Saw her get married and have a child of her own. My grandson. He's two years old. But never any contact. It breaks my heart, but keeping them safe has always been most important to me. So, I let them be and stayed hidden all these years in Mr. Paul's private paradise."

A man in a dark suit entered with what I soon realized was Jon Paul's urn. It was a beautiful metal and wood cube, unlike the typical urns I had seen before. Down to the container for his ashes, the Pope had style.

Samangja thanked the man, who nodded to us, doing a small double take at Walton. I couldn't tell if he was reacting to his celebrity or size, but he collected himself and left the room, serenely. Once he was gone, Samangja turned back to us.

"So, now you know my secret. You know that I could have indeed killed Mr. Paul. I was capable of it. But, I swear to you, on the soul of my daughter and my grandson, I did not kill him."

Samangja found our eyes with his and held the gaze long after Walton and I nodded and looked down. We said our goodbyes outside the funeral home, and left Samangja cradling Jon Paul's ashes in his arms.

We crossed him off our list of suspects.

Chapter 28

While Kentucky was playing Gonzaga back at the arena, Walton and I had time to grab a late lunch before the five-thirty game we were calling between the Sooners of Oklahoma and the Duke Blue Devils. I was excited. It would be a great game, and I wanted a solid meal in my belly to get me through it. This time I suggested going to Pika's. I hadn't stopped thinking about that burger, though more Mai Tais would have to wait until after the game.

We thanked Pika and headed down the stairs to the Mustang. I had parked it right under the restaurant. But Walton suggested we walk. The arena was only ten minutes away and, as always, the weather in Hawaii was absolutely perfect. I happily agreed. I was up for anything that allowed us to treat this like the working vacation we should have been on.

Back at the arena, the pregame vibe was nice. Many of the coaches brought their families and there was a friendly, festive atmosphere. In the stands, fans were drunk, sunburned, and happy to be hiding from the winters that were just getting started back home. It really was a great tournament.

I savored my last bite of burger and I was wiping my mouth when I heard Walton's phone chirp. "It's Nick. He's Facetiming me." Walton said as he clicked on the call and put his lips way too close to the screen.

"Hello, Video Wizard!"

"Hey, big red! I'm just here in the video truck and I was just wondering if you knew anything about a cataclysmic flood that swept across eastern Washington during the last ice age."

I couldn't believe my ears. Nick had just set up Walton to go off on a rant on his favorite subject. A topic that had dominated countless broadcasts over our years calling games together: the Missoula Floods. Once you got Walton started on this topic, it was almost impossible to get him to stop. Nick knew this as well as anybody. What was he doing?!

"Actually, Nick yes I do! I'm so glad you asked!" Walton said, positively beaming. The question had taken him right out of the funk he had been in since we left Samangja. "Nick, during the deglaciation that followed the last glacial maximum between 13,000 and 15,000 thousand years ago, something very interesting happened..."

I shook my head as the lecture was just getting started. I looked over Walton's shoulder at his phone and there was Nick, in the video truck, nodding along to a rant he had heard dozens of times before. I just didn't get it. He actually seemed interested. Then I saw a hand reach up and tap Walton on his shoulder. I turned and saw the impossible.

It was Nick.

Chapter 29

"Nick!" Walton said, looking from Nick on his phone to the Nick standing right beside him. "You're twins! Of course, this explains so much! You must be a Gemini."

"No, Bill. I'm not twins." He pointed to Bill's phone. "That's me there and this is me here. I did it, guys! I actually cracked the case!" Excited and quite pleased with himself, Nick led us back to the video truck while, on Walton's phone, he kept nodding along and smiling to a story Walton had stopped telling. Weird.

Nick sat us down at his workstation. Behind us, Stephanie poked her head out from behind her computer, made a noise, and went back to work. She and Bill hadn't talked since she berated him for his histrionics during this morning's game. Nick leaned over us, excited.

"So, you guys wanted to know if this guy was actually on this video conference when he said he was? No problem. Except, there was a problem. It was a private conference. Password protected. Investors only. Dead end, right?"

"Wrong! Be grateful for every dead end, for they oft lead to the hidden door!

Tell me, Video Wizard! Did you hack into the website?" Walton guessed.

"No. Again, big red, you overestimate my computer abilities. But, like I said, my dad invests with Rosenfeld & Moskos."

"So, you got the password from your father? Even better!"

"Hell, no," Nick said, laughing. "No way. My dad and I don't have the type of relationship where I can just call him up and ask for his important business passwords. But we do have the kind of relationship where my mom gives me their Netflix and DirectTV password. Turns out my dad uses the same password for everything: Jordan23GO@T."

"Like father, like son," Walton said, smiling. Nick, a native North Carolinian, was a huge Jordan fan. Except for his comeback years with the Wizards, which he considered "not canon."

Nick logged into the Rosenfeld & Moskos website and clicked on the video conference Arlo Paul had been on. "Okay, so I watched this thing a few times. Between games," Nick added pointedly over his shoulder to Stephanie, who didn't seem to care. "Pretty boring stuff." The page featured a dozen people logged into the same conference, each from their own computer. "See, twelve thumbnail videos all going at the same time."

"Kind of like the opening credits of the Brady Bunch, with three more Bradys." I said, smiling.

"Yeah. Sure," Nick replied, clearly not knowing what I was talking about and depressing me to no end.

"You can see everybody all at once like this, or you can click on one person and their feed takes up the whole screen." He clicked on Arlo Paul as he gave an impressive sales pitch for his reprehensible company.

"All you need is money and patience. The longer you wait, the more you make." I heard Arlo say for the second time that day. What a sleazebag.

"So, he's definitely there at five A.M." Nick said, pointing to the screen. "He's talking, responding to questions. No way to fake that. But then…" Nick fast forwarded the footage. "Right here, fifteen minutes later, he's done talking and the money dudes take over. They crunch the numbers for like an hour, and man, it's boring. My dad would eat it up with a dork spoon but I could barely keep my eyes open. And ol' Arlo here just nods along the whole time. Notice anything?"

Walton and I shook our heads. We didn't notice anything out of the ordinary.

"Exactly. In the moment, there's no way to tell anything's off. Especially when…" He minimized Arlo so he was just one of a dozen bobbing heads. "He's just a small face in a sea of faces. But, if I isolate his feed, record it and play it back at twice the speed…" Nick switched over to the iMovie application on his laptop which showed Arlo nodding at double speed. "Notice anything now?"

We watched again, getting excited. But we still didn't notice anything unusual.

"No?" I admitted.

"Of course not!"

Nick was really enjoying it, Walton not so much.

"Wizard, please get to the point! My friend is in prison while you sit here and play video games!"

"Okay, okay. See him scratch his nose there?"

We nodded.

"Now watch that nose scratch when I play the footage back at fifty times the speed."

He played the video again, this time super fast, and now we could clearly see Arlo would scratch his nose.

At exactly the same spot.

Exactly the same way.

Exactly every five seconds.

Chapter 30

"It's a loop!" Nick proudly shouted. "You can't tell at normal speed, especially if his box is minimized, which it would be when he wasn't talking."

"Did he have to be at the computer while this was happening?" Walton asked, excitedly.

"No! That's the whole point. He filmed himself, edited it to run on a loop and, after he gave his speech, overroad his camera feed with the loop of him nodding. It's like the digital equivalent of those glasses with the eyeballs painted on them."

"I love those glasses! I have many pairs!"

"Right. Well, it's totally easy. I do it all the time when my dad Facetimes to give me a long lecture about how I've most recently disappointed him. It can go on for hours, and sometimes I just need to check out for a little while."

"Wizard, hear me now." Walton turned to him, very seriously. "You must repair this relationship with your father before it's too late! Trust me, the clock is ticking on all of us! Tell your father you love him with all your heart! Do it today! Mom, too!"

Walton wouldn't let us continue until Nick promised to call both his parents that day and tell them both he loved them.

"How long did the loop run for?" I asked, trying to get us back on track.

"About forty-five minutes. Arlo was on the video conference at five A.M. That's ten o'clock in New York. He talked for awhile, and then made the loop from around five fifteen to six o'clock. There's a little glitch when he ends the loop, here. It's not much, it just looks like the feed lagged for a split second, but if you know what you're looking for, it's obvious."

He showed the footage in real-time and we saw Arlo's head jump a few inches, making him look a bit like Max Headroom, a reference I wouldn't even bother trying on Nick. Arlo interrupted the video conference to apologize, saying he had to step away for "some kind of emergency." That must have been when he heard Moses screaming.

"So, there you have it," Nick said proudly. "For forty-five minutes that guy could have been anywhere, doing anything."

Walton turned to me triumphantly.

"I told you BB was innocent! It was Arlo!"

"Let's not jump to conclusions, Bill. But yeah, this might be something."

"We have to go talk to Arlo right now!"

"Absolutely not!"

We froze like kids caught with our hands in the cookie jar. We turned to Stephanie who was finally paying attention to us. "You two have a game in ten minutes. When it's done, I don't care what you do. But for now, get your butts in those seats and keep your minds on the game."

Walton nodded. He took basketball as seriously as he took the investigation. Neither was more important than the other. Both were life or death. Confronting Arlo Paul and his vanishing alibi would have to wait for two halves of college basketball.

"Thank you, Video Wizard," Walton said, gravely. "I am in your debt. Whenever you need a favor, whenever that day may be, whatever hour you may call. I am your humble servant."

Nick beamed and looked to me.

"Don't get carried away, Nick. I'll buy you a burger at Pika's."

"Sweet. I hear that place is awesome."

Walton pointedly ignored Stephanie as he stormed out of the truck. Stephanie and I locked eyes and we shrugged together. I went over and stood in front of her.

"Stephanie, I understand your reasons for sitting this one out, and I appreciate them. I really do. But there's got to be some way you can at least pitch in a little bit. For Bill's sake. Say what you will, we're a good team. It'd be nice if we were all pointed in the same direction again."

"Thanks, Dave. But I'm not getting involved. Bill will understand. Eventually."

I nodded, putting my hands up in a gesture of surrender, and left the truck.

"Have a good game, Dave," Steph called after me.

"Thanks. You, too."

I left, sorry I wasn't able to convince Stephanie to re-join the team. I missed her input and support, and found myself convinced she wasn't telling us everything. She was hiding something. I just wasn't sure what.

Chapter 31

Oklahoma versus Duke turned out to be a blowout, only made exciting by the sheer dominance displayed by yet another talented group of Blue Devils. In June, most of the starting five would be on stage, shaking hands with the NBA commissioner, wearing a suit they would eventually come to regret. The team was fun to watch, and it was nice to stop thinking about death and murder for a couple of hours and just enjoy some basketball. Even Walton and Stephanie managed to get along during the broadcast. And that was after she insisted Walton finally take a shower and change out of his bicycle shorts and shoes before the game. Thank you, Stephanie.

After the game, Bill and I had to clear out to make room for the broadcast team covering the next game, but we took a moment to shake hands with the various friends and colleagues who stopped by to say hello, including a Naval officer with a crooked smile. He was wearing his service uniform. Khaki shirt and pants with a healthy amount of ribbons over his left breast. Everything was perfectly pressed and tucked in. His black boots shined. In military vernacular, he was squared away.

I shook his hand and then, after reading the nametag on his uniform, realized we had already met at Pope's party. It was Commander Kirby.

"Commander, I didn't recognize you out of your dress whites. Did you enjoy the game?"

"Yeah, my buddies and I were courtside, right beside you guys." He gestured to a few fellow Naval officers draining beers and having a great time.

"Commander Kirby! Welcome aboard," Walton boomed, shaking his hand. "Heckuva game you got to see."

"Well, I think my buddies enjoyed it more than I did. It's been a rough couple of days. I don't know what's worse, my friend being murdered or my other friend being arrested for it."

"It is indeed a travesty of justice," Walton said. "BB's arrest is utter nonsense. I assure you we are personally getting to the bottom of it. We're going to find out who really murdered the Pope, and free BB."

"Really? That's great. I thought I was the only one who thought he was innocent. I mean, there's just no way he killed the Pope."

"Thank you, brother Kirby," Walton said, wrapping him in a giant hug. "You, me, and Dave are the only three people on the planet who believe BB is innocent."

Commander Kirby looked to me. I shrugged unconvincingly.

"Look, I get BB comes off a little nuts," he said, reading my body language. "But I love the guy. He's a good dude and he's done a lot for me. It kills me that he's sitting in a jail cell right now."

"Agreed! And we will convince Detective Palakiko that BB is innocent!" Walton said, excited to have another ally.

"Good luck on that. Palakiko hates BB. Hates his guts. You know that murder charge they hung on BB a few years ago?"

"Yes! Unfounded! He was innocent! Exonerated!" Walton said. I mean, screamed.

"Yeah, well, Palakiko was the lead detective. One of his first murder cases. He was absolutely convinced BB did it."

"Preposterous!"

"Hey, I'm with you. But Palakiko did everything he could to send BB away. I think it's because Palakiko hates haoles."

"Haoles?" I asked.

"People who aren't from Hawaii. Usually white people. Definitely drug selling hippies, like our good friend BB." He smiled. "Which means Palakiko would rather take the side of a murdering Hawaiian drug dealer than an innocent haole who acted in self defense."

"Pasch! I knew there had to be a reason Palakiko was railroading BB. Of course!"

"Look, I don't know what went down with Pope..." Commander Kirby's crooked smile straightened out. "But I know Detective Palakiko has a reason for wanting BB in jail. He's been on his ass ever since that trial, trying to bust him for something. Anything. Maybe Palakiko didn't invent any of the evidence that put BB away. But he could have ignored some that might have cleared him."

"And it's hard for us to find out anything," I said. "Palakiko said he'd throw us in jail if we went anywhere near his investigation."

"Maybe he's trying to keep us away from the truth," Walton suggested.

We chewed on that for a second.

"Look, if there's anything I can do to help you guys, please, let me know."

"Thanks, Commander. We're actually going to follow up on a pretty good lead right now," I said. "Pope's son Arlo had a strong motive to kill his father, and we just found out he gave us a bogus alibi. We're going to confront him about it."

Walton held up his phone. "Arlo's at the Cowboy House."

"He texted you back?" I asked. "That's weird, I thought he didn't want anything to do with us after we accused him of murdering his father."

Walton smiled. "I told him I had second thoughts about turning down his investment opportunity. I said I wanted in and I wanted in big."

I laughed. Nice job, Walton.

"He thinks he's landed a whale, but I am not the whale! I am Jonah in disguise!"

"Can you get him to meet us somewhere?"

"He says he can't leave the house," Walton said as he texted back and forth with Arlo. "Said he's got calls and video conferences lined up all afternoon."

"Damn it."

I told Commander Kirby about the cops Palakiko left behind to keep Walton and I from doing exactly what we wanted to do. The Commander just smiled as his eyes lit up. "Oh, we can definitely figure a way around that. Come on, I'll give you a ride."

"Oh, I have a car. I can drive," I said.

"Trust me. I can get you there faster."

Chapter 32

Turns out Commander Kirby's "ride" was a US Navy Sea Ark Patrol Boat, a powerful gray machine full of engines and guns. Two giant .50 caliber machine guns mounted at the front and back certainly made an impression on the yachts we passed. We were cruising at thirty-five knots through the Maalaea Bay, taking the nautical version of the shortcut BB's flight took us on our first night in Maui. Once again, I wished I'd just driven. Thirty-five knots is about forty miles an hour. In a car, that's a smooth ride. On water, you feel like a pair of sneakers in a dryer.

"You feeling alright?" Commander Kirby asked me. He didn't have to yell. The engines were surprisingly quiet with the doors of the pilot house shut.

"Yeah," I lied.

I hated boats. Always have.

"Well, here's an anti-seasickness pill, just in case. Courtesy of Uncle Sam, so you don't get sick all over his beautiful boat." He gave me a single serving packet which I greedily tore open and swallowed with a swig from the bottle of water he also handed me. I started to feel better immediately. The pill was pretty darn good, and, knowing government spending, probably cost about three hundred dollars.

"Seaman First Class O'Connor! Please dispose of Mr. Pasch's refuse!"

"Aye aye, sir!" The young, blond, freckled, sunburned sailor steering the boat flipped a switch and turned on his heels with his hand extended like a cartoon butler. I placed the wrapper in his palm and he stowed it in a small container under the wheel. Then, after flipping a switch, he started steering the boat again.

"Thank you. Where you from, sailor?" I asked.

"Nebraska, sir. We don't get to see much water 'round there, so I thought I should join the Navy and come see what all the hype was about."

I smiled. Meanwhile, Walton had taken off his shirt and climbed on top of the pilot house to lie down and bask in the sun like an enormous cat. The man could relax anywhere.

"Commander, are you allowed to be giving out free rides in an official Naval vessel?" I asked.

"First off, call me Roy. Secondly, absolutely not. But I'm also not supposed to go see a basketball game when I'm on harbor patrol. And besides, BB is a veteran! We're coming to the aid of a fellow serviceman, even though he was only a pilot in the chair force." O'Connor chuckled "Seaman First Class O'Connor! What is so damn funny?!" Commander Kirby barked in his most official voice.

"Nothing, Commander!"

"Something making you laugh, son?! Do you think it's funny that the US Air Force is an equally valued branch of our armed forces, even though they just sit around in a chair all day while we are out here, standing tall, between the devil and the deep blue sea?!"

"No, sir!"

"So, you are only smirking because you are so pleased with the fact that you are an integral part of the most bad-ass fighting force in the world?!"

"Aye aye, sir!"

"A force that kicks ass from Pearl Harbor to Camp Lemonnier!"

"Aye aye, sir!"

"Seaman, do you even know where Camp Lemonnier is?!"

"Aye aye, sir! Africa, sir! Djibouti, sir! As close to the opposite side of the world as possible to our current location by water, sir!"

"Outstanding, Seaman O'Connor!"

It's funny. Hazing is weird. It's a tradition in every walk of life from athletics to the military. From fraternities to the kitchens of five-star restaurants. When it's done by bullies, it's hurtful, unhelpful, and should be totally banished from society. But, in my humble opinion, when hazing is done properly, with true affection for the person being hazed, I believe it can be a valuable part of the initiation process into a group or organization. Maybe it's a guy thing.

In my experience, there's something about being a twenty-year-old boy that makes you want to get yelled at by someone with experience at something you want to be great at. It's why rookies carry the veteran's bags to the locker room. It's why I happily sang the Syracuse fight song at full volume to test the microphones for the sportscasters I interned for out of college. So, while Commander Kirby mercilessly picked on Seaman First Class O'Connor for the entire journey, I knew they both loved every minute of it, and I knew that, if he asked him to, Seaman First Class O'Connor would run through a brick wall for Commander Kirby, saluting while he did it.

Chapter 33

While Commander Kirby was testing O'Connor on U.S. Naval history, Walton climbed down and moved to the giant machine gun at the front of the boat.

"Set target on all whaling ships!" Walton bellowed as he grabbed the gun and started swinging it back and forth, making me very nervous. "Today, we strike back for the blues, the sperms, and the humpbacks! For mother ocean herself!" Then he screeched like a humpback whale.

"Belay that order, Commander!" I said with my deepest voice.

He laughed. "Well done, Admiral Pasch!"

I saw Seaman O'Connor's eyes smiling through a straight face. He seemed both amused and concerned with Walton's antics. I had ridden that same fence quite often. Walton let go of the gun and sat down at the front of the boat, enjoying the splash from the waves that exploded off the bow every few moments. With the seasickness pill doing its work, I actually started to enjoy myself. Commander Kirby and I started talking basketball.

"Yeah, I played a little ball myself in high school. Virginia Beach. I wasn't bad. I was even thinking about playing in college but then..." Commander Kirby trailed off.

"What happened? Did you get injured?"

"Well, like I said, I was pretty good. Point guard. I could shoot all day and even made the all-city defensive team my senior year. The year we played Bethel High School in the first round of the state championships. They had this kid who had already quarterbacked their football team to the state championship that year. 1993."

Commander Kirby looked at me and grinned. 1993? I did the math in my head and then laughed.

"Iverson?"

He nodded.

"You played Allen Iverson in high school?!'"

He laughed along with me.

"Before the game, my coach pointed to him across the court and said, "Roy. You're on number three. Shut him down. And I said, "Coach, I got this." And I went out there and stood toe to toe with the great Allen Iverson." Commander Kirby paused for dramatic effect. If Seaman O'Connor leaned over any farther he'd fall over.

"And I played out of my mind. Played the best defense of my life." He smiled. "He scored forty-five points on me and we lost by thirty."

I laughed as Seaman O'Connor struggled to suppress a smile.

So, after that game, I stopped thinking about playing college basketball. Ended up at the University of Virginia and joined ROTC, which eventually got me nominated for Annapolis, and decided that sounded like a pretty good adventure. Meanwhile, Iverson did his whole Hall of Fame career thing. And…" He looked around and smiled. "I guess things worked out okay for both of us."

As we approached from the water, Haleakalā was monumental. The volcano was pouring smoke and steam into the air. Occasionally, lightning cracked in the clouds.

"Volcanic lightning!" Commander Kirby explained. "It's caused by static electricity. Pretty badass, huh?" It was ominous, and I tried to look away. I couldn't.

Commander Kirby instructed O'Connor to slow down as we approached the Pope's private dock, a simple but sturdy affair that was clearly well cared for. There was a beautiful sailboat tied to the other side. The boat's name, Ship of Fools, was written in pretty cursive on the back. Its sail was tied and stowed.

"You a betting man, Dave?" Commander Kirby asked.

"I've played my share of poker. I once took a grand off Jeff Van Gundy," I said as modestly as possible.

"Nice. Well, I bet you twenty bucks O'Connor can't park this thing without scratching the paint."

I looked to the terrified young seaman who was currently white-knuckling the wheel. "How many times have you done this, O'Connor?"

"Never, sir," he said.

Commander Kirby laughed. "He's not even supposed to be driving this thing. O'Connor's only been in the Navy a week!"

Commander Kirby thought that was hilarious. I wasn't nearly as amused, and strapped myself into my chair. Then, after a few tense moments, and more than a few expletive-laced instructions from his commander, Seaman First Class O'Connor eased the mighty patrol boat against the dock like Admiral Nelson himself.

"Outstanding job, Seaman! Outstanding!" Commander Kirby boomed as O'Connor blushed with pride.

"You are in charge until I return! Guard this vessel with your life!"

"Aye aye, sir!"

I gave O'Connor a thumbs up as the gang plank was lowered and Walton, Commander Kirby, and I stepped off the patrol boat onto Pope's dock. From there, it was a short walk to the private airstrip. Just a couple of minutes by foot. Roy led the way up a well-worn path and to the back door of the hangar that held Air Force Fun and the beat up old Land Cruiser. Roy got behind the wheel, flipped the visor down and dumped the keys in his hand.

"So, how are we going to get past the cops at the guard house?" I asked.

"Aw, that's easy. But, it doesn't do us much good if we're busted on camera while doing it."

We all thought about that for a second.

Then I smiled.

Chapter 34

It turns out Detective Palakiko had only left one cop in the guard house. After all, with Ahi and Ani's system, one person was all you needed to keep track of every single person who came or went. The cop was a well-seasoned patrolman in his fifties. Clearly, getting to spend your shift in a five-hundred-dollar ergonomic office chair was a cushy gig that went to someone with seniority. So, that sleepy old cop sat in that office chair all day. I doubt anybody but Arlo had come or gone from the house. I imagined that old patrolman was leaning back in that comfortable chair, just about to lose a halfhearted fight against a nap.

Then, at exactly five o'clock, every security monitor in the guard house turned black at the same time. The cop didn't notice, because, a few seconds before that, a boxy old Toyota Land Cruiser came screaming down the road, its driver honking the car's horn again and again before slamming on the brakes and skidding to a stop just a few inches from the boom gate. The old cop reached for his gun as a handsome naval officer jumped out of the vehicle screaming, "What the hell are you still doing here?! We've evacuated the entire area!"

"Evacuated? For what?!"

I learned a couple things that day. One, everybody trusts a man in uniform. Especially people who wear one themselves. It's instinctual. Secondly, it turns out hearing the word "evacuated" gets people's attention. It makes them far more concerned about their own personal safety than the safety of an old crime scene.

"The volcano! What the hell you think? The lava is about to spill over onto this side of the mountain! We only have minutes, maybe seconds!"

Hiding in the Land Cruiser, Walton and I were desperately trying to hold back our laughter.

"There's someone in the house," the cop said, already moving to his patrol car. "The guy's kid."

"I'll get him," Commander Kirby said. "Save yourself. Get out of here. Get as far away from here as you can and don't stop for anything! I pray it's not too late already!"

The patrolman headed to his car, but stopped just before getting in, nodding to the Land Cruiser.

"Wait. Why aren't you in some kind of official vehicle or something?"

I held my breath. Was this slapdash plan about to fall apart?

"I commandeered this piece of crap from a local after my official vehicle was burned in the lava! That's how fast it's moving! You want to be next?! My god! Here it comes!"

Commander Kirby pointed to the mountain, screaming. The old patrolman didn't even turn to look, he just jumped in his car and took off. We waited as long as we could, then Walton and I burst out laughing.

"That was fantastic! Way to stick it to the man, Commander!" Walton said as he unfolded himself from the trunk after Roy opened the hatch for him.

"An Oscar-worthy performance," I added, while popping up out of the back seat.

Commander Kirby took a mock bow as I checked the guard house and saw all the blank monitors. I pulled out my phone and called Ahi to thank him for cutting out the system.

"No problem, Dave. Let me know when you're out of there. We'll switch it back on and if Detective Palakiko asks, we'll just say it must have been a glitch. Screw him."

I thanked him and hung up the phone.

"Okay, we should hurry," Commander Kirby said. "That cop didn't look too bright, but it still won't take him long before he realizes the island isn't being evacuated. But, the good news is, when he finally does figure it out, he's going to keep it to himself. Trust me, Palakiko is the last person he'll want to find out about this."

We were heading up the house when Seaman First Class O'Connor ran up to us, out of breath. "Commander Kirby! We got a call from base saying you need to return immediately!"

"What's going on?"

"A bunch of machine guns were stolen from the armory."

"Again?!" Commander Kirby said, astonished. Then he looked up to the house and sighed. "Well fellas, I hate it when Uncle Sam needs me to actually do some work, but some idiot keeps stealing our guns. I'm afraid you're on your own."

He shrugged and got in the Land Cruiser. "Seaman O'Connor! Did you run all the way here to deliver that message?"

"Aye aye, sir!"

"Good man! See if you can beat your time running back."

"Aye aye, sir!" The kid ran off like his shoes were on fire. Commander Kirby chuckled and honked the horn.

"O'Connor! I was kidding! Get in the car!"

"Aye, sir!"

O'Connor sprinted back and got into the passenger seat as Commander Kirby turned to us. "Sorry, y'all will have to get another ride back to the arena."

"These two lonely travellers will find their way, Commander. It wouldn't be the first time my trusty right thumb got me home," Walton said, sticking out his left thumb. "Why don't people hitchhike anymore?!"

"Serial killers, Bill." I turned to Commander Kirby. "It's okay, we'll call an Uber."

"We absolutely will not! I refuse!"

"Go. We'll figure something out."

Commander Kirby saluted us, pointed the Land Cruiser in the right direction and took off down the road just as fast as he had arrived.

Chapter 35

Arlo answered the door with a big smile. "Walton! I knew you'd come around. It's just too good a deal. Dave Pasch, the man, the myth, the legend. We gotta get you involved, as well. You like making money, right? Course you do! Come on in, great to see you guys."

Wow. Arlo was a completely different person when he wanted something from you. I could see why he was a successful businessman. And, perhaps, a sociopath. It's a shame he didn't take after his father. And with the Pope, the charm was real. Arlo's felt like the karaoke version.

"So, how much do you want to come in for, Big Bill? Five Million? Ten? Go hard, Walton, just like your playing days. This isn't a business, it's a Xerox machine for printing money."

I wanted to strangle this guy. He wasn't printing money. He was pulling it from the pockets of struggling, young people whose only crime was needing help to pay for their education. Walton put up a giant hand.

"Arlo, I am sorry, but I misled you. I will never invest in your business. I find it abhorrent." Arlo's smile immediately fell from his face, like a marionette whose strings had been cut.

"Then why are you here?"

"To get the truth, Arlo," Walton said, moving closer. "We know you faked your alibi. You looped the video. We had a top, top computer expert analyze the footage." Walton kept moving forward, using every inch of his seven-foot frame to tower over Arlo, channeling his inner Maurice Lucas to intimidate him. Walton was as friendly a guy I had ever met but he could be scary as hell when he wanted to be.

"You lied to us, Arlo! Between five fifteen and six o'clock on Monday morning you could have been anywhere. And I know exactly where you were. You were down in your father's studio, murdering him!" Walton had literally backed Arlo into a corner. He was sweating, even though a perfectly cool breeze was coming in through the open doors to the patio. "Explain yourself!"

"I don't have to tell you guys shit," Arlo said, looking braver than he sounded. Walton nodded to me and I took over. We made a game plan on our way up to the house. Phase one was intimidation. Now it was time for phase two. My specialty: the bluff.

"Okay. If you don't want to talk to us, we'll call the cops and you can explain to them why you lied about your alibi," I said, pretending to dial 911 on my phone and praying to God he took the bait.

"No! Don't call the cops, please. Fuck!" Arlo said. "Okay. Okay! I did it!"

Walton and I stepped back, stunned. Arlo read our expressions.

"No, no no. I didn't kill my dad. Come on. No, I mean, yeah, I made the loop." Arlo was panting as if he just ran up a mountain. "Crap, guys. You fucking freaked me out. Let me catch my breath."

Walton, having gotten Arlo talking, acquiesced. He gestured to a collection of comfortable chairs right around where David Chang was carving pork shoulder two nights ago.

I finally took a second to look around. With the stage and all the furniture for the party gone, the Cowboy House was even more beautiful. The large living room was split up into lots of different sitting areas. Couches here and there. Comfortable reading chairs and end tables spread around. Plenty of plants and lamps.

Out on the porch, there was a bamboo fountain where water flowed into a wooden cup. I hadn't noticed it with all the noise from the party. The cup filled to the brim until the weight of the water made it fall and gently pour its contents into a reservoir of trickling water before slowly lifting back up to do it all over again. And again and again. It was comforting.

We all sat down. Walton and I looked at Arlo and said nothing, continuing the strategy we had learned from talking to suspects. The less you talk, the more they do.

"Okay, yeah. I made the loop. But just because those meetings are super fucking boring."

"Okay, then what'd you do for forty-five minutes?"

"Nothing. I just sat in my room," he said, looking anywhere but in our eyes.

"You just sat in your room. You made a video loop to get out of a boring meeting, to stare at the wall for an hour?" I said, as sarcastically as humanly possible.

"Arlo, you just lied to us again. And I do not like it," Walton said, leaning forward.

"Okay, okay," he said with a nervous look to Walton. "Look, I admit I made the loop. But can you just believe me when I tell you I didn't kill my father? I know we didn't exactly get along, but I wouldn't kill him. That's crazy."

I pressed him. "You have to convince us, Arlo, or we're calling the cops."

"No. Please, no cops," Arlo begged.

"Then start talking or that's exactly what we'll do," Walton said, instinctively attacking Arlo's weakness as he had done to so many defenses in his playing career. For some reason, Arlo was very worried about the police getting involved. I jumped in, giving the trapped man a way out.

"Look, we only care what happened to your father. Whatever else you may have been doing, no one else needs to know about it."

Arlo ran his hands over his face and nodded.

"Okay. I'll tell you the truth. I do have an alibi for that time because I wasn't alone in my room. I was with my girlfriend."

"Liar!" Walton yelled, standing up and pointing his finger at Arlo. "Ani and Ahi said the only people in the house were you, your dad, and Samangja! They did a complete and thorough search of the house before everyone went to bed!"

"I know, trust me, I know! I know all about the security. It was like living in a fucking prison. I knew they would search the house. That's why I snuck her up to my room during the party and hid her."

Arlo looked at us. Walton and I both had our arms folded against our chests.

"You don't believe me? Come on. I'll show you. After you," he gestured up the stairs.

"No, Arlo," I said. "After you."

I was keeping this creep where I could see him.

Chapter 36

Arlo led us to his room. There was a big bed to the right, under large windows facing west. I took a moment to soak in the breathtaking view of the ocean. A door was open to a bathroom on our left. It looked bright and spacious with one of those nice, stone sinks where water doesn't come out of a faucet, it flows off a ledge like a mini waterfall.

In front of us was an area Arlo had converted into a home office. A fancy office chair faced a beautiful koa wood desk that held a keyboard, two giant computer monitors, and a sleek printer. Arlo went over and got in the bed, which was suspended from the ceiling by braided ropes. Like a rocking chair on a porch. It was perpendicular to the entrance of the door. When you entered the room, you saw only the left side of the bed.

"Look, we were in bed, under the covers, waiting for them to do their search. Ahi and Ani knocked on the door, came in, and I just leaned up like this while I talked to them." Arlo rolled onto his side. "See? And she hid right behind me. They just wanted to make sure someone hadn't broken in and hid where they weren't supposed to be. So they checked the closets, under the bed. They looked everywhere, but they weren't going to search the crack of my ass."

Walton nodded. He was convinced, but I was confused.

"Wait, your father wouldn't let your girlfriend spend the night? Was he old fashioned or something?"

Walton and Arlo shared a laugh.

"Far from it. No, I had to hide her because she's kinda, you know, married."

Walton made a noise of profound disappointment.

"Yeah, I know, I know. You don't know the half of it, Big Bill. She's married to a freakin' cop. He was working the late shift in town that night. That's why she could come to the party. This stays between the three of us, right? You promised. I can't let my reputation take this kind of hit right now."

"Arlo, be more concerned with your character than your reputation. Character is what you are. Reputation is what people say you are. Do you know who said that?"

"My dad?" Arlo scoffed.

"No, it was John Wooden. But I love that you got the two confused. They were both great men and huge influences on my life," Walton said, tearing up.

"Look, man. It's not what you think. I love her. She's amazing and just, absolutely fucking gorgeous. Smoking, smoking hot. And smart, too! She's like a super successful realtor. We met at a bar in Wailea a few months ago. I took her back here to show off the place. It's kind of my move, and she went freakin' nuts for it. I mean, she really loved the place. She actually came up with this awesome idea to turn it into an Eco Hotel. I tried to convince my dad to sell it to her and her investors, but he fucking squashed the whole thing."

"Wait, Nalani Richardson?"

Arlo reacted. He was shocked I knew her name.

"I met her at the party. She was really nice," I said, taking out the business card she had given me.

"Yeah, that's her. She's super cool. And hot, right?"

"She's very attractive," I conceded.

"Well, I don't think 'super cool' people cheat on their spouses. Or break up marriages!" Walton said, piously.

"It's complicated, okay?"

"I hate to say it, Bill. But this actually sounds pretty reasonable. Arlo made the loop to hang out with Nalani while the bean counters crunched the numbers."

"Yeah. We just hung out," Alro smirked. "Hung out a couple times, in fact. Look, I know having an affair is wrong, but to be honest, it makes everything, like, ten times as hot. Guys, it's unreal."

"Enough!" Walton barked.

"Relax, Big Bill. Just a little locker room talk."

"Please! I despise that term," Walton said. "It's an affront to the sanctity of locker rooms. Sacred places where I have laughed and cried with some of the greatest human beings I have ever known. Spare me the slime, stick to the facts."

"Whatever. Jeeze. Yeah, I made the loop. Nalani and I... you know... and then, well, I guess I fell asleep. Yeah, that's right. I feel asleep for awhile. I woke up when I heard Moses screaming, and Nalani came running back in the room. Yeah, I remember freaking out because I thought I slept through the end of the video conference. I would have just been nodding and smiling like an idiot while people asked me if I had anything else to say. But I was able to log back in, excuse myself, and sign off. Then I went downstairs to find out what was happening."

"Wait. You woke up when you heard Moses screaming?" I asked, as some pieces of the puzzle started coming together for me. A second image was finally showing itself. An image where someone other than BB killed the Pope.

"Yeah. He screamed his head off."

"And then Nalani ran into the room?"

"Right."

"From where?"

"What do you mean, from where? From the house." Arlo froze. We all did.

"So, Nalani was somewhere in the house, by herself, during the time your father was murdered?"

"Arlo, you fool!" Walton boomed. "She killed your father before he could donate his estate to Hawaii! She knew you'd sell it to her, because she had you in the palm of her hand! She was using you the whole time!"

"No way! No! No, no." Then Arlo's wheels started spinning in overdrive. "Oh, no."

"What happened afterwards?" I asked, trying to keep him talking before he shut down.

"What happened? There were cops everywhere. That's what fucking happened. Her fucking husband was one of them. He was one of the first on the scene. We were up here freaking the fuck out. I kept Nalani hidden until things finally calmed down. Then, like six hours later, I was able to sneak her down to the garage, put her in the trunk of my car and drive her to her office."

"And thus, helping your father's murderer make a clean getaway," Walton said, shaking his head.

Arlo, for once, was speechless. I asked him one last question.

"What kind of car do you drive?"

"A Tesla Roadster," he said. "What does that matter?"

"Give me the keys."

Chapter 37

My heart was racing. But this time, I liked it. I was pumped up. Hot blood coursed through my veins. Chasing a lead and pulling a confession out of Arlo felt like, well… nothing else. There was nothing I could compare it with. Walton pulled me into this mystery kicking and screaming, but I wouldn't trade this feeling for anything in the world. And I wanted more.

It took me a second to figure out how to operate the Tesla, and even longer for Walton to climb into the tiny spaceship on wheels. The dashboard was like an Apple Store. Its huge screen was intimidating. Once Walton managed to sit down and get his seatbelt strapped on, I trusted my instincts and put my foot on the break while pushing the ignition. Bingo. The engine didn't roar to life. It hummed.

I found the button to open the garage door, eased the car out and rolled down past the guard house, letting gravity do most of the work. The old patrolman had returned and sheepishly waved as we drove by. I kept the darkly tinted windows up, letting him assume Arlo was inside the car. I gave the poor guy a friendly "honk" as we drifted by and, once we were on the main road, I let 'er rip.

Hotchie matchie.

We were doing 80 miles-per-hour in the blink of an eye. Then we really got going. We flew down the mountain, tires squealing as I got accustomed to the sheer torque generated by an electric motor that instantly read every signal my foot delivered though the accelerator.

"Watch your speed, Casey Jones!" Walton screamed.

I ignored him. I was in the zone.

Shifting wasn't necessary. Elon Musk had eliminated that. The engine just consistently accelerated, smooth as the bottom of a pair of dress shoes. I wasn't driving this car. It felt more like dancing. I was in a waltz with a machine. Turning the wheel was like spinning my beautiful partner, tapping the break a two-step, the accelerator pedal a plunging dip that made her squeal with delight. I wasn't in love. Oh no, far from it. This was vehicular lust. I felt young. As the speedometer surged, I felt the years slip away.

Thankfully, Walton was too busy holding on for dear life to connect his phone to the radio. No Grateful Dead on this ride. I turned on some music. I don't know if it was Pandora, Spotify, or some local station, but Arlo had the radio set to a house music channel. A techno beat that wasn't my usual cup of tea, but, in the moment, really hit the spot. I turned up the volume as impossibly fast drums banged faster and faster and even faster, until they dropped out completely, giving way to airy, trippy sounds until the beat kicked back in.

"Drums and Space, Dave! Drums and Space! What once was is again! Mickey! Bill! I hear you! I feel you!" Walton cheered as we flew into a long, straight stretch of road at outrageous speeds and total control.

In what felt like seconds later, our fantastic voyage ended at the address on Nalani Richardson's business card. An office plaza in Kahului Harbor on the north side of the island. Every office in the plaza faced the beach, the water only fifty yards away. Not bad. I pulled into the parking lot and, regrettably, turned off the car. My blood was still rushing from the drive. My hands ached from gripping the wheel. My jaw was sore. I had been clenching it the entire time. I got out of the car, took a deep breath, and shook out my limbs. I was running a bit hot, so I took off my windbreaker and tossed it in the front seat.

Nalani Richardson Reality was on the second floor of the office plaza. The sign was elegant and tasteful, an extension of Nalani herself. It was almost six o'clock and I was glad to see the lights still on. We were on a roll. In addition to the drive, I was still jazzed from our breakthrough with Arlo. Walton's passion and intimidation mixed with my cool intellect and powers of deduction were a powerful combination. We seemed to work better together solving crimes than we did broadcasting basketball games. I'm not sure how healthy that was.

"We're close, Pasch! I can feel it! I can smell it!" Walton said, excitedly. He slapped me on the back with a giant hand and I scooted forward a few steps. We walked up the stairs to the second floor. I took the steps two-at-a-time. Walton took them five-at-a-time and was upstairs in three paces. Lush clay pots bursting with tropical plants were scattered about, each blooming fragrant flowers. The door to Nalani's office was propped open, and as we walked in, we were greeted by a man sitting at the reception desk I can describe only as "glowing."

Our head of steam had run into a very cool bucket of water.

Chapter 38

"Aloha ahiahi. Welcome to Richardson Realty. I'm Sky, can I help you duders?"

Nalalni's receptionist wore his hair in long dreads, and his skin shone like polished stone. His teeth were beautiful, symmetrically perfect, as he smiled brightly to greet us. Walton and I softened immediately in his presence. His voice was like one of those calming rain sticks.

"Uh, hey. Hello. Hi. We'd like to speak to Nalani, please," I asked, politely.

"Ohhh, she's actually out of the office at the moment," said the chillaxed Sky.

"Can you please tell us where she is?" Walton asked. We were on our best behavior.

"Ohhh, I'm so sorry, but I can't give out that information. If you give me your number I'd be happy to have her call you the second I hear from her."

"Ah, shucks," I said, as an idea formed in my head. "We wanted to buy some property on the island and we leave town first thing in the morning."

"No we don't, Dave!" Walton interrupted, astonishingly.

"That's right, Bill. We leave tonight. How could I have messed that up?" I said, staring daggers at Walton until he finally understood. "We're on the red eye. Which is technically tomorrow. I know it's last minute but, before we left, we really wanted to put down a deposit on a property. A huge property. Enormous."

"Yes, we want to build a yurt," Walton added, insanely.

"Aren't yurts kinda small?" Sky asked, innocently. I hated lying to him.

"Most are, sure. But we are going to build a huge yurt. Giant yurt. We want it to be the largest yurt on the planet."

"Bigger than the one in Mongolia?" Sky asked.

Whoa. The beautiful man really knew his yurts.

"Oh yeah. Way bigger than that one. With a pool and a tennis court," I said.

"And a sweat lodge," Walton added. "For purification ceremonies."

"Nice. Of course. Sounds like an amazingly peaceful place."

"Yeah. Well, like I said. We're leaving tonight. I guess we'll maybe try another realtor? Can you recommend any in the area, maybe between here and the airport?"

Sky thought about it, weighing his two options. Would Nalani be more mad if he told us where she was, or if he cost her a big sale?

As always, the money won.

"You know, she's actually surfing right out there." He nodded to the beach behind us. "The sun's almost down. If you duders want to wait here, she'll be back in a half hour or so." Before he finished his sentence, Walton and I were already leaving the office, thanking the glowing, dreadlocked, model man.

"Mahalo, Sky!"

"Wait! Hey! Don't tell her I told you where she was!"

Walton and I assured Sky we wouldn't get him in any trouble, and headed down to the beach. Walton paused at the edge of the parking lot to take off his shoes and socks and roll up his pant legs until they were above his knees. I plowed on with my hiking boots. Boots on sand was not an ideal situation. Walton fared better than I did, his giant feet almost like snow shoes on the sand, but eventually we both made it down to the edge of the water and stood next to a little pop-up tent someone had set up. A blue, nylon cave about five feet tall. The tent was weighed down with a cooler and, despite the strong ocean breeze, still smelled strongly of marijuana. Walton sniffed the air like a wine connoisseur.

"Maui Wowie. How appropriate! A wonderful sativa perfect for riding waves both on the water and in the mind," Walton said, approvingly.

The sun was setting as we watched a couple dozen surfers catch the last few waves of the day. Surfing at Kahului Harbor seemed dangerous. This was no wide, clear ocean. There were rocks, heavy breaks, and many other surfers to navigate. And what was dangerous by day seemed to turn suicidal by dusk. I spotted Nalani. She was more than holding her own, carving a perfect roundhouse cutback on a particularly juicy wave.

In case you were wondering, I called some surfing competitions early in my career and I still know the lingo.

"Hey Bill, if she's an evil real estate person who killed the Pope to turn his house into a hotel…" I said, turning to Walton. "It's weird that she surfs, right?"

"Evil people can surf, Pasch," Walton said. "Trust me."

As it got darker, a group of surfers walked out of the water with their boards under their arms. Their bodies were athletic, an intimidating combination of Polynesian tattoos and muscles. They stuck their boards in the sand and got some beers from the cooler in the pop-up tent. The smell of Maui Wowie soon filled the air. We stood a few feet away, watching Nalani as she went back out into the ocean, in the near-total darkness, for yet another wave. Fearless.

"Hey brah. Back off."

I turned toward the surfers. They were all looking at us.

"Why don't you stop staring at the girl and get out of here?" Said the one holding the joint.

"We just want to talk to her," I said.

"Yeah, I bet you do, perv." They all laughed.

I sighed. "Let me guess. This beach is locals only?"

"Yeah. That's right. Maybe you two should get the fuck out of here," the biggest surfer suggested. "Just head east. That way. About 2,500 miles."

More laughter as the surfers lined up between us and Nalani. There were seven of them. Each more ripped and intimidating than the last. The biggest one, their apparent leader, stood right in the middle. My heart started racing.

"Our business here doesn't concern you hooligans! Now grab those redwood trees you call surfboards and move along," Walton said. "I am dear friends with the great David Nuuhiwa. A tremendous surfer and an even more tremendous human being. The man could surf circles around all of you on a toothpick!"

"What the hell are you babbling about, old man? You may be big, but trust me, you don't want to see what happens when I get you in the sand." The big surfer focused on Walton, instinctively going after the biggest threat. Go ahead, punk. Ignore me at your own peril. I clenched my hands into tight fists as the big surfer got in Walton's face.

"This is your last chance, big boy. You and your little friend need to back up and get out of here." All the surfers took a step forward, ready to fight. It was seven against two, but I didn't care. The old Dave Pasch would have backed down. He would have tucked his tail, pulled Walton out of there, apologized to the surfers, and ran back to the safety of his car, driving away as quickly as possible.

But I wasn't the old Dave Pasch.

I was Pasch.0. I was the guy who stopped taking shit from everybody and started standing up for himself. I was the guy who had done about 40,000 push-ups in the last eight months, and I stepped up and put every last one of them into the punch I threw into the face of the biggest surfer. I felt his nose break in a satisfying crunch as he fell to the sand. One down in one punch. Six more to go. I put my fists up, ready to fight. Ready to fight them all.

"Alright, who's next?!" I screamed as the entire world turned upside down. Instead of a brawl, I was knocked back by the shocked faces of the seven surfers and Walton.

"Pasch, what on earth are you doing?!" Walton screamed.

"Dude! What the hell?!" The big surfer sat in the sand, grabbing his nose and, impossibly, started crying.

"You friggin' punched him!" Another shouted.

"Somebody get some napkins, he's bleeding!" Said another.

"Call the cops!" The big guy said while tilting his head back, trying to keep blood from pouring out of his nose. It wasn't working.

"On it, bro!" A couple others had their phones out. One was already talking to a 911 dispatcher.

"What is your fucking problem, man? Did anyone get that on video? Fuck!" The big surfer suddenly didn't seem so big. What was happening? Walton looked down at me with profound disappointment.

"What?" I said. "Are we not fighting? I thought this was going to be a fight."

"Pasch, you fool! It was just some playful banter!" Walton said.

"I just wanted you guys to move because you were standing on my towel!" The big guy cried, pointing to our feet. I looked down. Walton and I had indeed walked up and stood right on their beach towel. Oh, God.

"They're just kids, Pasch!" Walton said as we backed up.

"What?! I thought they were, like, a surfer gang!"

"Fuck you, asshole. We're not a gang! We're in freakin' high school," said one of the surfers who seemed to turn from twenty-six to sixteen in the blink of an eye. They all did.

"I'm so sorry. It's dark. I can't see so well in the dark," I said, lamely.

"My dad's a lawyer and he is going to fucking sue your ass!" The big kid screamed as his friends comforted him.

Oh, Pasch. What have you done?

Chapter 39

The back of a cop car is never a place you want to find yourself. But that's exactly where I was. The arresting officer read me my rights and slapped the handcuffs on tight. Too tight. It was painful. I'm pretty sure he did it on purpose, but I didn't complain. I felt like I deserved whatever they wanted to throw at me. I felt awful. My knuckles throbbed, a painful reminder of my crime.

The cop car pulled away. I looked out the window as seven teenage surfers and Bill Walton gave me the finger. In the bright lights of the parking lot I could clearly see they were just kids. I saw Nalani finally coming in from the water, heading to her office. We locked eyes. She was shocked to see me in the back of a police car. I felt the same way. It was a short drive to the station. They brought me in through the back and processed me. I was shell-shocked as they took my fingerprints and my picture.

"Turn to the side!"

Flash.

Afterwards, they gave me a paper towel to rub the ink off my fingers and stuck me in an interview room. It was a sad, small room that Walton would say had very bad juju. I could smell the fear on the walls. I thought of all the desperate men and women who must have been there before me. The crimes they had committed. Had a murderer sat in this same chair? Yeah. Definitely.

I shuddered.

There was nothing in the room but two metal chairs and a metal desk with a disgustingly overfilled ashtray on it. The ashtray was metal. Everything was metal. I kept sliding forward in my chair and had to constantly push myself back. The front legs seemed shorter than the back legs. It was very uncomfortable, and I realized that was probably the point. I was there for awhile. Two hours? Three? I didn't know. They took my phone and my watch and there was no clock on the wall. When Detective Palakiko finally entered, I sank.

He didn't say anything at first. He just sat down and stared at me, smiling his reptilian smile. But I knew this trick. The less he says, the more I'll say. Uh-uh. I got myself in enough trouble tonight. I was keeping my mouth shut. Eventually, Detective Palakiko broke the silence.

"So. Mr. Pasch, what were you doing on that beach? Kahului Harbor is hardly a tourist destination."

I couldn't tell him we were there to investigate Pope's murder. So, in addition to punching a child tonight, I would also lie to a scary police detective. Here we go. Come on, Pasch. How many times have you convinced an audience that a boring, meaningless game was exciting? You can do this.

"Detective, I was there to go surfing and there was just a huge misunderstanding. I'm really sorry."

"Surfing."

"Yes."

Palakiko gave me a withering look. "If you were going surfing, where are your board shorts? Where was your surfboard?"

"Bodysurfing," I said. "I love to bodysurf. All I need is my body and the waves."

"Uh huh. And it also seems you neglected to bring a towel. So, after bodysurfing in the nude, which is illegal on Maui and frowned upon all over the world, you planned on getting back in your car soaking wet?"

"I was going to air dry. And, for the record, I planned to surf in my boxer briefs. It was a last-second thing. A spontaneous bodysurfing excursion."

A spontaneous bodysurfing excursion? Pull yourself together, Pasch!

"Interesting. And almost plausible." He chuckled mirthlessly. "Mr. Pasch, do you want to know what I think? I don't think you were on that beach to bodysurf. I think you and Mr. Walton were there investigating Jon Paul's murder, against my direct order."

"No!" I said, trying to return his gaze, which was very hard to do. "I was just trying to bodysurf and I ended up getting in a fight with that surfer gang."

"Surfer gang?" Detective Palakiko said, incredulously. "Those were children, Mr. Pasch. Wealthy children, might I add. They're from Oahu. They all go to Punahou for god's sake."

Punahou? That name rung a bell.

"Isn't that where Obama went to school?"

"Yes, Mr. Pasch. It is. It is a very good school and I assure you that, if you tried, you couldn't have picked a worse kid on the Hawaiian islands to punch in the face. You'd be in huge trouble tonight, even if you weren't, once again, interfering with my investigation!" The last few words he screamed. Palakiko went from zero to a hundred faster than a Tesla Roadster. He leaned forward. I leaned back.

"But I wasn't! I told you, I was just there to bodysurf."

"Mr. Pasch, I notice your little misunderstanding happened right outside Nalani Richardson's real estate office," he said, now perfectly calm. There was absolutely no way for me to hold back the shocked expression that reflexively took over my face. How did Palakiko know that? He smiled, knowing he struck gold.

"She was apparently in the water at the time of the assault. Not only was she at Mr. Paul's party Sunday night, but she had recently tried to buy his property and was rebuffed. Quite the motive. Were you attempting to talk to her about this when you decided to go around punching rich teenagers?"

Man, I thought Walton and I were good at this. Palakiko was better. Much better.

Deny, Pasch. Deny, deny, deny!

"No, sir. I promise we weren't investigating the murder. Just like you told us. We're here to cover the Maui Invitational. That's it. I just wanted to bodysurf to clear my head before the big game tomorrow. We're calling the championship. The Governor is going to be there and everything," I said, hoping I wasn't playing that card one too many times. The detective nodded, thoughtfully.

"Of course. I forgot all about your dear friend, the Governor. You know, I did reach out to her, through proper channels." He paused, then frowned. "It does appear she is a big fan of you and Mr. Walton."

Thank you Governor Kaluhiokalani!

"See detective? I wouldn't lie to you," I said, lying through my teeth. "I'm telling you, this was all just a misunderstanding. Is there any way you could get me out of here? Like I said, I have a big day tomorrow. I'd love to get back to the hotel and get some sleep." I smiled. Palakiko looked at me like a cat holding the key to the birdcage.

"No. You won't be going back to your hotel tonight. Mr. Pasch, you seem to think I am some kind of security guard and Maui is just one big all-inclusive resort where you can do whatever you want and it costs you nothing. You are sadly mistaken. You broke the law, Mr. Pasch. And when you break the law in Maui, you go to jail."

Palakiko stood up and looked down at me. "If you won't tell me the truth about what you were doing on that beach, I'm going to give you the night to think about it." Palakiko left the room and nodded to a big cop waiting outside the door.

"Lock him up."

Chapter 40

The big cop shoved me into a crowded jail cell. The red glow of Haleakalā in the distance, its presence like a beating heart under the floorboards, driving the entire island insane. A giant, tattooed man stood in front of me, telling me to stand up. His bloody knuckles dangled in my face. They were battered and bruised from the fight that probably got him arrested. I kept my head down, looking at my own hands. The knuckles on my right hand were bloody, as well. Did he pick me out of the herd because I was the other fighter in the room? The biggest threat? In a warped way, I was kind of flattered.

I stood up. He smiled. An ugly, yellow smile. This guy. This asshole. Guys like this had been picking on me my whole life. Guys like this tried to kill me on a cliff back in Seattle. They planned to shoot me and dump my body in the ocean over a bunch of stupid money. A rage exploded from deep inside my body. From my very soul. If I was going down, I was going down swinging.

"Listen up, you dumb son of a bitch! I've already broken one nose tonight. I'm happy to make it two!" I looked around the cell. "Or three! Or four!" I screamed at the top of my lungs, using every decibel of a voice I had spent decades training into an instrument of precision. "Anyone who wants to mess with me, get in line because it's gonna be a long, fucking night!"

"Dave Pasch!" A voice screamed.

"What?!" I yelled back as the cell door swung open.

"Come with me."

Oh, thank God.

I eased around the giant, who looked down at me with murderous eyes. I didn't know where I was being taken and I didn't care. They could drop me right into a fire. I just needed out of this frying pan.

The guard locked the cell door behind me. It was a different guy. Not the cop who put me in the cell. This guy was big, but he was more fat than muscle. He didn't have a nametag. I read somewhere that prison guards don't wear name tags. For obvious reasons, I guess. Nameless pointed me down the hall, and I headed in that direction, walking awkwardly. My feet and legs seemed like they belonged to someone else.

At the end of the hall, the guard opened a heavy steel door and pushed me into a large, octagonal room. Another guard, this one a stern, heavyset woman, sat at a big desk in the middle of the room. There were four steel doors leading in and out of the room, looking much like the four corners of a compass. We went from west to east.

The stern female guard glared at me as we walked by. She pressed a button and, with a loud buzz, the steel door opened. The guard prodded me into a hallway lined with cells, each one much smaller than the one I had just escaped. Barred cages about six by eight feet, each with a metal sink, toilet and desk. Each cell also had a metal cot with a thin blue mattress on top. They looked more like high school gym mats than a comfortable place to sleep.

There were no windows in here. I was hit by the odor of a strong, industrial disinfectant. A chemical, lemony bleach I didn't love, but preferred to the smells of alcohol, sweat, excrement, and vomit I had just left behind. All the cells were empty, save one. I could see someone lying down on the cot in the very last cell on the left. As we arrived at the end of the row, the person slowly swung their feet to the floor and sat up.

It was BB.

Chapter 41

The guard put me in the cell across from BB and walked away, his ring of keys a metal maraca against his thigh. Moments later, the steel door slammed shut and BB and I were alone together.

"You're welcome," he said, smiling.

"For what?"

"I got you out of gen pop, Dave!" He said, laughing. "Got you out of the tank! I've been in that stinkin' fish bowl before. Not much fun, is it?"

"It's horrible. How did you manage to get me out of there?"

"I know that guard. The one that got you out. I've been hooking him up with highly discounted, I mean, I'm talking practically free, weed for years. Dave, never charge full price to someone who can do you a favor. That's my motto. Word came in that you freakin' punched some kid, and Dicktective Palakiko stuck you in there like chum to the sharks. So, I called in my marker to give you a helping hand. And, you know, have someone to talk to. I'm going crazy in here. Well, crazier!" BB laughed his maniacal laugh.

"Thank you, BB. I mean it. You may have literally saved my life," I said, instantly hating the dirty old hippie a whole lot less.

"Ah, don't mention it. So, why in the hell did you punch a kid?" He asked, standing up and moving over to the front of the cell. I told him the whole story, down to the crunch of the kid's broken nose. BB laughed again. "One Punch Pasch!" I love it!"

"It's not funny," I said. Then started laughing right along with him. One Punch Pasch? I mean, it's not the worst nickname in the world. Feel free to use it.

For the next hour or so, I ended up telling BB everything that was on my mind. He was a great listener, and we had nothing but time. I told him about the cliff's edge in Seattle. The bikers. The guns. The hiking boots. The nightmares. My newfound confidence that apparently came with a side effect. Rage.

"BB, I feel so awful about punching that kid. I can't stand it."

"Come on, Dave. You messed up. Don't beat yourself up about it. That won't do you any good. You just gotta let it go, brother. You gotta get yourself clean."

"I'm not dirty, BB. Thank you," I said, sniffing my armpit to be sure.

"Not your body, Dave. You gotta clean your soul. Imagine your soul is like a sink. Right now it's got a bunch of dirty dishes in there. A lifetime of dirty dishes. You got a whole stack of dirty

Seattle dishes in there and now, right on top, there's a big ol' fat dirty frying pan with like, burned, encrusted grease all over it. That pan represents you punching that kid. Don't just stare at it. You gotta clean that thing, Dave. You gotta clean your soul dishes!"

"Clean my soul dishes?"

"Yeah, brother! Otherwise they'll just sit and start to stink and attract flies."

"Okay, BB. I'll bite. How do I clean my soul dishes?"

BB smiled. His gold tooth flashed. "Ho'oponopono."

"Okay," I said, not wanting to repeat and mangle that word.

"It's a very old, very sacred Hawaiian philosophy. No shit," he said, suddenly becoming serious. "It ain't about fixing or blaming or figuring out whose fault it is, you know, it's like the opposite of that. It's just a process of cleaning. Getting rid of the dirt. Letting it go. Ho'oponopono washes away hurtful memories. Negative thoughts. The dirty dishes in your brain sink!"

"How do I do it?"

"Okay man, Ho'oponopono uses magic words. Magic fucking phrases, okay? You ready?"

I nodded. At this point I was ready for anything. "What are the phrases?"

"I love you. I'm sorry. Please forgive me. Thank you."

I paused, disappointed. None of that sounded magical.

"Are you messing with me, BB?"

"No, man. Those are the four magic phrases."

I felt like a kid on Christmas morning who opened a giant present only to find a pair of socks inside.

"That's it?"

"That's it?! Man, that's everything! Say 'em, Dave. I want you to picture punching that kid in your mind and say the words."

"No, I'm not going to do that."

BB tried and tried to get me to say the four "magic" phrases, but I refused. The whole thing felt stupid. We went back and forth until he threatened to call the guard and have him bring me back to the drunk tank.

"You wouldn't," I told him.

"I motherfucking would, Dave. Say the phrases!" BB screamed, cheering me on more than berating me.

"Okay, okay, okay." I took a deep breath and looked up to the ceiling. It felt weird to look at him while saying the "magic phrases."

"I love you. I'm sorry. Please forgive me. Thank you."

I mumbled them quickly and without much conviction. BB didn't seem disappointed. In fact, he applauded. "Yeah, Dave! There you go! Now say them ten times in a row."

"No. This is silly. I'm not going to do that," I said, putting my foot down.

"Jerry! Jerry!!! Come get this guy and bring him back to the drunk tank!"

"The guard's name is Jerry?" I asked.

"I know! How Jerry is that?!" BB laughed.

The steel door squealed open and Jerry the guard, not the nine-and-a-half-fingered singer, walked toward us. "What up, Beeber?"

"Okay, okay. Fine, I'll do it," I quickly whispered.

"Nothing, Jerry!" BB winked at me, then turned to Jerry. "Sorry, man. We were just playing around." Jerry sighed, letting us know the playing around should cease and desist immediately, then walked away, closing the heavy steel door behind him. BB looked at me. "Come on. Ten times. And mean it this time. Put your back into it."

Okay, okay, okay. I took a deep breath.

"I love you. I'm sorry. Please forgive me. Thank you."

I said the phrases and repeated them nine more times. BB's skeletal grin grew wider and wider with each recitation of the phrases, which I said with increasing courage, conviction and volume. When I finished he applauded.

"Feel better, don't you?!"

I hated to admit it, but I did. I felt... lighter. I shrugged with what must have been a pretty goofy grin on my face. BB apologized for yelling at me and said the phrases himself ten times to make up for it. Then we said them together another ten times. Twenty times. Then, like push-ups, I just stopped counting. When we were done, BB laughed. The same laugh that drove me crazy when he piloted us into a volcano, suddenly seemed infectious. He laughed with his whole body. I laughed with him. Maybe I was just punch-drunk after a long, stressful night. But it really seemed to help. Afterwards, I sat down on my cot, feeling oddly relaxed and relieved for a man in a jail cell. I took a deep, cleansing breath. One that made me realize my lungs hadn't been operating at full capacity for awhile.

"Thanks, BB. I really appreciate this. I will... uh, try this."

BB smiled. "Hell yeah, brother. You just cleaned, like, a little dime-sized circle of that dirty pan. So keep at it. Keep cleaning."

I smiled and nodded. We were silent for quite a while. Basking in Ho'oponopono. Then I couldn't hold back my curiosity any longer.

"BB, can I ask you something?"

"Sure, man. Ask me anything. We got all night."

"Why'd you take the money?" I asked. "The hundred grand you took from the Pope. Why'd you do it?"

BB didn't answer. He just backed away from me and laid down on his cot. The only words I heard from him the rest of the night were four magic phrases. He said them again and again and, eventually, I joined him, saying them quietly to myself. I said the words along with him until I drifted off to sleep.

I love you.

I'm sorry.

Please forgive me.

Thank you.

Chapter 42

I slept hard that night. And I didn't dream. Surprisingly, the best night of sleep I had in eight months was on a thin blue cot in a jail cell. I woke up to the sound of the steel door squealing open, and approaching footsteps. I opened my eyes and saw that BB was already up. He was standing at the front of his cell. Through the bars, I could see Detective Palakiko leading two guards down the hallway.

"Open the door. Let him out of there. He's free to go," Palakiko said. I jumped off of the cot, eager to get the heck out of there. "Thank you, sir. Again, I apologize for everything."

"Not you," Palakiko sneered at me. "Him."

Palakiko looked to BB, who stared back in shock. The guards, who looked like they had just started their morning shift, opened the cell door. BB hesitated. He seemed to worry this was some kind of cruel trick.

"Get out of there!" Palakiko barked. "You know I don't enjoy doing this, so let's get it over with. You're free to go."

"What's going on?" I asked. "Did you arrest someone else?" My thoughts went to Nalani Richardson. Had Walton and I led Palakiko to the real killer?

"No, Mr. Pasch. If you must know, our investigation recently uncovered two voice memos Mr. Paul left on his phone at five twelve and five thirty-three Monday morning, both after Mr. Baxter came and went. In fact, the first memo referenced Mr. Baxter's visit. So, he clearly could not have killed Mr. Paul, who was very much alive after his departure."

"I told you!" BB said. "I fucking told you, Palakiko!" The detective made a gesture and the guards grabbed BB by the arms and followed Palakiko as he led them down the hallway. "Dave! Hang in there, brother! Good talkin' to ya! Keep cleaning your dishes!"

"Hey, Detective Palakiko! What about me?" I called after him. "When do I get out?"

The steel door slammed shut, bringing our little conversation to a firm end.

In the tomblike silence that followed, I had a lot to think about. I was certainly still worried about my future, both short- and long-term. Would I be bailed out soon? There would be major repercussions for me, and my career, if I was in jail during the championship game I was supposed to have been calling.

But what really dominated my train of thought was the shocking news that BB was innocent. I couldn't believe it. Walton was right the whole time. About everything. BB didn't do it, and, as a human being, he wasn't half bad. Actually, he was pretty great. Talking to him last night made me feel better than I had in a long time. I sat there by myself for awhile. I don't know how long. There were no clocks to tell me the time and no windows to tell me when the sun rose. I was getting antsy. I couldn't wait to get the heck out of jail.

And by the grace of God, and Bill Walton, I did.

Chapter 43

A cop led me out the front door of the prison, where I was temporarily blinded by the sunlight. It took my eyes awhile to adjust, and then Walton's giant head stepped forward, blocking out the sun and smiling down at me with equal radiance.

"There he is! Jean Valjean himself! Prisoner 24601! Dave, I am honored I was your one phone call from prison."

"Thanks for not picking up."

"My phone was on silent! I was in the middle of an amazing meal! Sushi night at Pika's! You wouldn't believe it. The wasabi is homemade!"

Stephanie was next to Walton, looking remarkably less happy. "Pasch! How is you getting arrested for punching a kid supposed to make my work vacation more relaxing and enjoyable?!"

"I'm sorry, I'm sorry." Before I said anything else, I dug through the bag of personal items the cops had given me and powered up my phone. Yup, I had missed many texts and calls from my wife last night. I stepped aside and called her, apologizing profusely and explaining what happened.

"You punched a guy?!" She gasped.

"It was a misunderstanding. Just a huge misunderstanding," I said, deciding to leave out the part about "the guy" being a high school student. Ah, to heck with it. No more lies. No more half-truths. "Honey, I punched a teenager. A big teenager."

I expected her to read me the riot act but her reaction was even worse. The quiet concern in my wife's voice was chilling.

"Dave. I'm worried about you. The nightmares. All those damn push-ups. Now this? You're punching children?"

"I know. I know. I messed up. But, as crazy as it sounds, last night I talked to someone about it and I think I took a huge step toward getting better. And I'm gonna get some more help when I get home. I'm gonna start talking to someone about how Seattle affected me. I promise."

We talked a little more, exchanged the important three words and then I hung up and walked over to Walton and Stephanie, who were now standing by the production van.

"Thanks for bailing me out of jail, guys," I said, not believing the words as they came out of my mouth.

"We actually didn't bail you out," Stephanie said. "Walton managed to get that kid and his father to drop the charges."

"Really?"

"Of course!" Walton said. "They agreed as long as you pay for all his medical bills and he and his friends got to watch the championship of the Maui Invitational from the front row."

"Which had me on the phone all morning calling in every last favor I had owed to me. And giving away many more. So, you owe me one, too. The heck with that, Pasch, you owe me ten," Stephanie said. "But, thanks to Walton, this fiasco won't go on your record and the network will never have to know about it."

"Thanks, guys. I mean it. I owe you both."

"Ours is a bond that requires no debt, my friend," Walton said, with a look to Stephanie that she ignored. "But really. A sucker punch? Pasch, please! You just cold cocked him! Unbelievable! How was jail? Did you see BB?"

I had been in a cell by myself for hours, and it took a moment for my brain to catch up to Walton's wandering, circuitous mind.

"Yeah. As a matter of fact, I did see BB. Right before he was cleared of all charges and released from prison by Detective Palakiko himself."

"What?!" Walton and Stephanie said in unison.

Once I finally assured Walton I wasn't kidding, he shouted an honest to God "hooray" to the heavens before picking me up and twirling me in a full circle. I made him put me down before telling him everything I knew about BB, Palakiko, and the Pope's voice memos.

"But Bill, it's weird. I talked to BB last night and he admitted to stealing the hundred thousand dollars from Pope. He just wouldn't say why he took it."

"Inconsequential! As I've told you from the start!" Walton said while shooing my concerns away with a flap of his giant hand. Stephanie and I got in the production van while Walton performed an extensive victory dance. You know the one. Performed by Deadheads all over the world. The twisting. The vague, unpredictable gyrating. The arms taking turns reaching into the sky as if swimming upstream in a river of weird.

I finally had my watch back, so I can tell you, with certainty, that the dance lasted seven minutes and twenty-three seconds.

Chapter 44

We finally got our dancing bear into the van as he pulled out his phone and repeatedly tried to call BB.

"It keeps sending me straight to voicemail!"

"His phone is probably dead, Bill. Plus, I'm sure he's going through a lot right now. He'll call you the second he can. Let him be," Stephanie said.

"I suppose you're right," Walton said, putting away his phone. "Oh, turn here. We're going to Kahului Harbor. BB is finally free. Now it's time to put away the real killer: Evil Real Estate Surfer, Nalani Richardson!"

"Absolutely not."

"Turn, woman, Turn!"

"No! You two clowns have a championship game in an hour and a half!"

"Plenty of time!" Walton insisted. "It's right back there! Execute a U-turn immediately!"

"It's not gonna happen, Walton. Your friend is out of jail. No more mystery nonsense. That's that."

"That is most certainly not that. We've just completed the first movement, our symphony is just beginning!"

"Let the cops do their job, Bill."

"But the cops aren't doing their job! Palakiko allowed his hatred of BB to cloud his judgement and let the real killer walk free for days!"

"And the second he realized BB couldn't have done it, he set him free. It sounds like this guy is honest and knows what he's doing." Stephanie looked at me in the rear view mirror, fire in her eyes. "Pasch, ninety minutes to game time. Is your head right or should I bring in a substitute? I can say you got food poisoning or something."

"No, no. I'm good, Steph. Nothing's gonna stop me from calling that game." She nodded at me. Right answer. We drove in silence for the rest of the trip, Walton pouting for Stephanie's benefit when he wasn't trying BB on his phone again and again every few minutes. His calls kept going right to a voicemail that was eventually completely filled with long, strange, rambling messages from Walton about freedom and vindication. The Grateful Dead and Neil Young were quoted liberally.

"Hey Bill, does Pika's do breakfast?" I asked Walton as the Hyatt appeared in the distance. The road to Pika's was just ahead on the left.

"Pika does a breakfast burrito that will make you moan with ecstasy. A hearty, yet elegant combination of eggs, bacon and cheese. They say breakfast is the most important meal of the day. David, this breakfast burrito will be the most important meal of your life. Guac is extra."

"Well, I'm in," Stephanie said as she made the turn.

"They're on me," I said. "Plus, I'd like to pick up my rental car. After breakfast I could use a little drive to clear my head before the game."

Stephanie nodded. "Make it a quick drive, Dave. I need your butt in the make-up chair at least ten minutes before air. You look like shit."

I relented. Whatever you say, boss. Moments later, we were at Pika's. I had Stephanie pull up to where I parked my car under the restaurant. But the Mustang wasn't there. I jumped out of the van and looked around frantically. No ruby red Mustang. My heart sank. Was it stolen?

"Dave!" Walton said, pointing.

I followed his finger to the car. Oh, no. I wished it had been stolen. The fate of that magnificent car was much, much worse. The Mustang was upside down, at the edge of the water, looking very much like a beached whale. It spun a few feet up and back every time the waves crashed in and out. Tourists were taking pictures. Some jerk attached the hook of his fishing pole to the bumper and pretended to be reeling it in. He was getting a lot of laughs.

Stephanie looked at me in shock as she pointed under the restaurant. "Dave! You left your car under there?! Why do you think the restaurant is on stilts?"

"I don't know!"

"The tide, Dave. It comes in every night and goes almost all the way up to the porch!"

"I don't know anything about tides, Stephanie! I grew up in Wisconsin! I hate the ocean! Can the next tournament we call please be nowhere near water?!"

I heard Walton and Stephanie's laughter behind me as I ran over to the Mustang. The windshield and windows had been smashed when the car flipped over. I felt extremely guilty for all the glass, oil, and gasoline I must have polluted the water with. I called Nick and had him arrange a tow truck as soon as humanly possible.

"Look, Dave, your car has crabs!" Walton pointed, and, indeed, a few hermit crabs were scurrying around the muffler. Walton and Stephanie found that absolutely hilarious. At least she had the decency to stop laughing when she saw the pained expression on my face.

"Sorry, Dave. I hope you got the insurance."

"You don't need the insurance when you use American Express, Stephanie! Plus I get SkyMiles because I use my Delta credit card!" What the hell was I talking about? Damn it, I really liked that car. "Well, on the bright side, we can still drive Arlo's Tesla," I said, thinking back to that magical drive to Kahului Harbor. But I could tell by Walton's expression, I wouldn't be driving the Tesla again any time soon.

"Sorry, Dave. I called Arlo to come get it after you got pinched by the cheese. It didn't seem right for us to keep it any longer than we had to. Plus, I couldn't figure out how to get my phone connected to the radio. It was too complicated!" Walton said, handing me back my Arizona Cardinals windbreaker.

"Dave, you can always drive the production van," Stephanie said, tossing me the keys. "You know, if you still want to clear your head before the game."

I looked to the big, white, boring cargo van and sighed.

"I'll walk."

Chapter 45

The Championship game is not always the best game of a tournament. Quite often, far from it. Many Super Bowls and World Cup Finals have let a run of exciting, single-elimination games go out with a whimper instead of a bang. With a seven-game series, like in professional basketball, baseball, and hockey, you're bound to get at least one or two good games in there somewhere. But when it's one game, winner takes all, you get what you get. Nerves can get the best of a team. In this case, they got the best of Kentucky. And we got another dominating performance from what was shaping up to be a special Duke Blue Devils team.

Kentucky was young, and there was little doubt that Coach John Calipari would get them turned around by the end of the season. If you ask me, he didn't mind an early-season loss like this.

I think it got the attention of his latest batch of budding superstars, and allowed him to start to do a little coaching. Be humble or you'll stumble. But Coach K already had a healthy mix of uber-talented freshman and experienced upperclassmen playing in midseason form. Today was Duke's day from the opening tip to the final buzzer.

Duke's players and coaches celebrated on the court with their families. It was nice, but by no means pandemonium. There was a long season ahead. The team knew how good they were, and had loftier goals for the season, but they had played well and were now whooping it up and giving hugs. Enjoying the moment.

Walton and I wanted to get out of there and confront Nalani, but we had a lot of people to greet after the game. The Governor came over to say goodbye, and I gave her my full attention. She had no idea how much she had saved my butt that week. Plus, she was truly a charming, brilliant lady and a heckuva basketball fan. I happily signed the Maui Invitational commemorative basketball her daughter was passing around for autographs.

I also shook hands with Sunny Sapolu, which turned out to be the name of the kid I had punched. And for the record, he was a big kid. Sunny was a 6'2", two-hundred-pound, star water polo player for the Punahou Buff 'N Blue, a mascot whose name represented "the golden isles in the midst of the blue Pacific."

I also met Sunny's father, the big shot lawyer, and all his friends that were on the beach last night. Thankfully, after enjoying the game from the front row, with all the complimentary food and drinks they wanted, and getting their picture taken with both head coaches, there were fewer hard feelings. Walton and Stephanie pulled no stops in helping smooth things over for me and I appreciated it. Sunny was even "randomly selected" to take a half court shot to win some free Maui Jim sunglasses. He missed, but Sunny seemed to be having a good time as the center of attention, despite the bandage over his nose. We all took a picture together, Sunny and I holding up our fists like boxers at a weigh-in. Walton stood behind us smiling, his arms stretched wide.

It was quite a crowd standing around us, as Walton and I held court. Once again, Commander Kirby stopped by. He was one of the people who kindly gave up his courtside tickets to make room for Sunny and his friends, but he still had nice seats for the game.

"Commander Kirby, are you evacuating the arena for a rogue earthquake?"

Instead of laughing at what I thought was a pretty solid joke, he just gave me a sad shake of his head. He apologized. "Sorry, Dave. I've been like this all day. I probably shouldn't have even come to the game. It's just hard for me to enjoy myself while BB's in jail."

"Well, then we have wonderful news for you," Walton said, overhearing. "Our BB bird has been set free! Free to fly once more! Pasch saw it himself while he was in jail for punching that high school kid!"

"Wait. What?" He said, looking at Sunny. "You what?"

"Oh, you know Walton. He's just talking nonsense. Haha. It's nothing. But the part about BB is true. He was released this morning."

"That's fantastic!" Commander Kirby said, his face breaking out in a relieved smile. Walton and I said our good-byes and headed out. We passed Coach K, who was lined up with his players and assistants taking pictures with the trophy, a large silver cup with fresh, flowering vines wrapped around it. We congratulated Coach K and he graciously thanked us. If there's a better gentleman and ambassador for the sport of basketball than Mike Krzyzewski, I haven't met them yet.

Chapter 46

As Walton and I left the court, we ran into Maki Sakamoto, Cal's seven-footer. He was watching the Blue Devils celebrate, standing in front of the Lahaina Civic Center's beautiful mural. It was magnificent, filling the entire wall behind one of the baskets. A colorful, art-deco depiction of Hawaiian life and basketball, a combination that perfectly described the Maui Invitational.

"Heckuva team." I nodded to the Blue Devils as we passed Sakamoto.

"Yes, they were incredible. It is hard to watch them perform so well in the championship knowing that, in a couple hours, I have to go out there and play in the loser game," Sakamoto said, referring to the game to distinguish seventh and eighth place in the tournament. And, to make matters worse, this year the "loser" game was being played after the championship. Another quirk of a quirky tournament. Because of the time difference between Maui and the mainland, the best games were played earlier in the day.

"Sakamoto, please! There are no loser games. The only game you lose is the one you don't play! Every game, every practice, every day of your life is a masterpiece in the making!"

Sakamoto smiled sadly. "I don't think this game will be my masterpiece. I'm not even starting."

"How is the best player on the team not starting?! That's absurd!"

"Bill, I'm sure Fast Eddie has his reasons," I said, trying to reel Walton in before he started Waltoning. We were there to cover the teams, not coach them.

"Coach Bianchi thinks the best chance we have against Villanova is a smaller, faster lineup. I may not agree. But it's his decision, he is the coach," Sakamoto said, diplomatically. "What can I do?"

"You can do everything, Sakamoto!" Walton thundered. "If you in the starting lineup makes the team better, then convince your coach you must start! Don't bend to the will of authority. Challenge it! Every order must be met with a healthy dose of skepticism. Anti-authoritarians are the lifeblood of a healthy society!"

"Bill, even if a player disagrees with the coach, they still have to listen to him," I said. "Otherwise it would be total chaos."

"Disagree! Strongly disagree! And, frankly Pasch, I resent your implication that chaos is a bad thing."

"Well, Bill. Did you ever disagree with John Wooden?" I smiled, thinking One Punch Pasch had just ended the argument in one fell swoop.

"I disagreed with John Wooden every single day! We battled all the time! About everything from facial hair to free throws! We debated ferociously, and, after he explained his position to me, I realized time and time again, he was right! But I never stopped pushing him and he never stopped pushing me right back! Conflict! Debate! That's what made us great! That's what made us champions!"

Walton turned to Sakamoto and put a hand on his shoulder. "You win the games, Maki. Not the great Fast Eddie Bianchi and his beloved 'system.'"

Sakamoto smiled. Walton's advice certainly seemed to make him feel better. If it were up to me, we'd find a player for Villanova and equally inspire him. You know, just to keep the scales even. But we didn't have time. After the next game, the tournament was over. Then Detective Palakiko wanted us off the island.

If we wanted to talk to Nalani Richardson, we had to talk to her right now.

Chapter 47

Walton and I rushed to the parking lot and headed straight for the production van, where we were surprised to find Stephanie leaning against the driver's side door.

"Where do you ding-dongs think you're going?" Stephanie asked.

"To take down an evil real estate surfer for killing my friend!" Walton said.

"Nope." She shook her head. "You have a game to call in an hour and forty-five minutes. You're not going anywhere."

"Stephanie, please! Her office is forty-five minutes away. We can be there and back in an hour and a half. That gives us fifteen minutes to pull a confession out of her. Fifteen minutes to truth! To justice! We can do this!"

I nodded. "He's right, Steph. We'll be back on time."

"Stephanie, Jon Paul's soul can't rest while his killer walks free. It's one thing to not help us, it's quite another to stand in our way!"

Walton's words clearly stung Stephanie. She crossed her arms.

"Okay. fine. Let's go."

"Yes! She's back on the team!" Walton said, triumphantly.

"No, no, no. I'm still out. I'm just coming with you to chaperone. I need to make sure you two get back in time for the game, and to make extra sure Iron Dave Pasch over here doesn't haul off and punch anyone."

I took the hit. And then I drove the production van. The behemoth handled like a cruise ship and accelerated like maple syrup pouring down a tree in February. But it got us there. Eventually. I parked at the beachside office plaza and Walton, Stephanie, and I stormed up the stairs into the office where Sky, Nalani's glowing receptionist, manned his post.

"Jesus, he's gorgeous," Stephanie whispered in my ear.

"Aloha 'auinalā, yurt duders. I thought you left town." Sky changed his calming tune as we stormed by him into Nalani's office. "Hey! You can't go in there, she's in a meeting!"

"Sorry, Sky," I said as I passed him.

"Dude," he replied, very disappointed in my complete lack of chill.

Walton dramatically swung open the door to Nalani's office to reveal her standing at her desk with a young couple who were signing some papers. "Congratulations, you two are now officially homeowners," Nalani was saying as we barged in. They all turned to us, surprised.

"Whoa. Is that Bill Walton?" The husband asked.

"Yes. He's buying some land on the island to build the world's biggest yurt," Nalani said, her voice dripping with sarcasm, before turning back to the couple and smiling. "Congrats again, you two. Feel free to call me if you have any questions." The husband shook Nalani's hand, the wife hugged her, and the couple exited past us.

"Sky! Be sure they get one of our Aloha doormats!"

"Totally, Nalani!" He called from the other room.

"Please. Sit." Nalani gestured to the couch and we all sat down. Her spacious office was brightly lit by the sunlight pouring in from the windows and tastefully decorated in minimalistic fashion. A surfboard hung on a rack on the wall behind her desk, looking like a work of highly functional art. Nalani closed the door and then sat facing us at the edge of her desk.

"Arlo warned me you would be coming to see me. He also told me that he's apparently going around telling people we're having an affair. I wasn't too happy about that, so please respect my privacy more than he did."

"Lady, how you treat the sanctity of your marriage is your business. We're here about what you did to my friend," Walton said, crossing his arms.

"Okay, let's just cut to the chase. I did not kill Jon Paul. Yes, I wanted his property. That was no secret. But he said 'no; and I moved on. You think I would kill him for it? Guys, who do you think I am? Come on. Look at me. I surf for God's sake," she said, nodding to her board.

"Evil people can surf!" Walton insisted. "They do all the time."

"Why don't you just tell us everything that happened that morning," I said. "From the moment you left Arlo's room," I added quickly, not wanting her to recount the torrid details of her affair. Infidelity made me sick to my stomach just thinking about it.

"Fine. I woke up around five forty-five to the smell of coffee. Samangja was making breakfast for the Pope, like he always did. It wasn't the first time I had spent the night there. My husband works the late shift a lot."

I winced.

"Arlo was asleep, with that loop thing still going on his computer, and I snuck down into the kitchen. Samangja gave me some coffee and toast. He had it ready for me. I'm an early riser and he always knows when I'm there. Samangja knows everything. And he never judged me. He has a way about him."

"Yes, Samangja is amazing. We all love him. But we're here for your story, surfer lady," Walton said, cutting her off.

"Okay, okay, I was drinking coffee and eating a piece of toast with cinnamon sugar and butter, just how I like it, and talking to Samangja. We were talking about the party and everything. And that's when we heard Moses Boulevard screaming his head off, when he found Jon Paul's body. I'll never forget it. I love Moses, he's amazing. I listen to that man's voice almost every day and I'll never forget hearing it in that moment."

Nalani paused. She seemed truly haunted by the memory. I couldn't help but believe her story. She took a deep, cleansing breath and continued. "Samangja told me to go back upstairs to

Arlo's room, and he called the cops. That's all I know. After that, I was either hiding under a bed or stuffed in the trunk of a car."

"Hey, Bill. When we left Arlo's room to go to the garage yesterday, we came down those same stairs," I said. "The stairs to get down into the studio were on the other side of the kitchen."

"That's right," Nalani said. "Samangja was in the kitchen when I came down and he was there when I went back up. I never went down to the studio. I couldn't have without Samangja knowing."

Walton and I looked at each other and shrugged. Her story certainly seemed reasonable, and was easy enough to confirm with Samangja. Nalani was telling the truth.

"Okay, thank you for your time. We should get going," Stephanie said, tapping her watch to Walton and me. "On behalf of frick and frack, I apologize for the intrusion."

Nalani walked us to the door, past Sky. We apologized for storming past him earlier and came clean, telling him we weren't really looking to buy land for the world's largest yurt.

"Ohhh," Sky said. It hurt me to disappoint him, but fortunately he readily accepted our apology. We said our farewells.

"Malaho, Sky."

"'A' ole palikir, duders!" He smiled his impossibly perfect smile. I think I saw a flash of light bounce off a tooth.

We stepped onto the balcony as a cop car pulled into the parking lot. We froze, like three deer caught in high beams. If Detective Palakiko was in that car, the jig was up. There was no way we'd be able to explain our way out of this, and the three of us would likely spend the night in jail, an experience I wasn't eager to repeat. But it wasn't Palakiko. Instead, a handsome, strapping police officer stepped out of the car and looked up at us. He smiled and waved to Nalani. She waved back.

"My husband, Kai," she explained.

None of us knew what to say. This was very awkward.

"I'll be right down, babe!" She called to him before turning to face us. "I still love him," she said, quietly. "But I also love being with Arlo." I frowned, not being able to hide my dismay. "I know, I know. It's wrong to be in love with two men at the same time. And I can't do it anymore. I'm gonna tell him it's over."

"Which one? Him or Arlo?" Walton asked.

She sighed. "I haven't decided, yet. But I will."

I shrugged. We headed down the stairs. Nalani called after me. "Remember, Dave. The day you want to leave it all behind and move to Maui, come see me. I'll fix you right up. Ocean-front property at land-locked prices."

"Thanks. And good luck, Nalani." I meant it. I was rooting for her.

Chapter 48

The seventh place game was, by far, the least attended of the tournament. And, so far, it seemed like fans were smart to stay away. Villanova was running away with it, destroying Fast Eddie's "small ball" lineup with a double-digit lead that just kept growing. Finally, desperate to mix things up, Fast Eddie put Maki Sakamoto in the game with ten minutes to go in the first half.

"FINALLY!" Walton howled as Cal's best player took the court.

Woosie Montague initiated the offense. Sakamoto posted up his man and called for the ball. Woosie dribbled. Crab dribbled. Probe dribbled. He dribbled between his legs as the shot clock wound down. Finally, with no time to do anything else, he chunked up a very desperate, very long, step-back three. It did not go in. It did not come close.

"Woosie Montague misses from the mysterious red line just shy of midcourt!"

"I thought you had to join a union to toss around bricks like that," Walton said. "I love all unions. And the Union Jack flag of Great Britain! Rule, Britannia!"

"Josh Whitney grabs the long rebound for Villanova and the athletic swing man wastes no time racing down the court, driving the lane and-- no! Rejected by Maki Sakamoto!"

"Yes!!! Sakamoto announcing his presence with authority!"

"Sakamoto's athleticism as he raced down the court reminded me a bit of Zion Williamson."

"Zion has tremendous talent, but has a long way to go before he lives up to his namesake, the incredible Zion National Park in Utah. Oh my, the beauty! Court of the Patriarchs! Towers of the Virgin!"

As Walton started listing his top ten hiking trails in the state of Utah, Woosie took the ball up for Cal. Right after he crossed half court, Sakamoto ran to the top of the key like he was going to set a screen. Woosie waved him away but the big man walked up to his point guard and ripped the ball out of his hands. I saw the referee raise the whistle to his lips. He almost called a foul, then realized it was impossible to foul your own teammate.

"Does it count as a steal if you take it from your own team?" Asked Walton, who seemed bemused by Sakamoto's actions.

"All eyes are on Maki Sakamoto as the shot clock is now a factor. He puts his head down and drives to the bucket-- no! He stops on a dime and spins the other way. He leaves his man in the dust and drains an open ten footer in the lane. What was that?!"

"A Dream Shake Hakeem Olajuwon would be proud to call his own! Artistry in the post I haven't seen since the glory days of my good friend, Kevin McHale! Footwork reminiscent of Fred Astaire! Alvin Aliey! The great Debbie Allen! Glorious!"

Walton, like Maki Sakamoto, was just getting started.

"How could this talent be kept on the bench?!" Walton screamed loud enough for Fast Eddie to hear. He gave Walton the stink eye.

Villanova, perhaps a little rattled, rushed the ball up the court and, instead of moving the ball around as they had been, settled for a quick, contested three that barely missed. It went in and out of the rim.

Momentum in sports is like a giant, heavy pendulum. When it starts to swing, it's very hard to stop. And the momentum of this game had been very much in Villanova's favor. Then Maki Sakamoto entered the game, and ripped the pendulum right off its frictionless pivot and threw it to the ground.

"Sakamoto with the rebound, takes it up the court himself, backing down his man in the post. He jukes right, spins left and gently tosses in a baby hook off the glass."

"The banks are open!" Walton yelled. He was in heaven. "Maki Sakamoto doing to the backboard what Alexander Hamilton did to the Bank of the United States in 1791! The great Lin-Manuel Miranda, we applaud you! Broadway awaits your return!"

"Sakamoto now guarding Villanova's inbound pass. He's smothering the small guard with his size and length."

Sakamoto called for his teammates to join his one-man full-court press. Moments later, he deflected the inbound pass and Woosie Montague grabbed the loose ball. Sakamoto put out his hands and Woosie, who honestly seemed a little freaked out, passed it right to him. Walton was openly cheering.

Sakamoto had the ball on the wing. He waved his teammates away and they spread out along the baseline. Two in the corners, two at the blocks. Sakamoto moved to the top of the key and backed his man down. When they double-teamed him at the free throw line, he backed both men down. When the entire Villanova defense collapsed on the big man, Sakamoto made a simple kick out pass to Woosie Montague in the corner. He was so wide open, he didn't know what to do. He held the ball for at least three seconds when Sakamoto finally yelled, "Shoot it!"

Woosie took a gather dribble and drained the open three.

Sakamoto looked at him, putting his hands in the air as if to say, "See?" Woosie smiled and nodded. Sakamoto urged his teammates to continue the full court press as he once again smothered the player inbounding the ball. Before they got a five-second penalty, Villanova called a timeout.

"Going to break, guys," Stephanie said in our ears. "Back in ninety seconds."

Sakamoto walked over to the bench sheepishly, ready to get yelled at, but Fast Eddie just stood there, shaking his head and smiling. Walton and I took off our headphones so we could listen in.

"Maki! What, you're my new seven-foot-tall point guard?" Fast Eddie yelled as his team sat down in their small chairs. "What the hell is going on out there?"

Woosie spoke up. "Coach. Maki gets the ball at the top of the key. The defense collapses on him. Leaves the rest of us wide open. And if they don't collapse on him? Shit. Green light. Big man scores. They're screwed either way. I like it, Coach." Woosie turned to his big man and extended his fist. Maki nodded and they bumped fists, or "dapped" as they call it now.

Fast Eddie nodded. "Okay, I love it. Let's do it. Keep that full court press till the end of the half, see how much of that lead we can chip away. If they ever actually inbound the ball past Sakamoto..." He winked at Maki. "I want Woosie and Prows to trap whoever gets it. We've got plenty of fouls to play with, so be physical. Come on, guys. Eat 'em up!"

The Cal players cheered. The horn sounded and they ran onto the court, full of energy and enthusiasm. It looked like they traded uniforms with a completely different team.

"Back in thirty seconds, guys," Stephanie called in our headsets.

Fast Eddie scrambled out to the middle of the court, sliding in his loafers, to whisper a last minute thought to Sakamoto. Whatever he told him, Sakamoto laughed. Fast Eddie patted him on the ass and strutted by our announcer's table on his way back to the bench.

"Fast Eddie's team playing defense? Passing the ball? It can't be!" Walton said, good-naturedly. "We're gonna have to start calling you Smart Eddie!"

Bianchi winked. This may not have been his "system," but he seemed smart enough to know when to shut up and get out of the way.

By the end of the first half, the score was tied. Amazingly, in only ten minutes, Sakamoto had fifteen points and ten assists, and when the second half started, the crowd had swelled. Social media was buzzing about Sakamoto's performance, and players and coaches from every team came out to watch. But Villanova did not go gently into the good night. The Wildcats came out swinging in the second half, and the game went back and forth, the two teams trading leads with almost every possession.

With Sakamoto orchestrating the offense from the high post, Woosie Montague was having his best game of the tournament, if not the best game of his life. Unencumbered by running the offense, he was blossoming before our eyes into a playmaking two-guard. Draining open shots when they were there and penetrating the lane for easy baskets if they weren't.

"Woosie drains yet another three! His sixth of the half!"

"Woosie Montague has found a wormhole from his hands to the back of the net! Before our very eyes, he's created a fourth dimension in the space-time continuum!"

"Bill, that's hyperbolic even by your standards, but the kid is red hot."

As hot as Cal was, Villanova refused to go away. Josh Whitney kept them in the game with an incredible run of hot shooting of his own, and, with twenty-five seconds left, Cal was only up by two. Then Woosie made the classic freshman blunder of fouling a player on a three-point attempt. Luckily for Cal, the ball didn't go in.

Villanova's Wright Ashford, a senior who led the NCAA in free-throw percentage the previous year, easily hit his first two free throws. The game was tied. During a Villanova substitution, Sakamoto moved over to Fast Eddie and gestured, "Timeout, Coach?"

Fast Eddie laughed. "For what? He makes this, we're down one. Take the ball that way and score," Fast Eddie said, pointing to the other basket. "Come on, Maki. Do your thing and make me look good."

Sakamoto smiled and went back to the block. Then Wright Ashford hit his third free throw. There were twenty seconds left in the game. Shot clock off. Cal down by one.

Sakamoto inbounded the ball to Woosie, who took the ball up the court. Then Woosie handed the ball back to Sakamoto at the top of the key and drifted to the corner to give the big man his space. Sakamoto backed his guy up to the free throw line. Ten seconds left. Nine seconds. Eight. Sakamoto made his move and the defense collapsed on him. They weren't going to let Sakamoto beat them.

"Sakamoto kicks it out to Woosie who takes the open three, no! It's an alley-oop!"

It was amazing. After passing the ball, Sakamoto quickly spun around his defenders and cut to the basket. At first, Woosie's pass looked too high, but Sakamoto jumped higher. He ripped the ball down from the heavens with both hands and nearly tore the rim off the basket.

"OH MY! WHAT A DUNK!" I'm not sure I ever screamed as loudly during a broadcast as I did in that moment. The arena erupted into pandemonium. I've never seen Walton happier. He stood up with his arms in the air. Eyes closed. Shouting to the roof of the arena.

"Daun ni nagete, Ōkī otoko! Daun ni nagete!"

"What's that Bill?"

"Dave, that's Japanese for, 'throw it down, big man. Throw it down!'"

I should have known. Walton can say "throw it down, big man" in forty-seven languages, including sign.

Villanova was out of timeouts. Wright Ashford tried to launch a desperate full-court shot at the buzzer, but, as he shot it, Sakamoto blocked it into the stands. It was one of those moments as a broadcaster I didn't need to say a word. The cameras capturing the reactions of both teams in victory and defeat said it better than I ever could. I also couldn't throw it to Walton because he left the announcer's table. He had captured the Cal mascot, put the giant bear head on his own, and danced into the stands.

And so, the seventh place game of the Maui Invitational turned out to be the best game of the tournament, and one of the greatest games I've ever seen. I will never use the phrase "loser game" again. John Wooden was right. Don't save your best for the big moments. Make every single day of your life a masterpiece. Success is the satisfaction of knowing you did your best, whatever the outcome. And looking at the smile on Maki Sakamoto's face as he embraced Woosie Montague, despite two loses, the Maui Invitational had been a very successful tournament for the California Golden Bears.

Chapter 49

After the game, we took the production van to Pika's. Once inside, Walton and I ducked away. We stuck Stephanie with the task of schmoozing the Network honchos who followed us over there. It's funny, the Maui Invitational always seemed to call for more network supervision than the games we did in Pullman, Washington. Needless to say, after being in prison and then calling two games in one afternoon, I was starving. We put in our order with the bartender. Three burgers, please.

I also got a Mai Tai. Walton was back to his usual, high alcohol kombucha. Ginger, lime, and rosehips. We got our drinks and saw Arlo Paul sitting by himself at the end of the bar. He was halfway through his own burger, angrily swiping through his phone.

"You okay, Arlo?" I asked, as Walton and I scooted down the bar to sit down next to him.

"No," he said, bitterly. "I'm far from fucking okay." He showed me an email on his phone. "Rosenfeld & Moskos turned me down. Fuckers. Everyone's turned me down. I put everything I had into this, and now I'm busted. I own millions of dollars of student debt and can't afford to hire anyone to collect a dime of it."

Walton and I looked at each other and shrugged. We didn't know what to say. It was like a Bond villain complaining that the death ray he was going to use to blow up the moon was broken.

"Maybe it's for the best, Arlo," Walton offered. "Have you ever thought about getting into wind? Windmill farms are very big right now. And not just in Holland! Harvest the wind, Arlo, and you harvest the future!"

Arlo looked at Walton like he was nuts. I recognized that look. I've made it many, many times before.

"Fuck wind, Walton. I'm not walking away from this. When I sell my dad's estate, I'll have the money to launch my company. I'm telling you, you guys should invest. I'm gonna make a killing and every asshole who turned me down is gonna look like a jackass."

"Uh-huh. How's the burger?" I said, desperately trying to change the subject. Arlo paused, a little thrown. Then he seemed to realize he had been ranting like a maniac. He smiled, happy to stop talking about a business that wasn't going well. He put down his phone and held up his burger.

"The burger is amazing. As always. Pika's a genius. You want to rank the top chefs in the world? Have 'em all make a burger and see how they do. I'm telling you, Pika would be in the conversation." Arlo laughed. I think it was the first time I had heard him make that particular noise. "Nalani is always trying to get him to serve those impossible burgers here. She's not even vegan, she just loves eating those things. Not me. The Impossible burger is not a burger."

"They're very good, Arlo," Walton said. "And good for you! They're filled with lots of protein, vitamins, minerals, and soy leghemoglobin, a tremendous plant-based source of heme iron. And believe me, you can taste it!"

"And they don't make you feel bad after you eat 'em," I offered, trying to be diplomatic.

"But that's the whole point!" Arlo insisted. "A burger's not supposed to be good for you. It's supposed to make you feel a little bad. That's what makes it a burger. Should I get a burger? Nah, I shouldn't. Aw, fuck it. I'm getting a burger."

I had to admit, he was right.

"It's not a burger if you don't feel guilty." He held up the beautiful, juicy double cheeseburger. "That's why I run every morning. To earn this burger."

"I'll drink to that," Walton said, and we all clinked our drinks together. Arlo drank some of his beer and turned to look at us.

"Do you guys think I'm an asshole?"

"Yes," Walton said without hesitation.

Arlo laughed again. This time even louder. I tried to say something nice, to smooth things over, but he cut me off.

"No, no. Forget it, Pasch. I know I'm an asshole. But... I want you guys to know, some of that stuff I said about my father? On the mountain? I want you to know it wasn't true. I mean, of course it wasn't. I was just pissed off. About a lot of things. And none of it was his fault." He paused, gathering his words. "My dad was a great man. A great guy. Obviously. I'm who I am because of him. But mostly, I'm who I am because of me. Does that make sense?"

"Perfect sense, Arlo," Walton said, putting a hand on Arlo's shoulder. "Your words about your father fill my heart. Thank you."

Arlo pushed his plate away and looked around the restaurant. "You know, Pika's is pretty much the only thing my dad and I ever agreed about. We loved this place. We'd come here all the time. Every special occasion. Birthdays. Christmas. Shit, tomorrow is Thanksgiving, isn't it? We would have come here together. Pika does an amazing Thanksgiving dinner."

Arlo got choked up. He had to stop talking. I didn't know what to say. I wasn't good at this kind of emotional stuff. I found myself wishing BB were here. Where the heck was BB? I figured he'd be right here at the bar, celebrating his freedom. I looked to the front door, almost willing him to walk in, and, at that exact moment, the doors opened.

But it wasn't him. A large group of people entered, happily chatting away. They were well-dressed, maybe fresh from a birthday party or some other big social event. They marched up to the bar and started putting in a rather large order for drinks, including a wide variety of elaborate cocktails. The bartender was swamped. "In the weeds," as they say in the restaurant industry. And he downright panicked when he pulled the tap for the draft beer and the only thing that came out was air and foam.

"Sorry, folks. I gotta go change the keg. It'll just be a minute."

"I got it, Benny!" Arlo told him. "You make the drinks, I'll change the keg." Arlo looked to us, explaining. "I basically grew up in this place."

"Thanks, Arlo. You're a lifesaver," the bartender said, while grabbing a cocktail shaker and mixing the first batch of drinks. Pika had just exited the kitchen with our burgers and saw the exchange. He smiled, thanking Arlo as they passed each other. Pika dropped the burgers in front of us. "See? I told you he's a good boy. He's got a good heart. Sometimes his brain just gets in the way."

While Walton said hello to Pika, I was able to carry our three plates of burgers and fries to the table in one trip, thanks to the nights and weekends I waited tables in college. I passed by Pope's table, which was still reserved in his honor, now adorned with even more pictures and flowers.

Some of the original flowers were already wilting.

Chapter 50

Stephanie was sitting at a table on the patio with a great view of the sunset. With the tournament over, the network honchos were heading to the airport. But we weren't going anywhere. Walton and I had pushed our flight back indefinitely. Despite Detective Palakiko's instructions, there was no way Walton was leaving the island before Pope's killer was found. And, if he was staying, I was staying. After all, we were partners.

My wife didn't love the news that I'd be missing Thanksgiving dinner. In fact, she was pretty damn mad. My first priority upon getting home would be to make it up to her, and my kids, any way I could.

As I approached the table, Stephanie was quietly enjoying the sunset, and I didn't disturb her. The horizon was being painted with a spectacular explosion of colors. A tropical combination of purples and pinks, ending in a deep red crimson. And then the colors disappeared, like a black velvet blanket being pulled over the sky. After the last sliver of sun fell into the Pacific, I put the three plates down on the table.

"Pasch, you hero!" Stephanie said, eyeing the burger and rubbing her hands together.

"Stephanie! Your first Pika burger," Walton said, as he joined us. "I'm glad I could be here for this momentous occasion." We dug in and, in moments, Steph's burger was almost gone. Rookie move. And hey, I had been there myself with my first Pika's burger. But now I was more experienced. I ate slowly. Savoring each bite. Enjoying every perfectly-toasted french fry. Stephanie was doing none of that. She devoured the burger, closing her eyes as she chewed. She moaned, sounding a bit like Meg Ryan in the movie When Harry Met Sally. I'm glad I was already having what she was having. Finally, less than a minute after she started, Stephanie finished her last bite.

"Well, hot damn," she said as she wiped her mouth. "That didn't suck."

"Steph, how about a burger for the Colonel?" I asked. "Is he on his way?"

Stephanie laughed. "No. They're still at the Wailea Golf Club. Apparently, for the first time in history, the Army/Navy game ended in a tie. Four days of golf ended in a tie. Can you believe it? It's too dark to keep playing so they went to a hardware store, bought a big metal trash can and put it a hundred yards out under the lights of the driving range. Sudden death playoff. First one in wins. So, I think you're stuck with me for awhile."

It got a little chilly on the patio. I put on my Arizona Cardinals windbreaker and zipped it up. Walton finished his burger, chewing thoughtfully, and turned to Stephanie. "Steph, I don't understand why you wouldn't help us solve my friend's murder, but I've just decided to forgive you."

"Thank you, Bill," she said, dryly.

"After dinner, Pasch and I will get back to work on the case. But now, it's time to forgive and forget. I've learned that life is too precious to waste a second of it fighting with someone you love. Let me buy us a round of drinks." I guess that meant I was buying dinner. Walton flagged down a waiter and ordered us a round of Mai Tais. Stephanie changed hers to a passion fruit lemonade.

"Steph, that's absurd. Have a Mai Tai with us. Pasch loves 'em. He's been drinking them all week."

"It's true," I said, holding up my empty glass.

"Not for me, thanks."

"Stephanie Walker, I insist. Drink a Mai Tai to toast our friendship!"

"No, Bill. I'm good."

"Come on, Steph." I said. "The tournament's over. You're officially on vacation. Have a Mai Tai."

"Guys, I really like that passion fruit lemonade. I'm good."

While the waiter stood there awkwardly, Walton and I went back and forth trying to convince Stephanie to get a Mai Tai when she finally lost her composure and shouted.

"Oh, my god. You idiots, I'm pregnant!"

Chapter 51

"Two Mai Tais and a passion fruit lemonade." The waiter said before gratefully bolting from the table.

"Can't you two take a hint?"

"I guess not," I said, laughing. How could I call myself an amateur detective after missing all those clues?! "Congratulations, Steph. That's great news."

"Blessings!" Walton said, raising his arms in the air. "Aloha nui loa, Stephanie!"

"Thanks, guys. I'm only eleven weeks. We're not supposed to tell anyone, yet. Least of all people I work with. So, chill. But Bill, that's why I couldn't help you guys. I wanted to. But I just couldn't risk anything like Seattle happening again. Not now."

"Of course! It all finally makes sense! And you did the right thing, Stephanie. Like Coach Wooden always said, family and love come first. And now look what love did! Another branch on the tree of life! This is truly a special occasion. Let us celebrate!"

Walton reached into his pocket and took out the huge joint Don Nelson gave him at Pope's party. He popped open the plastic tube and, before I knew it, the end of the giant joint lit up like Rudolph's nose on Christmas Eve.

"Whoa, Bill, I'm not sure that's good for the baby."

"I agree, Dave. It's not good for the baby. It's great for the baby!" He said, blowing smoke in our faces. I was furious and tried to get Stephanie to move to another table, but she didn't seem to mind.

"Stephanie, what's the matter with you? You won't have a drink but you're fine getting a contact high from Don Nelson's wonderjoint?"

"Dave, I could have a drink if I wanted to. I don't want one because I don't feel great. To be honest, a little bit of weed wouldn't hurt right about now," she said, turning to Walton. "A little bit."

Walton nodded and blew a single, perfect smoke ring in her direction before turning the rest of his combustion into my face. It was like the exhaust of a city bus.

"Stop it, Walton! The stuff rots your brain."

"Untrue!" Walton said. "Untrue! Marijuana does the opposite of rotting your brain, Dave, it ripens it! The human brain contains an endocannabinoid system that acts as docking ports for the micro crystals of cannabis! You see? Our brains were perfectly constructed to interact with marijuana! That can't be a mistake!"

Walton took another huge puff.

"Stephanie, help me out here," I said, then held my breath during Walton's exhale. "Tell him how stupid that stuff makes you."

"Are you calling me stupid, Dave?"

"Oh, no," I said. "You too?"

Stephanie shrugged and Walton shouted for joy.

"I like it, Dave. Weed helps me relax. At the end of the day, when I have fifty things bouncing around my brain, I can go home, put Ana to bed, smoke half a joint, watch a movie, and think about nothing else but that movie. It gives me tunnel vision."

"Because of the docking ports in your brain for the micro crystals of cannabis!" Walton insisted. "Dave, have some cannabinoids. Please."

Walton extended the joint toward me and I held up my hand. I was not swayed by their arguments. But, when I wasn't looking, Walton blew more smoke in my face. Stephanie laughed and leaned over to sniff some. Then Walton and Stephanie laughed together.

I hated being around stoners.

"Hey! We still don't know who killed Jon Paul," I said to Walton, angrily. "We shouldn't be sitting here toking up, we should be trying to solve the mystery!"

"That's exactly what I'm doing. I've done some of my best thinking while bouncing ideas off my good friend Mary Jane. Take a puff, Dave."

I shook my head.

"It could help," Stephanie said. "Seriously. Marijuana improves cognitive performance. It's a fact. Anxiety interferes with your quality of attention, so, when weed chills you out, your cognitive function improves."

"Because of the docking ports in your brain!"

"No thanks, guys. My brain is working just fine on it's own."

They giggled some more. Man, I was like Don Rickles to these stoners. I decided to ignore them and focus on the case. There had to be something I was missing. I turned my placemat around and drew a crude floorplan of the Pope's house on the back. I noted where everyone was and the times they came and went. Moses in the guest house. Samangja in his room, then in the kitchen making breakfast. Arlo and Nalani upstairs. Pope in his studio. BB in and out just after five o'clock. Pope recording voice memos at five twelve and five thirty-three. Found dead at six o'clock. Another blast of smoke came my way via Walton, but I was too busy to wave it away.

I added to my map. I even drew some of the foliage around the house. Added some of the wildflowers I remembered seeing. I drew the winding path through the bamboo grove, and the bridge over the koi pond. I thought about every suspect we had. Every interview we had done. There had to be an answer to a question I wasn't asking. Some piece of information hiding somewhere in the darkness beyond the spotlight of my mind.

I paused, looking out into the darkness of the ocean. I could hear it and smell it more than I could see it. The breeze on my face felt nice. Really, really nice. Man, I love Hawaii. I took a sip of my

Mai Tai. Holy smokes, that's a good drink. While I was distracted, Walton blew a few more smoke rings in my face.

"Come on, Bill. Be cool or someone's gonna call the cops."

I didn't even hear Walton's reply. Something clicked in my brain. I stood up, took out my phone and Nalani's business card and stepped away from the table. It took me a few tries to call her. I had quite a bit of trouble figuring out my phone. After a few misdials, and unintentionally opening the maps app a frustrating amount of times, I finally got the right number. Then, as it was ringing, I forgot what I was calling Nalani about. Thankfully, by the time she answered, I had remembered. I asked my question and her answer confirmed exactly what I was thinking. I ran back to the table.

"Guys..." I paused. What was I talking about? Oh yeah.

"I know who killed Jon Paul."

Chapter 52

I told Walton and Stephanie my theory. Walton was blown away, but I tried to calm him down and manage expectations.

"Slow down, Bill. Before we get carried away, we have to confirm everything with Samangja," I said. "Come on." I threw a handful of cash on the table to cover our tab. I had never done that before, just throwing cash on the table and leaving. I'll be honest, it felt really cool. Even though I left way, way too much. Arlo saw us running out of the restaurant and asked what was going on.

"Pasch knows who killed your father!" Walton said before I could stop him.

"Then I'm coming with you," Arlo said, jumping up.

"Wait, wait, wait. Maybe you and Stephanie should stay here," I said.

"No way, Dave," Stephanie said. "My husband is hitting golf balls at a trash can and I've been sitting by the pool all week, not drinking, and reading the same page of a book for three days. I'm coming with you." The look on Arlo's face told me he definitely wasn't staying behind. I relented.

We piled into the production van and headed back down the Honoapi'ilani Highway. I let Stephanie drive. I had a couple Mai Tai's and seemed to be feeling the effects more than usual. Walton connected his phone to the van's radio with an aux cord he kept in his pocket for just such an occasion. He played a mix of Grateful Dead studio releases. He didn't always listen to the live stuff, and, I gotta tell you, it wasn't half bad. I never realized it before, but St. Stephen is just a damn good song.

The same old patrolman was at the guard house when we arrived. Arlo leaned into the front seat and stuck his head out the window.

"Hey Ted, it's me. Can you let us in?"

"Sure, Arlo," Officer Ted said, as he yawned and opened the gate. His sleepy, half-closed eyes suggested we had woken him up from a nap. "Say, who's that with you, Arlo?" He said, looking into the van.

"Travelling companions!" Walton thundered, as we drove up to the house. "We're here to pay our friend's debt!" The big man didn't know the definition of the words, "low profile."

Stephanie parked the van and we ran inside the house. We found Samangja standing on the patio, his back to Haleakalā, looking west. To the ocean. We were all quiet for a moment. The only sound was the bamboo fountain, bubbling peacefully in the corner until the cup filled with water and clacked down on the rock. Splash.

We all found ourselves staring at the fountain. Maybe it pulled us in, maybe we were just postponing the conversation we had to have. But we all quietly stood there, watching the water slowly filling the wooden cup.

"Some call it a deer chaser. But I don't," Samangja said, following our gaze. "The sounds it makes is the rhythm of nature. A millennium every minute." He blinked, almost coming out of a trance. "I'm sorry, how can I help you?"

"I need you to confirm something Nalani Richardson just told me about the morning Jon Paul died."

Samangja paused, looking at Arlo.

"It's okay, Samangja. They know she was in my room that night."

Samangja turned back to me and nodded.

"At six o'clock, you were in the kitchen, making Pope's breakfast and talking to Nalani when you heard Moses scream." Samangja nodded. "What did you do next?"

"I called the police."

Walton sunk, collapsing into a chair. Samangja looked to me, confused.

"I asked Nalani to tell me exactly what Moses screamed when he found Jon Paul's body. She said she'd never forget that moment. And she said he just screamed. A pained, guttural cry."

Walton turned to his old friend. "Moses didn't scream, 'call the cops' or 'Jon Paul is dead.' He just screamed."

I took a step forward. "And you didn't run down there to see what was happening. Because you already knew what happened. You already knew Jon Paul had been murdered. Because you murdered him."

Chapter 53

"How could you?! How could you kill him?!" Arlo screamed. Stephanie and I had to hold him back.

Walton wiped the tears raining down his face. "Samangja, how could you lie to me? Was any of what you told us true?" Walton begged.

Samangja, suddenly looking even older and weaker, sat down in the chair next to Walton. "Everything I told you was true. Every single word. And I didn't kill Jon Paul. I promise you that." He looked around at each of us, landing on Arlo. "It's time you heard the truth. Three truths, in fact. I was going to wait until after tomorrow. After we scattered Jon Paul's ashes, per his request. He wanted it done right here. Three days after his death. He was insistent about that. And lately, Jon Paul had plenty of time to think about his final moments, because he was dying. That is the first truth. Please, have a seat. I will tell you everything."

Samangja gestured to a circle of couches and chairs by the pool. The glass dance floor from the party had been removed, and a light beneath the salted water lit the patio with a wavy, aquamarine light. It took us awhile to calm Arlo down and convince him to sit and listen, but he eventually relented.

"Arlo, your father was dying of cancer. You know he didn't like going to the doctor and he didn't go often enough. Not nearly. But, he knew something was wrong and he finally went. But, by then, it was too late. He was told he had a year to live, maybe more if he went through chemotherapy. But he refused. He didn't want to spend his remaining days weak from radiation. Only he, his doctor, and I knew. He wanted to enjoy his birthday without people knowing. After the party, he planned on telling everyone. Starting with you, Arlo."

"That's why he donated his estate. He knew he was dying," Arlo said, as the timing of Pope's generous offer suddenly made more sense.

"Exactly," Samangja replied. "He was facing death and he knew what would happen to the place he loved if you had inherited it."

I watched Arlo take that in. Eyes welling with tears before burying his head in his hands.

"And now, the second truth. The second truth is that late Sunday night, after the party, I received a text. It was a picture. I will show it to you." Samangja scrolled through his texts and then clicked on a picture. He passed around his phone, showing a candid shot of a young Korean family coming out of their house. A couple in their mid-twenties with a young boy, about two years old. They were a beautiful family, but something about the picture was creepy. It was shot from a distance with a long lens. The family didn't seem to know they were being photographed. There was also some writing on the picture I couldn't understand.

"What does that say?" I asked, as I passed the phone to Arlo.

"It's Korean," Samangja said. "Arlo, can you read it?"

Arlo nodded, explaining to the rest of us. "Samangja taught me. It says… if Jon Paul is alive tomorrow morning, they won't be." We sat in stunned silence. "It's signed, Kang. Kang?" Arlo asked.

"Mr. Kang. My old boss. Somehow he found me and used my daughter and her family to blackmail me into killing Jon Paul."

"So, you did kill him?" Stephanie asked, softly.

"No. But I went down to his studio early Monday morning with that intention. It was a horrible decision, one I hope none of you ever have to make. But, I simply could not let anything happen to my daughter or her family. So, I waited as long as I could. I lay awake all night, then a little after five thirty I went into the studio. Jon Paul was sitting at the control board, getting things ready for his session with Moses. He didn't even notice me until I smashed open the case holding the gun. I could have killed him with a knife, but I knew it would be less painful with the gun. After years of practice, I knew exactly how to do it."

Once again, the water from the fountain filled the cup and the handle gently fell against the rock. Water splashed and the cup raised again.

"I loaded the platinum bullet into the gun and walked up to my old friend. He was confused, of course. I told him everything. I showed him the picture, explaining the situation I had been put in. And then he smiled. He told me he loved me. And then he grabbed the gun in my hand. I didn't know what he was doing when he pulled the gun to his heart and pushed in the trigger."

"He killed himself?" Walton said, astonished.

"Yes. That is the third truth. Jon Paul killed himself, so I wouldn't have to. So I wouldn't break the promise I made to God that I would never kill again. And so, in our last moment together, he did the same thing he did in our first. He saved me. Before I went back upstairs to cook a breakfast I knew would never be eaten, I dropped the gun by the door and cleaned the gun residue from his hands. I didn't want people to think the greatest man I'd ever known had killed himself. And I wasn't ready to explain to the police why he did. I assumed it would have been an unsolvable crime. But, I didn't know BB had come and gone earlier that morning, and would be blamed for his death. The moment I found Mr. Paul's voice memos, I showed them to Detective Palakiko to clear him. And I was going to tell the police everything I knew. After tomorrow. After we scattered Jon Paul's ashes."

That explained everything. Well, almost everything. Once again, a missing piece of the puzzle was gnawing at me. Bugging me. Then it hit me.

"Wait. Why did the Korean mob want Jon Paul dead?"

"Because of guns, Mr. Pasch. Lots and lots of guns," Detective Palakiko said as he stepped onto the patio.

Chapter 54

"A very touching story, Mr. Samangja," Palakiko said. "I may not be able to arrest you for murder, but I will be bringing you up on charges for obstruction of justice."

"Detective! You can't be serious! How did you grow up in paradise to become such a curmudgeon?!" Walton shouted.

"Do you really want to push me right now, Mr. Walton? Here you are, yet again, with Mr. Pasch, ignoring the direct order I gave you. Your little tournament is over, yet you're still here and still interfering with my investigation!"

"More like solving it for you," I said before I could stop myself. I literally slapped my hand over my mouth. "Sorry, Detective. But, you kinda gotta hand it to us. We figured it out. Well, except for the part about the guns."

"Yeah, what's the deal with the guns?" Stephanie asked.

Palakiko paused, caught between being furious and wanting to show off. His pride won.

"A hundred machine guns were stolen from the marine armory at Pearl Harbor yesterday," Palakiko explained. "In addition to investigating Mr. Paul's murder, I was part of a collaborative effort between the military police, the Hawaii Attorney General, and police departments on every island to track them down. And I just found them under a tarp in Mr. Paul's private airplane hangar. Your friend BB has been stealing guns from the Navy and delivering them to the Korean mob using the so-called Air Force Fun. I was down there making my discovery when my man at the gate notified me of your arrival."

"Hold on, Detective. Did you have a warrant to search that hanger? We have a constitution in this country. A great one! Flawed, but great! You can't just waltz in wherever you want and start digging around for truffles, if you know what I mean," Walton said, getting in Palakiko's face. He was quite disappointed when Palakiko reached into his pocket and produced a warrant, signed by a judge.

"Okay, but where is your proof?! How do you know BB's involved? The door to that hanger is always left open. Anyone could have left those in there!"

"My proof is one of the voice memos Mr. Paul left himself just before he died. One that, ironically, exonerated Mr. Baxter just this morning. Here, you can listen to it yourself." Palakiko took out his phone and hit play. Walton instinctively put an arm around Arlo's shoulder when we all heard Jon Paul's voice again. It was chilling.

"Hey, Samangja. First thing Monday morning I want you to call…. man, I don't know. Call someone who can buy Air Force Fun off us. I don't care how much we get, just have it gone by Tuesday. Donate it if you have to. Actually, yeah. Donate it. Give it to Goodwill, for all I care. BB just came to see me. He was quite upset. Anyway, it reminded me about something I forgot to tell you last night… Believe it or not, somehow BB's gotten himself in trouble with some Korean mobsters. I'm sorry to bring them up, but it's true. But, it seems like if we got rid of the plane by Tuesday night, it would solve all of BB's problems. And I don't need that thing anymore. I'm not going anywhere. Okay, that's it for now. Thank you, my friend."

Palakiko smiled and put the phone back in his pocket.

"That proves nothing!" Walton insisted.

"It was enough to get a judge to sign a warrant. And the stolen guns in the hangar are enough to arrest Mr. Baxter." Palakiko spat out BB's last name. "I'm confident more physical evidence will soon follow, along with a full confession.

"Wait!" I said, "If those guns were stolen yesterday afternoon, then BB couldn't have done it. He was in jail!"

Palakiko paused, clearly unhappy about that loose end.

"Yes. Maybe he didn't steal them personally. But he was clearly involved. He was the one flying them to Korea. He orchestrated it. He was the mastermind. And I have him dead to rights. Come along, you two," he said to Walton and me. "You love being around my investigations so much, I want you to have a front row seat when I arrest your friend. Then, once Brian Baxter is back behind bars where he belongs, I'll put you on a plane myself."

Chapter 55

I was in the back seat of another police car, and I didn't like it. At least this time I wasn't in handcuffs. Palakiko put us in the squad car and took our phones so we couldn't warn BB. None of this seemed particularly legal, and Walton put up quite a fuss, but Palakiko was deaf to our complaints. Officer Ted, the old patrolman, drove, and Palakiko rode shotgun. When we pulled away from the Cowboy House, I looked behind us and saw Stephanie and Arlo following us in the production van. Samangja stayed back at the house. I was glad. He already played his role in this tragedy and he deserved some peace and quiet.

For the entire hour-long ride, Walton punished Palakiko, and everyone else in the car, with full-throated renditions of Grateful Dead songs. I was more than grateful when we finally pulled over to the side of the road around nine thirty. Palakiko told Officer Ted to keep an eye on us, then he led us all to a small shack built on the edge of the palm trees along the beach. This is where BB lived? I couldn't tell if I should feel sorry for him or be impressed. The shack was very humble, but it was on one of the most beautiful beaches I had ever seen. Beautiful and private, there was no one else around as far as the eye could see.

As we walked, Walton asked Officer Ted if he had heard about any volcano evacuations lately. Office Al looked back at us suspiciously, and I nudged Walton to keep him quiet. Stephanie and Arlo pulled up in the van and hopped out. Stephanie had her phone out and started filming Palakiko.

"Put that thing away," he ordered.

"No way, Detective. You detained my friends for no good reason and I'm going to make damn sure nothing happens to BB during his arrest."

"Fine. Film away." Palakiko sneered. "I assure you, this will be by the book. In fact, send me the video afterwards, I'll enjoy watching this again and again."

Then, knowing he had an audience, Detective Palakiko drew his gun, shouted "POLICE," and, quite unnecessarily, kicked in the flimsy door to BB's shack. He could have nudged it open with his pinkie. The door basically exploded.

Inside, the shack was spartan. BB seemed to own precious few things. A dresser with a hot plate and an electric kettle. A small table and chair with a metal bowl, a wooden spoon and a few old coffee cups. I didn't see a bed, and assumed he slept in the hammock strung up outside. There was a record player and an old stereo hooked up to a couple large speakers. A few crates of records. Only two things were on the thin walls: a folded American flag framed in glass and a Purple Heart hanging from a nail.

Once again, BB looked guilty as hell. When Palakiko kicked in the door, he had been tossing all of his belongings into a battered green Air Force duffle bag. BB dropped the bag, put his hands up, and started backing up against the far wall. His eyes flashed to a window, his emergency exit. He pivoted his foot to launch himself out the window, but Palakiko was on him in a flash.

"Brian Baxter, you're under arrest for arms trafficking!" Palakiko said as he slapped the cuffs on BB and read him his rights, knowing Stephanie was filming every move he made and would be giving the footage to BB's defense attorney. I wondered if Michelle Vignault would forgive BB and take this case.

"Arms trafficking? Shit. How'd you find out about the guns, Dicktective?"

"He means he's innocent!" Stephanie said, now putting her phone away and telling BB not to say another word.

"It's true?! You stole guns from the Navy? BB, how could you?" Walton said.

"Hold on, big man. I never stole no guns! I ain't never stole no fucking guns. I was just the pilot, man. I got them from here to there. I was UP-fuckin'-S."

"He's just trying to weasel his way out of this. Like he always does. I don't believe a word," said Palakiko.

"It's true, Dicktective!" BB turned to Walton. He seemed more interested in explaining himself to his friend, than the authorities. "Look, man. A buddy of mine swiped some guns and asked me to fly them to Korea on Air Force Fun. To be honest, I enjoyed it. An adventure, you know. And hell, it wasn't like it was the first time I broke the law."

"He didn't say that." Stephanie turned to BB. "Dude. You might want to shut the hell up until you have a lawyer present."

"Ah, fuck that. I need to get this off my chest." BB turned back to Walton. "We did it again this summer and that was a little less fun. It was just a bad vibe, man. Then he told me he wanted to do it again. On the day before Thanksgiving."

"That's today," Palakiko said.

"Wow, detective. I'd applaud, but my hands are cuffed. Fucking Harry Bosch over here. Look, Bill, I told my buddy I didn't want to do it no more. Honest. I told him I was done. But he said there was too much money at stake to back out."

"Let me guess," I said. "A hundred thousand dollars?"

"Bingo! One Punch Pasch with another knockout! Yeah, man. That's why I stole the money from Pope. Borrowed. I tried to buy my way out. But, man, I stole that money for nothing. My buddy said if we didn't fly those guns to Korea, we'd both be dead!"

"Wait, how did you guys plan on landing a plane full of machine guns in South Korea?"

"We didn't," BB said, winking at me.

"Then how'd you deliver the guns?"

"Pasch! That has absolutely nothing to do with what we're talking about. Stay on point!"

Did Bill Walton just say those words?

"Pope confronted me at the party about the missing money and I told him everything," BB said. "I had to. I couldn't lie to that man. He forgave me. Of course. And said he'd handle everything. Pope figured he'd get rid of Air Force Fun. No plane. No gun runs." BB laughed sadly. "Hell, even I thought that would do it. So, I told my buddy it was over."

"Your partner was at the party?" I asked.

"Yeah, man. He freaked out. Then, later that night, he called me and said we were back on. Said the Koreans would take care of the Pope. Shit. I realized right then and there what my dumb ass did. That's why I went there at five o'clock that morning. To warn Pope. To get him out of there. I offered to fly him anywhere in the world. But Pope turned me down flat. Wouldn't budge. I was worried, but I convinced myself he'd be safe enough at the Cowboy House. Man, I still don't know how those bastards got past Ani and Ahi to kill him."

He didn't know.

We told BB what happened to the Pope. About the cancer. About Samangja. About Pope grabbing the gun and… everything.

"Holy shit. For real?"

We all nodded and let him process the information. It was a lot to take in. In the silence, my mind drifted back to the party, running down all the people that were there. Then, I finally found the last piece of the puzzle. The one that put the entire picture together. It just wasn't a picture I wanted to see. I didn't want it to be true.

"BB. Was your 'buddy' Commander Kirby?"

BB froze. He didn't say anything. But a familiar voice did.

"Dang it, Pasch. I was standing out here praying you wouldn't figure that out. Because I know BB would'a kept his mouth shut."

I could almost hear the crooked smile.

Chapter 56

Commander Kirby entered the shack and pressed a Sig Sauer P226 against Detective Palakiko's temple. The gun was standard Navy issue, indicated by the white anchor on its short barrel. Commander Kirby held out his hand, and Palakiko furiously surrendered his gun. Old Officer Ted came in afterwards, his hands behind his head, being prodded by three men holding machine guns. I recognized them. The men and the guns. The men were the friends Commander Kirby had been sitting courtside with at the Oklahoma/Duke game. The machine guns, M16 rifles, were the ones they stole from the armory while Commander Kirby and O'Connor gave us a ride to the Cowboy House on the patrol boat. They were all wearing black. Boots, jeans, hoodies. The rogue Navy men certainly looked the part of gun running smugglers.

"Commander Kirby, no! Not you!" Walton cried.

Kirby shrugged and flashed his crooked smile. "Sorry, Walton. I really am. But this whole situation has gotten out of hand. I swear, everything was peaches and plums a week ago, then all hell broke loose. And now, y'all need to come with us. I'm sorry, but I don't really have a choice. I'm not exactly working for reasonable people."

"You're making a huge mistake," said Detective Palakiko. "But, if you let us go right now, you'll be out in ten years. Maybe five."

"I think what Detective Palakiko is saying is, if you let us go, we'll forget this ever happened," Stephanie said, staring him down.

"Absolutely not," insisted Palakiko. "He pulled a gun on a police officer, he's got to go to jail."

We all looked to Palakiko.

"What?"

Unbelievable. This guy was going to follow the rules right to our graves.

"Sorry, Detective," Commander Kirby said. "Right now, the US Navy outranks the local police."

"You're not the Navy," said Palakiko. "You're pirates."

Commander Kirby and his men laughed.

"Pirates? I like that. And maybe you're right. We did go outside the rocks and shoals on this one. Hell, maybe I should get an eye patch and a parrot. I'll take a hard pass on the peg leg, though. Alright boys, stack 'em, pack 'em and rack 'em!"

Kirby and two of his goons kept their guns trained on us while the other took his time carefully tying our hands behind our backs with short lengths of rope. Kirby personally took each of our cell phones and smashed them under the heel of his boot, and led us outside to the production van.

"I wanna thank y'all for bringing a vehicle large enough to hold us and all our hostages. Very thoughtful of you," Kirby said. "Make 'em comfortable, boys!" His goons laughed. Kirby didn't smile. "I'm serious. Come on, guys. Let's do this like gentlemen. We're not damned pirates, despite what this cop may think of us."

Kirby and his pirates loaded us into the back of the van. And I'll give it to them, they were nice about it.

Chapter 57

The ride was bumpy. And crowded. Walton, Stephanie, Arlo, BB, Detective Palakiko, and I were jammed in the back of the cargo van. Oh, and Officer Ted. Almost forgot about him. I think he fell asleep. Kirby and his goons sat up front. I remember thinking the seats of the production van were uncomfortable. I didn't realize how good I had it until I was stuffed in the back like human cargo. We couldn't see our captors, but we could hear them. And we could talk to them. It wasn't hard to get Kirby talking. The man loved to spin a yarn.

"Guys, you gotta believe me. I didn't wake up one morning and decide to steal guns and sell them to the Korean mob. I'm no criminal mastermind. One thing just led to another. See, it all started with a whole bunch of machine guns that were being replaced with the newer models. Happens all the time. You know how it is in the military. Out with the not that old, in with the new and more expensive. And I was given the task of melting down the old guns. And that's exactly what I was gonna do.

"But... then I got to thinking. What if I don't melt 'em down? What if I just tuck 'em away somewhere, melt down a bunch of empty boxes and sell those perfectly good guns to someone else? Look fellas, I don't play chess. I can't think ten moves ahead. I live in the moment! I play checkers. I see an opportunity and I jump. And, as it so happens, I know a few people. You know, the kind of people who know some people who know some people and, eventually, I find out that some gentlemen in Seoul would love to give me a nice, big chunk of change for those useless old machine guns. Plus, I was good buddies with a pilot who had access to a private jet, who flew missions just like this for the freakin' CIA. Well, I couldn't turn down that opportunity. Easiest two hundred grand I ever made."

"Hey, asshole! You said you made a hundred!" BB barked.

"Oops. Sorry, beebs," Kirby said.

"Commander," I said, using his title as sarcastically as possible. "How did you guys land a plane full of machine guns in Korea?"

"We didn't."

"But--"

"Pasch! Nobody cares how they ran guns into Korea! It was a heinous crime! We don't care how the criminal sausage was made!"

That's not true. I cared. I cared very much. The riddle was driving me crazy. But, I held my tongue while Kirby went on. And on.

"So, BB and I brought 'em the guns and I had a nice pile of cash nobody knew about. And I enjoyed myself. I'd go on these amazing first-class vacations. Courtside seats at the Maui Invitational for me and my friends. And, hey. Running guns was fun. We had a good time, didn't we, BB?"

"Yeah, it was pretty fun," BB had to admit. "The first time."

"There you go!" Kirby had crawled to the back seat so he could lean over and see us as he talked. I looked up and there was his big, crooked smile. I wanted to knock it right off his face. "And I was done after that one time. I promise you. But, those gangsters wanted more guns this summer. And you do not say 'no' to these people. Hell, when I told them the deal was off because Pope was getting rid of the plane, they said they were going to kill me! Well, obviously, I freaked the hell out. And I started talking. You guys know I don't hate the sound of my own voice." He winked.

"And boy, I started saying anything and everything I could think of to save my life. I even told them a story I heard about an old Korean mobster I knew. An assassin who washed up in Honolulu twenty-five years ago. Yeah, I had heard bits and pieces of Samangja's story over the years. I didn't know everything, but I knew enough to get them interested. Very interested. The only other thing they needed to know was his phone number."

"You bastard! You got the Pope killed!" BB screamed.

"I'm sorry about that. I really am," Commander Kirby said. "But they were going to kill me. I loved the Pope, but I love me just a little bit more." The commander sighed. "I really am sorry you all had to get involved. Damn sorry."

There wasn't much more to say after that. Even for Commander Kirby.

Chapter 58

I knew by the turns we were taking, back and forth, up through the mountains, that we were getting close. I felt the tires go from rough mountain road to smooth runway, and then I could see Air Force Fun out the back window of the van as we stopped in Pope's hangar. Commander Kirby and his goons opened the back doors and kept their guns pointed at us as they helped us to our feet.

"Where are you taking us?" Stephanie demanded.

"I'm sorry to say only halfway to South Korea," Commander Kirby said. "Then, unfortunately, we have to drop you out of the plane." He held up a hand, stopping our chorus of voices. "No, no. I know, I know. If I let you go, you won't say a word. Sorry, I can't take that chance. Hell, if I let Palakiko go, he'd arrest me on the spot. Ain't that right, Detective?"

After a pause, Palakiko nodded.

Our heads sunk. Stephanie and Arlo cursed the detective, but at that point I almost had to respect Palakiko's zealous adherence to law and order. Almost.

Commander Kirby and his goons prodded us up the rolling staircase into Air Force Fun. Once inside, Kirby had us turn around and sit on the floor. The door was open, and I had a clear view of the hangar where Commander Kirby and two of his goons started loading crates of guns in the baggage compartment under the plane. One goon remained behind to guard us. I looked around. If the circumstances had been different, I would have really enjoyed being on board Air Force Fun. It was something else.

We entered in the back of the plane, into what was once the coach section. But, it definitely wasn't coach anymore. All the seats had been taken out and the giant, open space looked more like a living room or a really cool basement. The walls of the plane were wood paneled and the giant middle cabin was separated, on both sides, with closed doors that led to the front and back of the plane. There was carpet. Not sad, thin commercial airline carpet. It was a fluffy, burnt orange shag.

There were comfortable looking couches under the windows, a fully stocked bar with stools bolted into the floor, and a dining room table with swivel chair seating for a dozen people. There was even a red felt pool table. For a brief moment, I wondered how you played pool at ten thousand feet without the balls just rolling willy nilly all over the place, but even my curious mind had its limits. I put that mystery aside as there were more important things to focus on.

What grabbed my attention at that moment was a stretch limousine that was pulling into the hangar. Even Commander Kirby seemed to be surprised by its arrival. He and his men aimed their guns at the car as it stopped, and a very distinguished Korean man came out of the limousine, holding his hands in the air.

"Please, put your guns away. Commander Kirby, we have not met, but I am your employer, Mr. Kang."

So, this was the famous Mr. Kang. He was short and heavyset, almost round, but the man radiated strength, wealth, and power. His gray hair was perfectly trimmed and combed, like a politician's. He wore a very nice black suit, obviously custom tailored, and his wrists and fingers glistened with diamonds and gold. Commander Kirby told his men to lower their guns and respectfully greeted Mr. Kang.

"I didn't know you'd be coming with us, sir," he said, nervously.

"The less people who knew, the better," Kang said as he waved his men out of the limousine. His protection, his muscle. Six men in light gray suits and matching gray overcoats, who moved with quiet, lethal precision as they exited the limo. I wondered if Mr. Kang had color-coordinated his entourage. Their light gray outfits made him, in his black suit, stand out like ink on a page.

"I assumed you could give us a ride."

"Of course. Can we help you with your luggage?" Kirby said, eager to please a man who could make him rich, or have him killed, with a snap of his fingers.

"We have no luggage," Mr. Kang said, smiling. "Just some cargo we need to take back home with us." He waved his hand at the car like a game show host. His men opened the trunk and pulled out a tiny, frail, scared, old man.

It was Samangja.

Chapter 59

It was heartbreaking to see Samangja in the hands of those soulless killers. Then I remembered he used to be one. Samangja didn't put up a fight. He seemed resigned to his fate.

"We are escorting my old friend home to die on Korean soil as he should have done many years ago."

"Commander! Some chatter coming in on the radio," one of Kirby's goons said, pushing in an earpiece he had connected to a walkie talkie. "Cops are looking for Palakiko and this hangar was his last known location. They're sending a car to check it out. Half hour, tops."

"Okay, let's move this along!" Commander Kirby said, turning to Mr. Kang and his men. "Gentlemen, I believe the first class compartment will suit your needs. Please ignore my guests by the door, they won't be making the entire trip."

Mr. Kang's men circled Samangja and followed their boss up the stairs into the plane. Walton reacted when he saw Samangja.

"Samangja! No!" Walton cried.

"Bill, please. It is okay. We have made an agreement. If I go quietly, my daughter and her family will be safe," Samangja said, as he passed us. "I only pray you can save yourselves."

They walked on, past the bar and the pool table, and through the door to the front of the plane. As it opened, I saw another spacious area with comfortable seating for twelve people. Six fluffy recliners on each side of a wide aisle. There was another door on the far end of that cabin which, based on the length of the plane, must have led to the cockpit.

Commander Kirby ran up the stairs and into the plane. He unceremoniously flipped Palakiko over, went through his pockets, found his handcuff keys, and uncuffed BB. "Okay, buddy. Time to go to work. Get this bird fired up."

"No fucking way, brother," BB said. "I ain't flying shit. Fuck you. You can shoot me, I don't care."

"Okay, okay. That's fair. But I'm not going to shoot you, BB," Commander Kirby said, smiling. Then he pointed his gun at Walton. "I'm gonna shoot Bill Walton. Then I'll shoot him, and him, and him, and her. Then, just to really piss you off, I won't shoot Palakiko. Now get your ass in the cockpit and get this plane ready to fly, or I swear to God, I will shoot one of the top ten centers to ever play the game. In three, two, one... oh at the buzzer!"

"No, no, no, no, no! Okay! I'll do it! Shit, man. Fine! Fucking asshole," BB said as he stood up and walked to the cockpit. "Hang in there, guys," he called over his shoulder.

"Commander, you've made a huge mistake," Walton said, very seriously. "I am not a top-ten center. Top twenty-five? Maybe. Top twenty? Debatable. There are just too many great men ahead of me on that list. Dave Cowens. Wes Unseld. Patrick Ewing, who just needed a little more help during his time in New York. And let's not forget the legend, George Mikan, whose talents must not be forgotten by time! Then there's Dikembe Mutombo! Walt Bellamy! Benjamin Wallace! Arvydas Sabonis! The list is staggering! The Gasol brothers!"

"Bill, Bill, Bill!" Commander Kirby was finally able to cut him off. "Bill, I'd love to debate the list with you, I truly would, but after we're in the air, okay?" Commander Kirby said before turning to the goon who had been watching us. "Davy, come with me. We need all the help we can get loading these last crates in."

As they left the plane, Walton laughed.

"Davy? Your name is Davy? And you're still in the Navy? Let me guess, and you probably will be for life?"

"What the fuck are you talking about?" Davy said, stopping at the door. He was in his early twenties and clearly had no idea what song Walton was referring to. We had found another depressing divide in the generational gap. Walton seemed positively disturbed.

"Young man, I sincerely encourage you to listen to the works of Billy Joel. He's a tremendous talent, especially the early stuff.

Start with The Stranger then, Davy, be sure to listen to the titular track of Piano Man."

"Whatever," Davy said, before running down the stairs as BB started the engines. I struggled against the ropes that held my wrists behind my back.

"Guys, I feel like our chances for survival will plummet the second the plane leaves the ground," I said to my fellow captives.

"Oof. Bad choice of words, Dave," Stephanie said.

"My bad. And Stephanie, I'm really sorry we got you into this. Especially now that you're, you know..."

"No need to remind me, Dave!" Stephanie snapped back. I noticed her fingers moving around, messing with something.

"Trying to get loose? Any luck?"

"No. These knots are tied tight. These Navy guys didn't skip knot tying class. But I did manage to get my ring off. Remember the heartbeat ring my husband gave me for our anniversary? Well, for the past hour I've been tapping out an S.O.S. in Morse code. I only hope Elvin can tell the difference between my heartbeat and "please come save my ass."

Even under the circumstances, I had to chuckle.

"Wailea Golf Club isn't too far away. They're close, I just hope they get here in time."

And then, we heard the click-clack of golf shoes on cement.

Chapter 60

Colonel Cabrera had once again come to our rescue. Back in Seattle, we were stranded on an island when he arrived, impressively, in a Black Hawk helicopter. This time he arrived in a different vehicle. The Army/Navy game came to the rescue in a golf cart. The Colonel and his friends had no idea what they were running into when they found Commander Kirby and his men loading crates of M16s onto the plane. The two groups of men paused for a second, each completely shocked to see the other.

Then the hangar erupted in gunfire.

It sounded like firecrackers in a trash can. And I was inside the trash can. I could still see out the open door of the plane as Kirby cracked open one of the crates and tossed guns to his goons. They started shooting the M16s as the Colonel and his friends dove for cover and returned fire. One of Commander Kirby's men went down. A kneecap shot that wasn't fatal, but watching the man writhing around on the ground in agony, he may have preferred that it was.

One of Mr. Kang's men came out of the first class cabin and carefully closed the door behind him. He took out his gun and moved toward the open door of the plane while keeping himself clear of the windows. He stopped at the edge of the door and shouted, "Commander Kirby! Mr. Kang wants to know what is happening!"

"I don't fucking know! Four dudes just pulled up in a golf cart and started shooting at us! Craziest fucking thing I've ever seen! Tell Mr. Kang to wait inside, we'll handle this!" The gangster nodded and made his way back to the first class compartment.

He didn't get there.

Out of the corner of my eye, I saw Palakiko smoothly slide his hands under his legs. Then he ran up to the gangster from behind and choked him with the rope that still bound his hands together. Before suffocating him completely, Palakiko slammed the gangster's head against the bar, knocking him unconscious.

"Throw him down, Palakiko! Throw him down!" Walton said, cheering him on before we all hushed him. The detective rummaged through the bar and found an old paring knife. Palakiko put the knife in his teeth and cut himself loose. Then he slapped the handcuffs BB had dropped on the shag carpet onto the unconscious gangster, securing his hands behind his back.

"Palakiko! Quick, cut me loose!" Walton shouted over the gunfire that still filled the hangar. Commander Kirby and his last two men standing had taken cover behind the engine block of the old Land Cruiser, shooting blindly at all the open doors of the hanger with an endless supply of firepower. Thankfully, the Colonel and his friends seemed to have redeployed outside the hangar, out of my field of vision and, hopefully, the field of fire.

"The rest of you stay where you are and keep your heads down," Palakiko instructed as he cut loose Officer Ted.

"Why release Officer Ted and not me?!" Walton bellowed. "What's he gonna do, write them a parking ticket?!"

And then the sleepy patrolman picked up the gangster's revolver. A stainless steel Magnum Research BFR which was, with apologies to Dirty Harry, the most powerful handgun in the world. Officer Ted casually stepped to the open door of the plane and fired two shots. And with two thunderous booms, Commander Kirby lost his other two men. At thirty yards, Officer Ted blew holes in their chests you could pass a basketball through. Davy did, in fact, spend the rest of his life in the Navy. He never got the chance to listen to Billy Joel.

Officer Ted turned to me and read the stunned expression on my face. "Marines," he explained.

"Oorah!" Walton hollered.

Then, insanely, Palakiko stepped out of the plane, onto the top of the rolling stairs and held up his badge. "POLICE! Commander Kirby, you are under arrest! Drop your gun, immediately!"

"Detective! Get down!"

Is what I would have shouted if Commander Kirby had given me the chance. But he didn't. He had already raised his Sig Sauer and fired. Palakiko took it in the chest and fell down the stairs.

Officer Ted went right after him, firing until his gun clicked, empty. While Commander Kirby dove for cover, Officer Ted grabbed Palakiko and dragged him behind the limousine. In the same moment, Commander Kirby traded places with them. He closed the baggage compartment and ran onto the plane. Panting, he picked up a phone from its cradle by the door.

"BB! Get us in the air in sixty seconds or I start shooting people!"

"Fuck you, asshole!" I could hear BB reply in the earpiece. Nevertheless, the old plane started moving out of the hangar, slowly at first, then picking up more and more speed as she went. In a flash, as we went by, I could see two members of the Army/ Navy game taking cover outside. I heard the Colonel yell, "Don't shoot! My wife is in there!" I looked over at Stephanie who was still tapping away at her ring. If I knew Morse code, I'd know she was tapping P-L-A-N-E, P-L-A-N-E, P-L-A-N-E over and over again.

Commander Kirby, feeling brave in the face of their ceasefire, leaned out of the plane and jauntily waved goodbye before closing and sealing the door. "Holy shit, who were those guys?! And what happened to him?" He said, nudging the gangster's body with his boot.

"He tripped, and BB's handcuffs fell onto his wrists," Walton explained, dryly.

Kirby laughed. "Fair enough. Enjoy your flight. Once we get in the air I'll come back here and give you some peanuts or something. I promise we'll do this as civilly as possible." Kirby paused, trying to think of something else to say, then just shrugged and headed to the door to the front of the plane. He knocked, and, after a pause, the door opened and he went in. Before the door closed and locked behind him, we could hear him smoothing things over with Mr. Kang, who was furious.

Meanwhile, BB had us on the runway and gaining speed in a hurry. I saw the trees passing by, faster and faster and faster until they were gone. Replaced by nothing but sky. We had lifted off. I felt a sinking feeling in my gut that had nothing to do with our sudden burst in elevation. We had just left our rescue party on the ground behind us. I could tell Walton, Stephanie, and Arlo had similar thoughts. Things weren't looking good for us. Not by a long shot. Then, quite by surprise, the door to the back of the plane opened.

"Hey, babe. Sorry I'm late."

Chapter 61

It was the Colonel. His clothes were torn and covered with black grease. He took out a pocket knife and cut us all loose, starting with his wife.

"Colonel, it is great to see you," I said as he untied me. "How in the world did you get on the plane?"

"Well, I couldn't exactly use the front door, so I had to work my way up from the landing gear. I hopped on when the plane was leaving the hangar. Thankfully, the Army does our hostage rescue training on big old birds like this one. There's a ladder in back so the flight staff can get supplies from the cargo area during the flight. I know these old 737s like the back of my hand," he said, then looked around at the bar and pool table. "Though this rig has clearly had a few alterations."

We couldn't hear Commander Kirby and Mr. Kang yelling in the first class cabin, so we assumed they couldn't hear us. Though we kept our voices down, just to be safe. We all stood up and moved around, massaging our wrists and getting the circulation going in our legs again.

"What's the plan, Colonel? Did you happen to sneak a Blackhawk helicopter up through the bottom of the plane with you?" I asked.

"I'm afraid not. If we want to get home, we have to take this plane. What's the sitrep?"

"Five gangsters with guns. A chatty gunrunning pirate with a gun. An old mob boss who may or may not have a gun. One friendly in the next compartment, and another one flying the plane," Stephanie said, giving her husband the "situation report."

"And what do we have?"

"Well," Stephanie said, looking around. "We have me, you, a pocket knife, a paring knife, two basketball announcers and…" She paused, looking at Arlo.

"A useless asshole," Arlo said, shrugging.

"We'll see about that."

"Colonel, Pasch can more than handle himself in a fight," Walton said, patting me on the back both literally and figuratively. "And if any of those guys is tougher than Kareem Abdul-Jabbar, I'll happily jump into the ocean myself."

"Noted," the Colonel said. "What happened to him?" He said, pointing to the unconscious gangster who started coming around and making noises, until a swift kick from the Colonel's golf shoe tucked him back to sleep.

"Palakiko took him out and took his gun before he…" I paused, realizing I didn't know the fate of the detective. "I mean, he was a pain in the ass, but I certainly hope he's not dead."

"Yeah, he looked pretty bad. But he's down there right now with my friends. If anyone could keep him alive until the medics show up, it's them. Now forget about that. Let's keep our minds right here, right now. What do we know about the mob boss? I have to assume he's in charge up there."

We nodded and told him everything we knew about Mr. Kang, who flew across the ocean to collect an old debt.

"Okay, then it's just a question of priority. What would you say he values more, surviving this trip or seeing us dead?"

We thought about it. It didn't seem like he cared about us one way or another.

"He wants Samangja to die on Korean soil. That's all he cares about," I said.

"Good. We can work with that." Then the Colonel laid out his plan, giving us each instructions and, for the next few minutes, we focused on our assignments. Everyone had something to do and we did it quickly and quietly. When we were finished, we gathered at the door to the front of the plane.

Then, we politely knocked.

Chapter 62

We stood in a half-circle behind Walton, who was holding the unconscious gangster up to the peephole of the door, making sure to keep his eyes, which were closed, out of its field of vision. I hoped they didn't notice he had suddenly grown taller. Walton was lifting him a few inches in the air. One of Mr. Kang's men said something through the door in Korean. We turned to Arlo.

"He wants to know what took him so long."

"Do you know Korean for, 'I had to take a shit?'" Stephanie whispered back.

Arlo put his hand over his mouth to muffle his voice and did a passable job imitating a man he had only heard speak once. He turned to Stephanie, smirking.

"That's actually one of the first phrases Samangja taught me."

The door opened to reveal one of Mr. Kang's men. He was relaxed and smiling, just the way the Colonel wanted him. Seconds later, the man was neither relaxed nor smiling. He was unconscious with a blue golf tee protruding from his left eye. The Colonel dumped him on the ground behind us, where Stephanie and Arlo quickly dragged him away and tied him up. The Colonel then put his hands in the air as Mr. Kang's remaining four guards jumped up, drew their guns, and formed a protective shield in front of their boss. Commander Kirby stayed in his seat. He seemed content to sit back and see how this played out.

"Whoa, whoa, whoa, whoa. Everybody relax. Just relax," the Colonel said in a calming voice. "Mr. Kang. You look like a smart man. You all do. And smart men don't shoot guns in planes. Let's just put away the guns and talk."

Mr. Kang said something in Korean. It sounded like "wondo." The men put away their guns. The Colonel smiled. "There you go. Thank you."

Then the four gangsters reached behind their heads and pulled out swords. It turns out, Mr. Kang said "hwando," the Korean word for sword. Each gangster now held a one-handed sword with a curved, razor sharp, twenty-inch blade. They had been hiding them in scabbards that went down their spines. Just like the one the Colonel found on the gangster Palakiko knocked out. The sword the Colonel now had tucked down the back of his pants. The Colonel kept backing up, his hands in the air. "Whoa, whoa. Easy, fellas. Easy."

Two of Kang's men advanced, while the other two stayed behind to guard their boss. Damn. We were hoping all of them would advance on the Colonel. That was the plan. The reverse of what the Spartans did in the Battle of Thermopylae. Instead of tunneling a superior force into a narrow gap, we wanted to bring them out into the open. With one little surprise. Well, two surprises: Me, and top twenty-five center of all time, Bill Walton. We were hiding on either side of the door, holding pool cues in our hands. Each cue had been broken in half over Walton's knee and carved into a spear with the Colonel's pocket knife.

I steeled myself for what the Colonel told me to do next. What he taught me to do. Showing me exactly where to plunge the cue, right into the back of their necks at the base of the skull. I couldn't believe I was about to do this. But I had to. Our lives depended on it. The Colonel passed by us as he backed up, luring the men into our trap. I looked down. I saw the tip of a black shoe step into the doorway. I gripped the two cues tightly, one in each hand, and then...

"Junji!"

Mr. Kang yelled, and the men stopped immediately. Like well-trained dogs. I saw Arlo sink, shaking his head at me. Silently telling me our plan wouldn't work. Mr. Kang was too smart to let his men fall into our trap.

"Okay, guys. Plan B." The Colonel said.

Plan B? We had never gone over a Plan B. What was Plan B? Then, I realized what Plan B was. Plan B was total chaos.

Walton loved it.

Chapter 63

The Colonel screamed, took out his sword, and took on the two gangsters in front of him. The Army had clearly trained him how to fight with a sword. However, the two gangsters seemed better trained to stand there holding a big, scary sword and look intimidating. By the looks on their faces, they never had to do much more than that, and, even two against one, they were no match for the Colonel. In hand-to-hand combat, he was an artist. Fighting with graceful fury. The gangsters retreated toward the cockpit door as the Colonel pushed them farther and farther back into the cabin.

Walton and I joined the fray, storming into the cabin holding our pool cue spears. He roared, "HOKAHEY!" A battle cry made famous by Crazy Horse. Walton was something of a battle cry aficionado. I had heard him use that one before while using the restroom.

Mr. Kang's remaining two men surged forward to take us on, and I quickly found out that a pool cue spear is no match for a sword. The gangster that came after me chopped them both in half with one swing. I dropped the useless sticks and grabbed his sword by the hilt, doing everything in my power to make sure he wasn't able to pull it back for another swing. We struggled. Fighting for my life, I banged the hand holding the sword against the wall of the plane until the sword fell to the ground.

"Ha!" I laughed. A victory bark. A victory that was short-lived as the gangster turned and punched me right in the face. I was knocked backwards across the aisle, falling into one of the cushy first-class seats. The gangster looked around for his sword. He found it under a seat and picked it up. When he turned to face me, my fist hit his chin like a wrecking ball on a condemned building.

Boom.

The gangster went down in a heap.

"One punch Pasch!" Walton shouted. He was looking at me over the man he was fighting. "Walton! Pay attention!" I said, as the gangster almost stabbed Walton in the chest with his sword. At the last second, Walton stepped aside and deflected the sword with the two pool cue spears he held together in one hand. If the Colonel was an artist in hand-to-hand combat, Bill Walton was Rembrandt.

Walton had an enormous advantage in size and reach over his opponent. He easily fought off the sword-wielding gangster, dodging another thrust and answering with a sharp elbow to the man's face. Then Walton stepped back, snapping punches into the gangster's face from a distance the man couldn't begin to respond to, even with a twenty-inch blade. Walton poked the man with his pool cue spears like a picador in a bullfight, leaving little holes all over the man's body from his shoulders to ankles. Soon, the gangster's light gray suit was polka-dotted with blood. Walton's footwork, as always, was impeccable. He always told me, no matter how big a guy was, it all started with his feet. The difference between scoring and getting your shot blocked wasn't in the seven feet of your height, it was in the inches of your footwork.

Walton stepped, and slid, and spun, and turned, and pummeled the gangster. The pool cue spears were like drumsticks in his hands, and the Korean gangster was the snare. If there was a referee, he would have stopped the fight. If we were at Madison Square Garden, the crowd would start booing, accusing Walton of holding up a lesser opponent in attempts to sell a bad fight.

"Walton! Stop dancing with this guy and put him out of his misery!"

"I'm trying, Pasch! I can't use my full reach in here! I'm hitting with more accuracy than power. I could use a little help!" Walton said, as he sent another jab that backed the gangster up toward me. Then Walton swung. A big, wide, right hook. The hair on his knuckles grazed the wood paneled walls of the plane. He was going high so I went low. Well, not that low. Frankly, I just took one big step forward and kicked the guy right in the nuts with my hiking boot. Our two blows landed at the same time and launched the guy about a foot into the air. He slammed against the wall of the plane. The now-possibly-neutered gangster fell to the ground. He was down for the count. They could count to ten, twenty, thirty, heck, they could use a calendar. This guy wasn't getting up for awhile.

Around the same time, the Colonel was finishing his own fight. He lured the two gangsters into the back of the plane, where Stephanie and Arlo were waiting by the door to smash them over the head with liquor bottles from the bar. Jameson and Bacardi. The gangsters fell to their knees, dropping their swords. After that, it was all over. The Colonel took out one gangster, hitting him on top of the head with the hilt of his sword. By the time he turned to take out the other, Stephanie had already incapacitated him with a savage kick. And that was after she punched him in the face with a left hook, leaving behind what was becoming her signature: a slicing cut across his right cheek from the sharp diamond of her wedding ring. This particular gangster was lucky to get just one. There was a biker sitting in jail back in Seattle right now named Handsome Billy who, after facing Stephanie in a fight, would never be called handsome again.

I looked around the cabin. In the fray, Commander Kirby had run into the cockpit and locked the door behind him. I couldn't believe it. We did it. We took out five sword-wielding gangsters. Well, six, including the one Palakiko knocked out. I was relieved. I was exhilarated. For a very brief moment.

"May I please have your attention?" Mr. Kang said, calmly. He stood in front of the cockpit door, holding a sword against Samangja's throat.

Chapter 64

"I commend you all on your actions this evening," Mr. Kang said. "Well done. We clearly won't be dropping you into the Pacific during this flight. You will all make it to Korea safely. And then you will be killed. So, please, enjoy the rest of your flight." Mr. Kang knocked on the door to the cockpit. "Commander Kirby, please open the door."

"Don't let him get in that cockpit," Arlo whispered. "My dad flew this plane with all kinds of people doing all kinds of crazy things. The cockpit and my dad's private bedroom in the back are basically safe rooms. If he gets in there and closes the door, we're done."

The door to the cockpit opened, just a crack, and Commander Kirby peeked out. He then opened the door wide and welcomed

Mr. Kang inside. Samangja paused outside the door. He clearly knew what Arlo knew about the cockpit.

"Come now, Johnny. I can't kill you, not yet," Mr. Kang said, using Samangja's old name. "Johnny Soon-Park will die in Korea as he should have years ago. Then I will kill your daughter and her son and her husband and their friends and their neighbors. And before they die, I will carefully explain to each and every one of them exactly who sentenced them to their excruciatingly slow, painful deaths."

"No," Samangja said. He begged. "Please, we had an agreement."

"Yes, we did, Johnny. We made an oath, you and I. But what's an oath to a man with no honor? It is nothing. It is less than nothing, like you. And so, I will kill your daughter myself. With this very blade."

Mr. Kang briefly lifted the blade to show it to Samangja. And a second later, Mr. Kang had no head. Samangja was so fast, my brain couldn't register what happened. I had to guess, based on the result. And so, Samangja must have ripped the blade out of Mr. Kang's hand, spun around and cut off his head in one swing. But I didn't see it. All I saw was Kang's head fall to the ground, and Samangja holding the sword in the air, like a golfer holding the form of his follow through, waiting for his ball to land. Mr. Kang's body remained standing for about as long as it takes for a golf ball to travel three hundred yards. It just stood there, his blood painting the cabin walls red, before collapsing in a heap.

"Holy fucking shit!" Commander Kirby yelled, frozen in shock.

None of us moved. Well, one of us did. One of Mr. Kang's guards. The one I thought Walton and I took out. He was more resilient than I gave him credit for. Tragically so, because he took out his gun, a Magnum Research BFR just like the one Officer Ted used to blow holes through Kirby's men. Officer Ted was a great shot-- he did it from thirty yards away. I don't know what kind of shot the gangster was, because he was only a few feet from Samangja when he raised the gun and fired. Inside the enclosed space, it sounded like an atomic bomb. The bullet tore through Samangja's tiny body and buried itself somewhere deep in the plane's instrument panel.

"Oh, fuck!" BB screamed. Alarms rang out from the cockpit as the plane lurched into a nosedive. The Colonel was right. Smart men don't shoot guns in planes. We all fell forward as swords, guns, and people slid towards the front of the plane. BB leveled us off as Commander Kirby slammed the cockpit door shut. Walton screamed. In a fit of rage unlike anything I had ever seen from him, Walton slapped the gun out of the gangster's hand, lifted him over his head and slammed him to the ground. The gangster was knocked unconscious, but this time I wasn't taking any chances. I dragged him to the back of the plane and asked the Colonel to tie him up with the rest of Mr. Kang's men. Then I ran back to where Walton was cradling Samangja in his arms.

"Samangja, I'm sorry. I'm so sorry," Walton said, giant tears raining down his face.

"It's okay, Bill. My daughter is safe. With Kang dead, there will be war. And then someone else will be in charge. Someone new. Someone young. Someone who won't care about a tired old assassin or his daughter. I just hope God can forgive me for breaking my promise. I swore to Him I would never kill another man."

"I'm sure he'll understand, Samangja," Walton said.

"Call me Johnny."

He smiled, then closed his eyes for the last time.

Chapter 65

We carefully wrapped Samangja's body in some blankets and gently placed him on Jon Paul's bed in the back of the plane. The Pope's bedroom on Air Force Fun was simple and comfortable. The only decoration was a framed picture on the nightstand of the Pope, in his younger days, happily smiling with his wife, Tandy, and a one-year-old Arlo. His first birthday party.

Then we dumped Mr. Kang's body in one of the lavatories. I don't know who did it, but someone put his head in the toilet. I would have moved it, but I was distracted when the plane banked hard to the left, slowly turning a hundred and eighty degrees and then leveling off. We were heading back to Maui. Then the plane made an awful sound. The worst sound a plane can possibly make.

Nothing.

No engines. Silence. The lights went out and the emergency lights came on as we felt the plane start dropping like a stone. BB's voice came over the intercom. "Uhhh, lady and gentlemen, this is your captain speaking. We're going down, y'all."

The cockpit door flew open and Commander Kirby stepped out, smiling. "Hey, friends! How we all doing tonight?!"

We rushed him, each of us holding some form of sword, pool cue, or jagged bottle in our hands. "Whoa, whoa, whoa! Hold on! Listen to me! Just listen to me! Hey!" Kirby got our attention, shouting in his biggest, most official Naval officer voice. "Do you really think I would have dropped you in the Pacific Ocean? Come on, y'all. I was putting on a show for Mr. Kang. He and his men were the ones I would have dropped in the ocean, not you guys! I love you guys!"

"Wait," I said. "You threatened to drop us in the ocean before Mr. Kang even showed up."

We all rushed forward.

"Okay, okay, okay! Okay, I would have dropped you in the ocean. But that was then, and this is now! Things change! And right now I'm the only guy who can save your lives!"

We stopped in our tracks.

"How?!" The Colonel shouted.

"Hey, Pasch, you wanna know how we got those guns into Korea?" Commander Kirby asked.

"Uh, not at this particular moment, Roy."

"Trust me, Pasch! You're gonna want to hear this!" BB shouted through the open cockpit door. "And we have a few minutes before we crash into the ocean and die."

"Sounds great, BB," I said, sarcastically. "Okay, Commander. Go right ahead."

"We never landed in Korea with a plane full of guns, because by the time we landed in Korea, we had dumped 'em. BB would fly low, I'd open the door of the plane and just push the crates out. They'd land on a little island east of Korea, Ulleungdo. Kang's men would be waiting for them."

"They catch 'em like pop flies. Can of corn, Pasch!" BB yelled. "Can o' corn!"

"That's insane," The Colonel said. "The guns would be destroyed on impact, I don't care how low you were flying."

"We did this twice, Colonel. The guns arrived in perfect condition." Commander Kirby looked at me. It took me a second but I finally got it.

"Because they used parachutes."

"Bingo! One Punch Pasch with another knockout!" BB yelled.

"One Punch Pasch?" Stephanie asked.

"It's a nickname that's kinda going around. You can use it if you want," I said.

"Here's the deal. I know where the parachutes are. I stowed them away myself. Not even BB knows where they are," Commander Kirby said. "So, if we work together, I can get us all strapped in and off this plane before it crashes. Deal?"

We paused. It was hard to trust a word coming out of the guy's mouth.

"Y'all better figure this out soon! We're going to be too low to jump in a hurry!" BB yelled.

"Okay, deal! It's a deal!" Walton said for us all.

"Fantastic! Y'all wait by the bar. I'm gonna go down and send the parachutes up through the dumbwaiter. It's the quickest way," Commander Kirby said, then started to run to the back of the plane.

"Hold on! I'm going with you," The Colonel insisted. "Just to be sure you don't try anything."

Kirby looked disappointed. He was clearly going to try something. Then, he shrugged and led the Colonel to the back of the plane.

Alro led us to the dumbwaiter and explained, "There's a kitchen under us. They could make anything you wanted and would send it up right through here."

After a couple of minutes that felt like hours, in an airplane that had turned into a hunk of falling metal in the sky, we finally heard a whoosh and a ding. Arlo opened the rolling door of the dumbwaiter to reveal four parachutes. As many as would fit at one time. We took them out and sent the dumbwaiter back down. After a few trips we had enough parachutes for everybody, even Mr. Kang's bodyguards, who were still tied up on the floor in varying degrees of consciousness.

"Okay, Stephanie first," The Colonel said, running into the cabin behind Commander Kirby. He personally strapped Stephanie into a parachute then strapped on his own.

"Okay, folks, this is your captain speaking. I can finally see the coast up ahead of us. We're about a mile out. Don't freak out. The wind is in your favor, if you just keep heading toward the lights, you'll make it. Probably. If not, I hope you can swim."

The Colonel nodded. "He's right. When you're out there, it'll look like we're too far out, but you'll make it." He looked to Stephanie. "You'll make it, I promise. Remember, these are cargo shoots. There's no ripcord to pull. They'll open when you jump."

Commander Kirby led us to the door in back of the plane, just behind the wing, then shouted. "BB! Tell us when!"

"Fuck man, like five minutes ago! I'm doing everything I can up here, but we're under 8,000 feet and dropping! Fucking jump, dudes!"

The Colonel nodded to Stephanie. "I'm right behind you." Then he grabbed the red lever on the door, pulled it up and pushed it out. The door violently slammed against the side of the plane. We were low enough that the plane was no longer pressurized, but wind still roared through the cabin. We all steadied ourselves on the nearest thing bolted down. Arlo held onto Walton.

Stephanie stepped up to the door and turned to us. "This is the last time I let you two pull me into a fucking mystery!" Then she jumped out of the plane. I'm not sure she heard our apologies. Thankfully, her parachute opened immediately and the Colonel stepped up to the door to go after his wife.

"Before you hit the ground, bend your knees!" The Colonel advised us. "And run through the landing." We nodded, and he leaned forward to jump.

"Wait! Colonel!" I found myself yelling. "Who won the Army/Navy game?!"

The Colonel looked at me like I was crazy.

"Sorry. Just curious. And if these parachutes don't work, I'll never know."

He smiled. "Those damn anchor clangers got us, Pasch. But hey, you can't win 'em all!"

And the Colonel was gone.

Commander Kirby helped Arlo as he nervously walked to the open door and gave him some encouraging words before he jumped.

"Commander! Help us get Kang's men out of the plane!" Walton shouted over the noise of the open door.

"I got a better idea!" Kirby said as he strapped on a parachute. "You do that yourselves while I get a five-minute headstart. See you around, fellas. And hey, no hard feelings!" And, with that, Commander Kirby gave us one last crooked smile along with a form-perfect salute as he fell backwards out of the open door of the plane.

Chapter 66

Walton and I lunged for Commander Kirby, but he was gone. His parachute was open and we saw him angling north, up the coast from where we all agreed to congregate. I had to stop Walton from diving after him without a parachute. He was furious that Kirby was getting away, but I finally convinced him to help me strap parachutes to Mr. Kang's men. I cut the ropes binding their hands and feet and Walton strapped a parachute to each gangster and unceremoniously threw them out the plane one by one. Then we ran to the cockpit.

"Okay, BB. Time to go!" I said.

"What are you guys doing? Get the hell out of here! Jump!"

"You too! Come on!" Walton pleaded. "You've done all you can do, BB. Now let's fly!"

"No can do, brother. I let go of this stick, the plane is going to crash right into Wailea." He pointed to the town straight ahead of us on Maui's southwestern coast, the lights of its 6,000 residents glowing brightly in the night sky.

"Okay, fine. Then dump it into the ocean," I suggested.

"That's the plan, man. You guys jump, then I'll pull up the flaps and be right behind you."

"Just do it now! We'll jump together!" Walton shouted, grabbing BB and trying to pull him out of his seat. But he couldn't. He slipped right off. Walton looked at his hands. They were red. I looked down at BB and realized the front of his shirt was in ribbons. Dark blood oozed through the hand he pressed against his stomach.

"Yeah, the fucker got me, too. Heck of a shot! Took out Samangja, me, and the plane with one bullet! Must have been a hollow point. Powerful little fuckers. Turned my guts from an innie to an outie!" He said, laughing a laugh that quickly turned into a cough as he started hacking up blood. He wiped his mouth with his arm. "I'm fucked, brothers. All I can do now is make sure this bird don't land on anyone's head."

"We're close, BB! We're so close. Can't you just land at Pope's airfield?" I asked.

"No chance. It's on the other side of the mountain. No way I'd make it. I just gotta make sure this baby lands in a safe spot. Pope wouldn't want his plane to hurt nobody. And it won't. Not on my watch."

"Fine. I'll dump the plane, and Pasch, you jump with BB and take him to a hospital," Walton suggested. "Kula Hospital is close and it's fantastic. They treated me with great tenderness and care after I was stung by hundreds of bees while harvesting wild honey."

"A hospital? Man, I wouldn't make it to the door of the plane!" BB said, squashing Walton's insane plan. "Hey, Pasch. Here. I want you guys to hold onto this for me," he said, digging into his pocket before handing me a nickel.

"What's this for?"

"It's a mystery, Pasch! But I know you'll figure it out. Hell man, y'all figured out everything else," he said, smiling, his gold tooth now stained with blood. "Now you guys gotta jump right now! Ten more seconds and parachute or no parachute, you'll splatter on the ground like bird shit! Please, guys. This is my last fuckin' request and shit."

Walton started to protest and then surrendered. He bent down, hugged BB and whispered something into his ear. The two old friends laughed and Walton hurried out of the cockpit. I paused, trying to figure out what to say. I couldn't think of anything. I still don't know what I could have said in that moment. Sometimes there are just no words. So, I just nodded. As I put the nickel in the pocket of my windbreaker, I felt something else in there. It was the plastic tube holding the joint Don Nelson gave me at Pope's party. I smiled and handed it to BB.

"Well, thank you, brother! Perfect timing! Very Jerry," he said, popping open the plastic container, sticking the joint between his lips and lighting it with a battered old Zippo from his pocket. "Now go! Go, now!"

I nodded and ran to the front of the plane where Walton was waiting for me, his eyes red with tears. I numbly stood there while he strapped a parachute on my back and pushed me out of the plane just ahead of himself. The air hit me like a locomotive. I started spinning. I didn't know which way was up or down, until the parachute opened and I went from falling to floating in the blink of an eye. All the blood rushed from my head to my feet, and I got dizzy. A memory flashed in my brain. My dad catching me in midair by the back of the shirt when I fell off the porch of our new house.

I looked over and saw Walton's parachute had opened, as well. He gave me a sad thumbs up as we floated toward the coast, toward the lights of Wailea. But, there was another light that guided us. A light whose power dwarfed the little town of Wailea. We were heading toward Haleakalā. Volcanic lightning shot up from the crater, cracking and sizzling in the black smoke billowing up into the sky.

I saw the plane, and the volcano, and knew what BB was going to do. I knew how he was going to make sure the plane didn't hurt anybody when it crashed. Brian "BB" Baxter flew Air Force Fun right into the volcano. The plane barely made it over the lip of the crater, and then angled straight down. I flinched. I thought there would have been a spectacular explosion. But there wasn't. The bubbling lava just swallowed the plane whole without so much as a gurgle. The old plane just disappeared.

Air Force Fun was gone. And so was BB. And Samangja. As I floated down, I wept, my tears falling thousands of feet into the ocean below.

Epilogue

The next day was Thanksgiving. Arlo greeted Walton, Stephanie, the Colonel, and me at the front door of what was now his house. We headed out to the patio where Ani and Ahi stood with Moses Boulevard. Stephanie and the Colonel stopped in their tracks. We had purposely not told them a global superstar would be there. We introduced them to Moses, who was as nice and charming as ever. By Stephanie's expression, Walton and I may have taken a few steps in the long journey back to her good graces.

"Still keeping Moses safe, I hope," I said to Ani and Ahi as I greeted them.

"Safer than safe, man. These dudes caught her," Moses said, nodding proudly at his two bodyguards.

"Yeah, you guys were pretty busy last night, so I guess you hadn't heard," Ahi said. "We caught Ellen Pishkin."

334 | JAMES KIRKLAND

"Caught her trying to climb up the side of the hotel at four in the morning, like Spiderman," said Ani, still amazed at the tenacity of Moses' stalker.

"She's messed up, man. I hope she gets some help. But, just in case, I'm keeping these dudes with me at all times," Moses said. "Home and away. They're gonna hook my house up like this. Just like the Pope had it."

"Fabulous news!" Walton beamed. "Another victory for the Swiss Guard, or, should I say, the staff of Moses! But this time, not turning into a snake but instead finding snakes in the tall grass!"

I moved on. I nodded to Michelle Vignault and Lala Kapule, the Pope's lawyer and business manager, and went over to talk to Arlo. I felt bad. He was just standing there by himself.

"So, will Nalani be joining us?"

He shook his head. "We broke up. Well, I guess it's more accurate to say I picked up the phone this morning and she broke up with me."

"Oh. Sorry," I said.

"Yeah, well. It's probably for the best."

I nodded. It definitely was.

I was surprised to see Governor Kaluhiokalani arrive. She was by herself. Her security detail waited outside. I went over to greet her as Detective Palakiko came in. His arm was in a sling. Kirby's shot had apparently hit more shoulder than chest, missing everything vital and, much to the chagrin of his doctors and nurses, Palakiko walked out of the hospital this morning. After all, the tenacious detective still had work to do. We asked him about the hunt for Commander Kirby.

"Still at large. And now the Navy is missing a patrol boat," Palakiko said, exasperated. "It went missing about the same time an ensign went AWOL. Some kid named O'Connor."

Oh no. It was true. O'Connor would run through a brick wall for Roy Kirby. He would also apparently steal a patrol boat for him. I tried convincing Palakiko to go easy on the kid if and when he ever found him, knowing I was wasting my breath.

"Everyone, I want to thank you for coming," Arlo said, getting our attention. "I found the instructions my father left to Samangja about how he wanted this to go, and he'd like us all to have a drink together before spreading his ashes," Arlo said, his voice cracking.

Arlo went into the house. I was expecting him to come out with some old bottle of scotch. Or maybe a hundred-year-old bottle of champagne or something. But instead, he wheeled out a cart of short, ice-filled glasses and two cocktail shakers. "Everyone, please come get a Mai Tai."

I had to laugh. I loved Jon "The Pope" Paul's style. And I loved his Mai Tais. I wish I had a chance to know him more. I'll always be grateful Walton pulled me away from that party at the Hyatt so I at least got to meet him once. If ever so briefly.

After we all had a drink in our hands, Arlo raised his glass.

"It's been three days since my father passed away, but it feels more like three years. So much has happened since then. And it's all given me a lot to think about." He paused, trying to rein in his emotions. "I realize I haven't always been the man my father raised me to be. It seems sometimes I ran away from his example, instead of following it. My father left behind an incredible legacy. And last night, somewhere between jumping out of an airplane and landing on the beach, I realized that my father's legacy is also me. It's who I am and it's what I do with the rest of my life. For that reason, Governor Kaluhiokalani, I invited you here because I have decided to execute my father's will exactly as he wanted. The Cowboy House, and all its land, will go to the state of Hawaii, as he intended. Effective immediately. Ms. Vignault, I hope you can help me arrange that."

Michelle nodded, smiling.

Arlo raised his glass high in the air. "Tonight we'll drink to Samangja and BB. But now, we drink to my father. To the Pope."

"To the Pope!"

As we drank, the bamboo fountain clacked. The timing was incredible. I smirked. It was like the Pope was downing his own drink from the other side. Then we put our glasses down to applaud Arlo. He awkwardly accepted our congratulations. It looked like he'd have to get used to being a nice guy.

"Congrats, Arlo. I mean it. That's really great," I told him after picking my Mai Tai back up and taking another sip. It was delicious. Arlo had nailed it. Just like his father.

"Thanks, Dave. I'll probably regret this tomorrow. I just gave away a ton of money. But money's not everything, right?"

"Yeah, well. You've still got your business. Maybe you'll find some investors?" I said, not really meaning it. Arlo laughed. "Nope! In the spirit of the day, in my dad's honor, I also forgave all the student loans I bought up. So, I am officially broke. I have absolutely nothing. Cheers!" Arlo chugged his entire drink.

"I'm not so sure about that," Palakiko said.

We all turned to the detective as he took out his phone. "There were other things that demanded my attention at the time, but I had planned to forward this to Ms. Vignault when I had time. I hope you'll forgive the delay."

"What is it?" Michelle asked.

"The last voice memo Mr. Paul left before his passing. The second memo that exonerated Mr. Baxter." Palakiko, for the first time, said BB's name with reverence instead of disdain. Last night, after we landed, Walton and I found him and told him everything that happened on the plane. Well, not everything. I left out the part about the joint I gave BB. I was sincerely worried Palakiko would charge me for distribution of a controlled substance. Palakiko hit play, held the phone in the air, and, for the last time, we all heard Jon Paul's voice.

"Hey, Samangja. I was sitting here thinking about Arlo. Giving away the estate last night must have hit him pretty hard. And I just refused to help him with his new business, the thing with the college debt. When we talk to Michelle tomorrow, remind me that I also want to change my will to leave Arlo something. Something special. I want him to have Pika's. He'd own it. He'd run it, and he'd make a good living from it. I already talked to Pika and he loves the idea. Best of all, Arlo would be great at it. I know it. I love him so much. I just wish he'd stop trying to make millions and start trying to make himself happy. Okay, that's it. Thank you, my friend. Hey, I love you, too."

It took awhile before any of us could speak again. If Samangja was there, he would have been passing around tissues, but he wasn't there, so we all had to settle for wiping away our tears with our shirts and sleeves. I'm not one to hug, you know that about me, but I walked right up to Arlo and wrapped him up in a great big one. One that grew even bigger when Walton wrapped his long arms around both of us.

"Arlo, you truly honor your father today," Walton said. "And you honor the name he bestowed upon you, Arlo Ziggy Jerry Paul. Blessings!"

"Do you think that would hold up in court?" Palakiko asked Michelle.

"I'll make sure of it. Thank you, Detective."

Moments later, Walton lifted the Pope's urn high over the railing of the balcony and turned it over, scattering the Pope's ashes. The wind was strong that day. It carried Jon Paul's ashes far and wide over his beloved tropical paradise and out to sea, to the waves, to the Pacific, to eternity.

We were silent for a long time. Everyone processing the moment in their own way. I said a silent prayer. After a few minutes, we slowly started mingling again. Everyone was clearly affected by the moment.

"Okay, everybody. It's time to go to Pika's," Arlo said, wiping away tears and guiding us to the door. Everyone hugged him on their way out. Walton and I walked to the van with Stephanie and the Colonel. We chatted, talking about the season that lay ahead of us. It seemed crazy, but it was just getting started. Walton and I would be calling our first regular season game at Arizona State that weekend, which, lucky for me, was close to home. I'd spend as much time with my family as humanly possible.

"Time goes by so fast," I said. "Before you know it, we'll be calling the Pac-12 Tournament again."

"Oh, did you hear?" Stephanie said. "They moved it to Las Vegas."

"Las Vegas?!" Walton thundered. "An amateur basketball tournament in a desert surrounded by gamblers? What could go right?! Oh, but just think! The access to such remarkable natural wonders! The Valley of Fire! Pyramid Lake! Fly Geyser! Red Rock Canyon! The glory! The majesty! I can't wait!"

"At least it'll be warm. And dry. With no oceans!" I said, stopping before getting in the van to look up at Haleakalā. "Thanks BB," I said. "Rest in peace."

"Throw a nickel on the grass, save a fighter pilot's ass," The Colonel said to himself as he got in the van. I stopped him. "Wait. What was that? What'd you say?"

"It's just an old Air Force thing. Something you'd say at a pilot's funeral. Kind of a little song you sing."

I got out BB's nickel and smiled. "Can you teach us?"

Moments later, Walton, Stephanie, the Colonel and I, with nickels in our hands, sang a tribute to our fallen pilot.

"Throw a nickel on the grass, save a fighter pilot's ass! Oh, Hallelujah, Oh, Hallelujah! Throw a nickel on the grass and you'll be saved!"

Then we threw our nickels on the grass. The Pope's perfect, manicured grass.

I love you. I'm sorry. Please forgive me. Thank you, BB.

That night at Pika's, we enjoyed a Thanksgiving feast I'll remember for the rest of my life. Arlo was right, Pika was a genius.

Each course was better than the last, and was served with love by the chef and the restaurant's new owner. I must have had a half-dozen Mai Tais.

The next morning, Walton and I flew back home. Whenever we flew, Walton always took the aisle. Even in first class, he needed the extra leg room. That left me with the window. I looked down as we flew over Haleakalā. The smoke had cleared. The lava had stopped. Last night, as we slept, the mighty volcano went dormant once again.

May it rest another four hundred years.

Aloha.

The Bill Walton Mysteries
will continue in Las Vegas...

ABOUT THE AUTHOR

James Kirkland was born in NE Portland, Oregon
and received a BFA in poetry at Emerson College.
He now lives in Los Angeles with his cat where he
works as a novelist, and actor. His first novel
Friend of the Devil: The Bill Walton Mysteries was
published in 2019 by Meathouse Publishing. His
cat is named Chompsy.